THE
HOUSEWIFE'S
SECRET

BOOKS BY ANNA-LOU WEATHERLEY

THE
HOUSEWIFE'S
SECRET

ANNA-LOU WEATHERLEY

bookouture

Published by Bookouture in 2024

An imprint of Storyfire Ltd.
Carmelite House
50 Victoria Embankment
London EC4Y 0DZ

www.bookouture.com

ISBN: 978-1-83790-965-0
eBook ISBN: 978-1-83790-964-3

For Qefs, and anyone trying to break free

'Three things cannot be long hidden: the sun, the moon and the truth'

BUDDHA

PROLOGUE

I shouldn't even have been there.

It wasn't my usual dispensary, but I needed to pick up a prescription, and I'd spotted a parking space slap bang outside, so on a whim, I'd pulled in. The heat felt humid and oppressive that day, like a thick, heavy overcoat weighing me down. The freakishly hot dry spell we'd been experiencing in the UK finally felt ready to break though, and I could sense a rainstorm wasn't too far off the horizon.

I'd been standing in the pharmacy queue for around ten minutes – though it felt like longer – when a rush of warm air hit me as the automatic doors opened and a young woman with a pushchair walked through them. A small child was tottering behind her – a little girl – no more than two or three years old. She moved the buggy right past me with a harried, 'S'cuse me,' and a waft of her cheap body spray.

'Stay close, Dolly,' she instructed the child. 'Don't go running off now, d'ya hear me?'

Dolly. I felt myself stiffen at the name, flicked my hair from my face. It was beginning to stick to my skin. The little girl was carrying a doll – *Dolly was carrying a dolly* – upside down in one hand, the toy's nasty, acrylic yellow hair dragging along the floor as she stomped behind her mother in a pair of purple glittery wellington boots and a bright pink tulle ballerina skirt.

I briefly turned my attention back to the pharmacy queue, resisting the urge to exhale loudly. The heat was making me irritable and the sensor-operated doors that kept opening and closing next to me, affording me a blast of artificial heat on top of it, really weren't helping.

The woman in front of me in the queue tutted loudly before looking round at me and rolling her eyes. I raised my eyebrows sympathetically before turning my attention back to Dolly and her mum, who was now inspecting products at the make-up counter, testing coloured lip glosses and eyeshadows on the back of her hand. The grubby pushchair was next to her, blankets and hastily opened packets of rice cakes spilling out of the under basket, and her market-stall-dupe-designer handbag was stuffed haphazardly on top of the hood. I felt a flicker of envy in that moment – I wanted to be a mother too – but I also felt something else, a sudden sense of unease which manifested as an unpleasant prickle on my skin – though I couldn't say why exactly.

The store security guard – a short, stocky man with no neck who carried himself with an air of authority – began slowly patrolling the aisle. He looked uncomfortable in his thick black uniform and high-visibility vest, and the lack of space between his head and shoulders only appeared to compound this.

The young woman was leaning over the pushchair when her phone rang. I continued to watch her, wondering what it was about her that had ignited my interest and unsettled me at the same time. I couldn't put my finger on it, but it was definitely *something*.

The move was lightning fast and seamless – to the untrained eye at least – as she slid the lip gloss into her pocket while simultaneously retrieving her phone from it. My eyes immediately began searching for the security guard. Instinctively, I felt compelled to warn her that he was close by.

The queue finally began to move then, and so I duly shuffled forward, but not too much.

'Excuse me, madam.'

She swung round sharply, startled.

'Can I ask you to step aside for a moment...?'

I was holding my breath as I watched them; had to remind myself to breathe.

She cancelled the call I suspected she was pretending to take and looked at him blankly. 'Can I help you?'

Security Sid visibly braced himself, like a soldier about to go into battle. 'If you could come with me to the office, madam...?'

Dolly was still playing a little way behind them. She was singing to herself and pulling faces, oblivious to her mother's predicament, to anything other than her naked, plastic, dead-eyed companion.

'Why? What for?'

I imagined she'd been hit by a rush of cortisol at this point and that her breathing had rapidly increased, sensations I was, regrettably, all too familiar with. I started to feel her unease by proxy.

'We can talk about it in the office.' He looked pleased with himself, and I swallowed dryly. I have a special kind of contempt for store security guards.

'Go into...? I ain't going into no office,' she said. 'What 'ave I done?'

'Madam, if you'll just come with me...' He began rounding on her so that she was forced to take a couple of steps backward.

'I ain't done nuffink,' she protested, but her body language was leaking, and I could tell her confidence was beginning to wane.

'I *saw* you...' Security Sid said with an edge of exasperated resignation. 'That lipstick in your pocket... Let's not make a scene, eh? Let's just go into the office and sort this out quietly, the nice way.' He pointed to a sign on the wall behind her, and she turned, glancing at it over her shoulder. Her hand was on her hip now, and her chin was raised in defiance. The queue began to move again, but I was rooted to the spot.

'We can check the CCTV footage in the office if you like. The cameras never lie...' He continued to move in on her.

'Don't touch me!' Her voice rose a few octaves, alerting others in the queue, who automatically turned to see what the commotion was.

'Did you see that?' The young woman suddenly made direct eye contact with me, wrong-footing me for a second. 'And... Dolly?' She stopped mid-sentence and glanced around her. 'Dolly... where is she? Where's my baby?'

I turned around, doing a slow 180 to see if I could locate the little girl and... I saw something, a flash of that horrible synthetic yellow hair in my peripheral vision. Dolly was still happily jabbering away to herself as I watched her totter through the automatic doors and out onto the pavement. Fear shot through me like an arrow, piercing my guts.

I reacted instinctively before I'd even had time to think, to process, because if I had, I would have remembered to stay invisible, not to draw attention to myself and remain just another faceless housewife going about her business, but it was already too late.

'Stop! STOP!'

The car was rapidly approaching as I launched myself in front of it. In that moment, I thought I saw *his* face, there, in among the horrified onlookers as it clipped me, those small, dark eyes flashing before me, his lips parting into that slow, crooked smile...

And then everything went black.

ONE

DARCIE

'Well-behaved women rarely make history.' Hugh Abberline slaps his wife Anita's exposed thigh playfully as she knocks back the remainder of the amaretto in her glass. She's barely maintaining a grip on my Asprey crystal, and I imagine it slipping from her flimsy grasp and smashing all over my expensive tableware any second. Not that it would especially matter if it did. I could easily replace it – and the plates too – a thousand times over if I wanted. It's remarkable, really, *how things change*.

'Now, who was it who even *said* that?' Hugh says, though he poses the question largely to himself. 'You know, that famous old black-and-white screen actress...'

Our guests, Dr – well, *Mr,* to use the correct term for a surgeon – Hugh Abberline and his wife, Anita, are, amusingly, a little drunk. Though I don't really drink alcohol myself – at least not anymore – watching others shed their self-consciousness has become something of a substitute for the real thing, like getting pissed by proxy, minus the hangover and chronic self-loathing the next day. And I certainly *don't* miss that. Besides, now I think I might have good reason to abstain.

I cast my eyes over the clean plates around the table and

feel a flutter of satisfaction. The evening is shaping up well. The lamb-and-sage ravioli with a bone marrow consommé has been a resounding success. Not bad for a girl who once upon a time relied upon her wits for her next meal. Doing a quick mental calculation this morning while I prepped the fish starter, I estimated that it's taken me the best part of a week to source, shop, prepare and finally cook tonight's meal for four, coming in at around £126 per head – and that's not even including wine. I know I shouldn't do this, break down the cost of everything – and I certainly don't need to, not now anyway – but old habits die hard, if they ever do at all.

'Greta Garbo!' Anita spits the name triumphantly from her plump lips.

I kind of like Anita, even though she once had a fling with my husband. Admittedly, it's a strange, somewhat uncomfortable feeling to know that she has intimate knowledge of the man I'm married to, even if it was eons ago now.

I watch her as she casts her large blue eyes over Gabe's face with a generic full-lipped smile and try not to wonder if she's thinking about a time when they once made love. A little of her Châteauneuf-du-Pape sloshes over the rim of her glass as she throws her head back in laughter, and I wipe it away with a napkin along with the image of them together in my mind. I suppose we've become something loosely resembling friends, Anita and I, though largely at her behest. A few months back, we started attending a yoga class together and have met up for coffee where I found myself enjoying her company more than I should, or certainly more than it's wise to, for me at least.

Anita's husband, Hugh, is a neurosurgeon – he fixes people's brains for a living and possesses a pretty active one himself. He and Gabe were at medical school together and share an ease around each other that only friends with longevity seem to possess. Even ones who've slept with the same woman. I'm sure Gabe told me it was he who'd introduced Hugh to

Anita in the first place, now I think of it. 'She was much more his type,' he'd told me. Anyway, they work together at St Catherine's after Hugh secured a prominent position at the prestigious hospital a couple of months ago.

I glance over at Gabe and feel my heart jump as our eyes briefly meet.

It's really no surprise to me that my husband's specialty is the heart. I tease him that he literally 'mends broken hearts' as a day job. He certainly fixed mine. Before I met him, I wasn't sure I even possessed one – or not one that functioned properly anyway.

I begin to clear away the empty dishes from the table to appreciative murmurs.

'That was bloody exquisite,' Anita sighs, sitting back in her seat and crossing her long legs. 'And seriously, I just can't get over this incredible apartment...' she says, looking around her in wide-eyed appreciation, or perhaps envy, though I prefer to think the former. She's right though – there's no doubt that this apartment *is* incredible, all £1.7 million of it. I still struggle to believe it's mine – *ours* – though I've struggled more with *how* it came to be ours.

'I particularly love how you've utilised the space,' she enthuses. 'Did you get professionals in to help you with the design process?'

'No,' I say, inwardly embarrassed that the thought had never even occurred to me. Sometimes I forget that I have money in the bank.

'Well, you obviously have a fabulous eye! The colours you've used are *so* sympathetic to the era, yet with the juxtaposition of the modern interior... it really works. And it's *such* a great building in *such* a wonderful location as well... Must've cost a *fortune*.'

I recognise Anita's compliment as a roundabout way of asking how much we paid for the place, a question I'd incidentally pre-empted. I've nothing to gain by not telling her – and I've nothing to hide really, not about that at least – but my concern is that she'll go on to ask *how* we could afford it. And that's the part of the conversation I'd rather not have, because then, by default, I'll be forced to mention *her*. Dr Carmichael – my therapist – told me I shouldn't be reticent if people ask about my 'windfall' – as she'd put it – and I shouldn't feel guilty but had also, and somewhat paradoxically, added, 'You have no obligation to tell anyone *anything* if you don't want to, Darcie.'

Thankfully, however, Anita doesn't wait for me to answer.

'I am intrigued though. What made you decide to buy an apartment and not a house?'

Our open-plan converted apartment, complete with mezzanine level, occupies the entire ground floor of an imposing Victorian residence, and it was the feeling of space and light that appealed most to me when we viewed it. Frankly, the fewer rooms the better. I don't like the sound of doors closing behind me.

'I've always loved that New York studio loft apartment vibe, I suppose,' I reply, which isn't even a lie.

She nods with gravitas.

'And easier for the housekeeper to clean I'm sure – not many stairs.'

I don't tell her that I don't have one of those – a housekeeper. I keep this frankly shocking revelation to myself lest it invite more questions.

'Mae West,' Gabe suddenly pipes up. 'It wasn't Greta Garbo; it was Mae West who said, "Well-behaved women never make history."'

I glance over at him, impressed, and he flashes me a warm smile. I love the way my husband looks at me. I don't think I could ever tire of it, or of the way it makes me feel. I so desperately want to tell him the news – our wonderful news – but I can't, not tonight, not yet. I have an appointment with my gynaecologist tomorrow morning. I'll tell him once I've had absolute confirmation and the all-clear. For now though, it remains a secret – *and I'm pretty good at keeping those.*

'"It's not the men in my life... it's the life in my men..." now that *was* Garbo, wasn't it?' Hugh says.

'Well, whoever said it,' Anita interjects, 'they were absolutely correct, weren't they, Darcie?' She shoots me a conspiratorial 'sisters together' sort of glance and raises her empty tumbler. 'To the lives in our men!'

'The men in our lives – *who save lives,*' I say, raising my glass of sparkling water in response.

Gabe squeezes my leg underneath the table; runs the tips of his fingers gently upwards of my thigh, causing my skin to prickle.

'In fact,' Anita says, pouting, the edges of her voice amplified by expensive wine, 'come to think of it, I may be the only person in this room who *hasn't* ever saved a life!'

I feel my happy buzz instantly evaporate. *Why had I gone and mentioned saving lives?*

Anita clearly senses my discomfort. 'Oh, come on, don't be so modest!' She prods me with a freshly manicured fingernail. 'You're a national bloody hero you are!'

I shake my head, will her not to go there.

'You made headlines when you saved that little girl's life, didn't she, Gabe? *National* headlines.'

Gabe squeezes my thigh again, this time in reassurance. He knows I don't like to talk about that incident, though perhaps not for the reasons he thinks. I hadn't wanted or courted any form of publicity or even recognition from that day outside the pharmacy, didn't want my name and face plastered all over the papers and social media. But that's exactly what had happened anyway. Some teenagers had captured the entire event on their phones – some nine months ago now – and had posted the footage on TikTok and Instagram. It had quickly gone viral, racking up thousands of 'views' and 'likes' and bloody 'shares'. It hadn't been long before the press had got wind of it, and then, well, it seemed to take on a life of its own. I might've remained anonymous if Anita hadn't seen it on social media and had some kind of misplaced need to identify me.

Realising that the press weren't about to allow my good deed to go unpunished, I finally acquiesced to their incessant requests and gave them a brief telephone interview, one I'd hoped would satisfy them enough to leave me alone, only this seemed to exacerbate the public's interest in the story, and some weeks later I was told that I'd only gone and been nominated for one of those 'Pride of Britain' type awards where ordinary members of the public are recognised for various displays of altruism and acts of bravery. Mortified, I couldn't think of anything worse and politely declined, despite Dolly's mum's persistent, even angry, demands for me to attend. I just wanted the whole thing to go away.

'I need the little girls' room.' Anita stands abruptly, a little unsteady on her towering Louboutin heels. 'Too much wine!'

Hugh guffaws. 'Too much of a good thing...'

'Can be wonderful!' We all sing the words collectively.

Anita's heels clack loudly against the polished wood floor as she struts off.

'Oh, turn the music up – I like this one,' I say to my husband as I make my way to the kitchen sink and begin rinsing the china plates by hand – the gold leaf will ruin in the dishwasher otherwise.

Purdy – my miniature chocolate dachshund – barks suddenly from her bed, causing Hugh to jump. Her ears and tail pricked, she scoots from the kitchen down towards the front door.

Gabe laughs. 'She's got quite a voice on her, hasn't she? Great little guard dog though... even if she has got a Napoleon complex!'

'Bit late in the day for the postman, isn't it?' Hugh remarks, checking his watch.

Purdy is patrolling the front door, whining, sniffing and scratching at the letterbox.

'Probably junk mail,' Gabe says, stretching in his seat, the contours of his well-defined chest visible – to me at least – through his pale blue shirt. Suddenly I can't wait for our guests to leave.

'Ooh, Tchaikovsky!' Anita announces brightly as she returns from the bathroom. 'I love a touch of classical.'

It's actually Chopin, but I can't bring myself to correct her – it wouldn't be polite, and she might ask me how I know, which again will force me to think of *her*. Plus, it's somehow reassuring to know that Anita too is also, in her own way, pretending to be something she isn't.

'So... haunting.' She begins to twirl around the kitchen in tipsy, over-animated ballet moves.

Purdy is still barking loudly at the front door.

'I think the dog prefers Mozart,' she says, throwing herself back into her chair.

I abandon the dishes, briefly drying my hands with a dish-cloth to go and investigate whatever it is that's got her all excited.

'It's indicative of the breed,' I call back to Anita as I stoop to pick up the envelope from the doormat. 'The postman thought she was the size of a German shepherd when he first heard her bark—' I stop; stare at the word 'Darcie' written in black ink on the front. Odd, I think, checking the clock on the console table. It's 9.22 p.m. Who would be hand-delivering me a letter at this time of night? The correct spelling of my name instantly suggests the sender must be someone who knows me. Nine times out of ten, people assume I spell Darcie with a 'Y'.

'What's this then, eh, Purds?' Intrigued, I glance down at

her at my feet, her upstanding tail wagging as she looks up at me with her usual judgemental expression.

The cream bonded paper feels thick between my fingers as I pick it up, expensive. For some reason, I bring it up to my nose and sniff it. It even smells expensive, musky and creamy, like old ladies' hand lotion. My initial thought is that it must be an invitation of some sort, though I can't think who the sender might be, given I have few, if any, friends and rarely get invited to anything.

I open it and unfold the note inside.

A flush of confusion ensues before an explosion of adrenalin hits me square in the solar plexus. I feel my breathing increase suddenly – short, sharp shocks of cortisol like tiny stab wounds to my body – as I read the two handwritten words on the page: *FOUND YOU!*

I stare at them, my fingers beginning to lightly shake. Instinctively, I go to open the front door, to check if whoever delivered the note is still there – they can't have gone far – but...

'What's that you got there, baby girl?' Gabe is suddenly behind me, his arms snaking around my waist.

I screw it up in my hand. 'Oh... it's nothing.' I smile breezily. 'Just more bloody junk mail.' I discard it in the rattan wastepaper basket by the door. 'So,' I say, turning into his embrace, 'are we ready for dessert then?'

TWO

It's the first – and only – thing on my mind when I awake the following morning – that damned note. Despite doing my level best to convince myself that it was just some marketing campaign doing the rounds – albeit one with potentially sinister overtones – I can't prevent my thoughts from tormenting me – who else could've sent it but *him*? But that's absurd. I've been telling myself my recent social-media infamy doesn't mean he can find me – I'm unrecognisable now compared to the person I was back then, and my surname has changed.

The memories I have of that time in my life are, by and large, pretty sketchy. Sometimes I think none of it ever actually happened and that it was all just some horrible nightmare.

Dr Carmichael, my therapist, had given it a name: 'dissociative amnesia'. She said that I'd blocked out some of the details because of the trauma I'd suffered.

I feel a miserable mix of frustration and dread as I dress in my dog-walking uniform of leggings and a long-sleeved top, throw on a running jacket and trainers. I scrape my hair up into a messy bun on top of my head and stare at myself in the mirror. It's taken reaching my fourth decade to finally arrive at the place I find myself today – a solvent, successful, sober wife and – dare I tempt fate and say – maybe yet a mother? These are things I'd once deemed unlikely, if not impossible, at least until I met Gabe anyway. *Please God, don't screw everything up now. I'm begging you, please...*

I turn away from my sombre reflection and feel cross with myself. I should be focusing on the – hopefully positive – news that I'm praying to receive at my doctor's appointment.

To say that stupid note ruined my evening last night would be an understatement. I couldn't properly focus on anything after I'd opened that envelope – not my guests or their conversation, nor the painstakingly prepared fancy dessert that I could barely swallow a mouthful of, and not even my Gabe as we fell, naked and entangled, into bed together once the Abberlines had finally left during the early hours (with Anita clutching her Louboutins drunkenly in one hand and one of my Asprey crystal glasses in the other).

We'd made love, something I'd hoped would distract me from my increasingly moribund thoughts, but miserably it hadn't. My husband has mastered my body, studied it carefully, ergo the sex is incredible, the best I've ever experienced. Yet I'd faked an orgasm, something I've never done before – not with Gabe anyway – have never needed to, which fills me with more self-loathing, but I knew, no matter how attentive his touch, that I was never going to get there, not after reading that note, and I didn't want him to suspect that anything was wrong.

I'm seriously contemplating contacting Dr Carmichael as I place Purdy's collar and lead around her neck, grab my keys and phone, and zip them up in my pocket. Therapy had been painful enough in the first instance, despite being long overdue, but it had helped – it really had – which made me regret not having made the leap years ago. I suppose fear had always prevented me, yet ironically it had proven to be the biggest fear itself in the end.

It was *her* unexpected 'gift' from the grave that finally forced me into seeking professional help, although when I look back on it, Dr Carmichael kind of found me. I really hadn't planned to tell her the whole sordid story though – that was never my intention. I suppose it was that six degrees of separation thing, because when it came down to it, I couldn't really talk about *her* without any of the rest of it. It was all so intertwined somehow.

The note! It's still in the wastepaper basket! *Shit!*

Gabe is at the breakfast table when I make my way downstairs, chewing on a piece of soggy sourdough while simultaneously watching a film that's playing on TV. It's a rare morning off for him, and he's dressed for an early game of golf in a crisp pair of white trousers and a navy-blue polo shirt. He looks almost ridiculously handsome.

'Is it just me, or is Kevin Costner always wearing some kind of uniform in all his films? Look.' He points up at the screen with his sourdough. 'He's a pilot in this one...'

'That's a US naval uniform,' I say, 'not a pilot's. Anyway, can't say I've ever noticed, but then I'm not really a big Kevin Costner fan – he's not my type.'

'No?' He looks over at me with that delicious, boyish grin that makes me want to squeeze his cheeks. 'And who *is* your type, *Mrs Bonneville?*'

I drop my head to one side; tap my lip with my finger. He's fishing.

'Hmmm, now let me think... well, he's tall, taller than me anyway, though that's not especially difficult, and he's got all this crazy dark curly hair like noodles, and he's smart and funny and sexy, and he has a *huge...*'

His eyes widen, and I laugh. 'Like you even need to ask me that! What you doing watching a film this time of the morning anyways?'

He wrinkles his nose. 'I've had enough of the news. Frankly, there's enough misery in the world. I don't want to kill my buzz just before my game.'

I doubt that'll be a possibility. Gabe is always in a good mood – even his bad moods are good. He's pretty damned near perfect, or at least I think so.

'So, who do you think's going to win today's game then?' I ask breezily. 'Are you on form?'

'Baby, I'm *always* on form.'

'Modest as well,' I muse with a smile.

'Probably Matt to be fair.' He sniffs as he looks up at me. 'But even if I lose, I win because I get to take my beautiful wife out for lunch afterwards.'

'Lunch! You've booked us lunch?'

'Bertollini's if you fancy it, *bella ragazza?*' He raises his eyebrows comically.

'Really? You booked Bertie's?' I clasp my hands together with a little appreciative gasp. '*Ooh, grazie mille, mio caro marito.*' Gabe loves it when I speak to him in Italian. He was impressed when he discovered I'm fluent. In truth, it's perhaps the only good thing to have come out of my upbringing.

'At 1.15 p.m.,' he says, absent-mindedly brushing away invisible crumbs from his pristine polo shirt. It's as if he intuitively knows we may well have something wonderful to celebrate today. I imagine his reaction – the look on his face – as I announce the happy news I'm pretty certain I'll have for definite by then, and this momentarily distracts me from the wastepaper basket.

I watch him as he sips his black coffee then starts reading his phone while ruffling his thick mop of curly hair. Sometimes I just can't believe my luck. Because that's what it was, meeting Gabe – pure and simple, right-time-right-place good luck. And I sure as hell had needed some of that in my life.

His soft curls smell clean and lemony fresh as I kiss the top of his head. I was hoping he might leave for his game of golf before me, allow me to fish the note out of the bin and dispose of it properly, just to be sure, maybe even check the doorbell camera footage, but he's showing no signs of making tracks, and I need to get a move on if I'm to get all my chores done before my appointment.

'You're my favourite husband,' I say, making a heart shape with my fingers, and he squeezes my backside as I turn away from him. I want to bend down and snatch the note from the bin as I open the front door, but he's still watching me, and I bottle it, tell myself that he won't go looking for it, probably hasn't even given it a second's thought.

There's a sharp chill in the January air this morning, which I suppose is to be expected, but I wish I'd worn another layer now. I bury my gloveless hands into my kangaroo pocket as Purdy and I enter the woods, the bright morning sunlight cutting through the trees like lasers making black lace patterns over the leaves, the cold earthy scent of the mulch beneath my feet reaching my nostrils.

Purdy turns to check I'm still here behind her like she always does – and like I always am. She's been my loyal companion for five years now, before the gods looked favourably upon me and I met Gabe. I suppose I don't have what you'd call many 'real' friends – perhaps with the exception of Gina, wherever she is – though this is largely through choice. Friends become confidants over time, and I don't trust myself almost as much as I don't trust others. Life has taught me that it's safer to keep people at a distance; there's less potential for heartbreak and disappointment – on both sides.

My breath is visible like cigarette smoke as I exhale, and there's a light dusting of frost on the ground. I check the time on my watch. It's 7.42 a.m. My gynae appointment is at 9.30 a.m., meaning I have enough time to walk Purdy, go home, have a quick shower and grab a light breakfast, though I've no real appetite this morning.

I pass another dog walker – a neighbour – who I recognise, and we exchange a polite nod.

'Beautiful morning,' she says as Purdy greets her dog in the way that dogs do. 'Cold but crisp – just how I like it.'

'Yes, it's lovely, though I wish I'd worn another layer now,' I reply, bristling.

Today *will* be a lovely day, I tell myself unequivocally as she ambles off. *It was all years ago now.*

Instinctively, I place a hand on my belly as Purdy and I walk deeper into the woods, a cut-through off the main pathway – a route we sometimes take. Do I feel different this time? It's difficult to tell. Perhaps I've been a little hungrier than usual, my breasts a touch more tender. Or maybe I'm just imagining it because I want it so bad. The home pregnancy test I'd done had shown a positive result – but I'll believe it's actually real when a doctor tells me, even though I know those tests are almost one hundred per cent accurate and—

Suddenly the air feels eerily still around me as we approach the small clearing, and something in my peripheral vision instinctively causes me to spin round. I stop dead.

I spot something to my left, a shadow moving between the trees, the sound of twigs snapping as though crunching under-foot. My heartbeat begins to accelerate; becomes amplified in my ears.

'Hello?' I call out, my voice belying the sudden fear that flushes through me. 'Is someone there?'

I don't so much as blink while I await a response.

After a few moments, when one doesn't come, I feel my heart rate gradually settle back into a normal, steady rhythm and almost burst out laughing at my own jumpiness. It was probably just Purdy, bobbing and weaving through the bushes and branches. *It was nothing...*

THREE

DAN

Fiona's been talking at me for a full minute and a half when Gwendoline Archer swings open the door to my office. I'm about to leave the nick for two whole weeks' holiday, and some overdue paternity leave, so Fiona and I have a lot to organise, but Gwendoline is the sort of super who only interrupts in an emergency, so I'm instantly unsettled. Seeing I'm on the phone she nods at me silently and mouths, 'A word – my office!'

'I've *finally* finished packing the suitcases,' my harried-sounding wife continues. 'There's five of them, plus the buggy and the Moses basket and...'

'Five! Flipping hell, Fi. We're only going for a fortnight!'

I can hear our latest addition to the family – our seven-month-old son, Jude – cooing in the background. My son is a happy little chap; he chuckles whenever he sees me, although Fiona reckons he's laughing *at* me and not *with* me.

I am looking forward to spending some quality time with my 'accidental' family. I say accidental because both our kids have been a surprise, albeit happy ones. January might not be considered the ideal month for a 'staycay' I realise, but the opportunity to house-sit Fiona's friend's beachfront pile in

Sandbanks while she's away on business was a no-brainer, and I have ten days' leave carried over from last year that I'll lose otherwise. Besides, I don't tan easy anyway.

'Fi...'

'We're going on our holibobs. Yes we are, oh yes we are!' Her voice is high pitched as she continues talking to Jude, as if she's inhaled helium. 'Mimi's on her way over already, just in time to help with the last few bits before we all head off.'

Mi-Sun, or Mimi as she's known to us, is an old family friend of Fiona's who sometimes helps with childminding when our work schedules clash, which is admittedly quite often given mine and Fi's respective professions. Fi's already taken on more than a few commissions from her editor at the newspaper since Jude's birth. I'm pleased Mimi will be joining us in Sandbanks. Hell, we may even get to go on a few date nights, like real married couples do apparently.

'Fi, I... Listen, I'm sorry, I've got to cut you off. Archer's—'

'I'll see you at three then, yeah?'

I instinctively nod, but no words follow to give it any credibility, and I'm not sure why.

'Dan...?' Her voice suddenly drops an octave or two. 'You *will* be back by three, *won't you?*'

'See you then.'

I hang up quickly.

'Everything OK, ma'am?' I say as I enter Archer's office.

'Ah yes, Dan.' She's straightening out the various objects on her desk, moving her laptop a millimetre to the left in line with her phone then positioning her silver pen carefully next to it. My boss, Superintendent Gwendoline Archer, affectionally known throughout the nick as 'Cupid', has the worst case of OCD I've ever known, or maybe it's the best case? I suppose it all depends which way you're coming at it.

'I just wanted to say bon voyage, wish you a happy holiday.'

My bullshit detector immediately kicks in. Why the urgency just to wish me a happy holiday?

'Thank you, ma'am. We're looking forward to it, and I—'

'There's a misper just come in actually,' she casually interrupts. 'A thirty-seven-year-old woman, Darcie Bonneville... last seen walking her dog this morning. The husband – Gabriel Bonneville – called it in. Uniform attended, but I've sent Davis and Parker down there to do an initial risk assessment.'

'Splendid,' I reply, not wanting to ask why she feels the need to tell me in the first place. Mispers come in practically every day, and there's no one more qualified than my second in command, my dearest and trusted 'work wife', DS Lucy Davis, to investigate. She works extremely efficiently with DC Parker, a promising young detective with sharp instincts that he hides beneath a slightly hapless façade.

'It's looking a little suspicious though, I must say.'

Must she? I don't need to know. I'm officially on leave. I tell myself just to say my goodbyes, turn around and walk out of her office, then head off home to somehow squeeze five full-sized suitcases into the boot of my Ford Focus. But instead I find myself asking: 'Suspicious? How exactly?'

Not even a beat passes.

'She was walking her dog in Ravens Wood around 7.30 this morning – her usual route apparently. Well, the dog returned home – without its lead – but the owner didn't.'

'The dog made its way home alone?'

'Yes, apparently it was sitting on the doorstep, whining, when the husband returned from a game of golf around elevenish. He's a doctor, a consultant cardiologist down at St Catherine's and... Anyway, leave it with us. You go off now – have a well-deserved break with your little family.'

My *little family*? Is she being sarcastic? I think to pull her up on this remark, but my mind has already jumped ship.

'When was the last communication – from Darcie I mean?'

'When she left the house – well, apartment actually – to walk the dog. Nothing after that.'

'Her phone's off?'

'Ringing out apparently.'

'And there's no obvious reason to think she would decide to go off-grid: no argument, no mental-health issues, history of depression, family, work, financial problems...?'

Archer shakes her head, though her pristine hairstyle remains unnervingly static.

'Husband claims they're blissfully happy, only been married eighteen months, still in the honeymoon phase I should imagine. He's supposed to be taking her for lunch today; booked a restaurant, Bertollini's; says she should definitely have returned home by now.'

Well, that answers one question at least. Bertollini's is a very exclusive – and expensive – restaurant that overlooks the river. It's popular with the rich and famous, which is probably at least two reasons why I've never been there.

'The husband says it's entirely out of character, that they're in regular communication throughout the day usually, and that she seemed perfectly normal, happy even, when she left.'

'Maybe the dog ran off and she went looking for it – got lost? Ravens Wood is a big place... Perhaps she lost her phone or keys in the search – went to a neighbour's, or a friend's house?'

'It's possible,' she replies, quickly adding, 'but the husband doesn't think so. Even if that was the case, then surely she would've just gone straight home, found a way to contact her husband or waited for him to get back from his game of golf? She knew he'd be home before lunchtime, in time to change for their lunch date. He seems convinced that she may have come to harm, and, well, I don't need to tell you what's going to happen if he's right.'

No, she certainly doesn't. Middle-class consultant's wife

vanishes on dog walk? It'll be breaking headline news in a matter of hours. And then we could be talking full-scale manhunt, forensics, helicopters, dogs... a huge operation involving a large volume of people and multiple agencies.

The issue with mispers is that you have to investigate all the possible scenarios – gather as much information as possible before you can level it up to something more high risk. Technically, anything – and nothing – could've happened to this woman because anything *does* happen to people, and being in this game, nothing surprises you. The trick is not to jump to conclusions or speculate, to keep an open mind, explore all possibilities and conduct a proper risk assessment, erring perhaps, though, on the side of caution.

I check my watch. It's 12.25 p.m. This lady has been uncontactable since 7.30 this morning, so coming on for five hours. It's not an awfully long time in the grand scheme of things, but it's enough to set off alarm bells in the circumstances.

'What time did the husband call it in?'

'Around midday,' she says. 'A little after he came home and found the dog... Apparently, she was only dressed in a light running jacket and leggings when she left for the walk, and it's a cold day, which would suggest she had no intention of staying outside for any great length of time.'

'What about friends, family...?'

Archer shakes her head again. 'She's a bit of a home bird apparently – not many friends, and no family either. Her mother's dead, and there's no father, no siblings... Husband's adamant she's had no recent problems, no enemies, or none he's aware of anyhow.'

I nod. It's admittedly odd but still not enough to conclude she may have come to any harm. And I'm always dubious when I'm told someone has no enemies. *Everyone* has enemies, even covertly; in fact, they can be the most dangerous type.

'No other personal items with her except for the phone?'

'Just her house keys – no money, no handbag or purse. That's it.' She glances at me; pauses. 'Anyway, like I say, leave it with us and have a good time. With a bit of luck, she'll be home by the time you reach... Where is it you're off to again?'

'Sandbanks, and thank you, ma'am.' I nod, turn to leave. 'I'll do my best.'

I try – I swear I really do – not to ask the question as I open the door to exit her office. In my head, I'm halfway home, already singing 'Oh I do Like to Be Beside the Seaside', albeit off key, but it's already slipped from my lips before I have time to consider the possible outcome of being in possession of the answer. 'What's the address?' I ask. 'Just out of interest...'

FOUR

Gabriel Bonneville looks at once hopeful then crestfallen as he swings open the front door. I assume this must be because he's expecting us to have found his wife already and, therefore, don't take this lacklustre greeting too personally.

'Gabriel Bonneville? Dr Gabriel Bonneville?'

'Yes.' His voice is calm, but his expression betrays him. He looks washed out with worry.

'DCI Dan Riley.' I flash him my credentials.

'Detective *Chief* Inspector?'

'Can I come in?'

'Of course.' He steps aside from the door. 'Please...'

Money: it's the first word that comes to mind the moment I enter the huge open-plan pristinely furnished apartment – these people must have lots of it.

'*Gov*?' Lucy Davis blinks at me like I'm an apparition. 'What are *you* doing here? Shouldn't you be...? I thought you were...?'

'I was... I am. But I thought I'd swing by, see how much you're missing me already. Is Parker here with you?' I glance over her shoulder.

'I thought you'd be on the motorway by now – you, Fiona and the kids...'

I check my watch. It's 1.23 p.m. Technically, I'm not even late yet.

'Gabe, this is my boss.'

He shakes my hand solidly, a reassuring start.

Dr Gabriel Bonneville is, I'd say at a guess, in his early forties, a similar age to myself. Tall, slim but well built, with a full head of dark curly hair, he's a striking-looking individual with bright-blue eyes and an instantly easy, approachable demeanour. Looks a little on the youngish side to be a consultant cardiologist though, which makes me think he must be exemplary at his job.

'Boss?' Parker hurries over. 'I thought you were—'

'I am,' I sigh. 'I just wanted to drop by and speak to Mr Bonneville here – find out exactly what's been happening.'

'Please... it's Gabe,' he says, 'and I'm sorry to have had to bring everyone out like this. It's just that with Purdy being on the doorstep and... well, it's freezing out, and she wasn't wearing particularly warm clothing when she left, and her bag and car's still here, and her phone's just ringing out, and she hasn't replied to any of my texts... We had a lunch date booked today at 1.15 p.m., and she'd definitely have called me if she couldn't make it and... and I just don't know. *I can't think where she's got to.*' He's talking quickly though his tone is soft, almost apologetic. 'I thought... I *hoped* that maybe you were her, at the door.'

I nod, somewhat apologetic myself.

'You did the right thing by calling us when you did. The sooner we can look into this, the sooner we can get to the bottom of it, OK? Perhaps you can sit down?' I say. 'I'd just like a quick word with my colleagues before we have a chat, if that's OK with you?'

He manages a cursory smile as I pull Davis to one side.

'So...?'

Davis's body language isn't exactly filling me with confidence. I can tell by her micro mannerisms, the way she's gently swaying, distributing her weight from one foot to another. I've seen her do this before: she's spooked.

'I dunno, gov,' she says. 'Something's not right...'

I'm suddenly aware of a dog – a tiny chocolate-brown dachshund – down at my feet. I'm wearing my 'civvies' as we say, and the dog, somewhat bravely, starts sniffing at the embarrassingly ancient Adidas trainers I'm wearing.

'This him then – the dog that was found on the doorstep when he got home?'

'Yes,' Davis says.

I bend down and tickle its head.

'Purdy... and he's a she. He found her when he came home around 11.15 this morning with no lead... and no wife.'

'Hmm...' It's the dog part I'm struggling with the most. People treat their dogs like their children; no one loses their dog without raising the alarm – or their wife, come to mention it.

'He says Darcie left here at around 7.30 a.m. and she's usually home somewhere between 8.15 a.m. and 8.30 a.m. tops. He's out playing golf with a pal down at Dunstain Green. Left a little while after her, around 7.50 a.m., and took the car – his own. Hers is still on the driveway.'

'The Evoque? The white one outside?'

'Uh-huh.'

'So he says he returned home around 11.15 a.m. and found the dog on the doorstep – and no sign of Darcie. He tried calling, but her phone's ringing out. He thought about going down to the woods to look for her but was reluctant to leave in case she'd lost her keys or something and returned home while he was out searching for her. He left it a little while longer, then he called 999.'

'Could she have returned home and then left the house again to go somewhere else before he came back? Anything from the initial search of the apartment? One has been done, hasn't it?'

'Uniform gave the place the once-over when they got the call-out before radioing it in, and it's possible, gov, but her handbag is still here and her purse is in it, her driving licence, and husband says her passport's here... and none of her clothes or any personal items are missing either apparently.'

'And they were on good terms when she left – no argument, nothing like that?'

'Not so he says...'

'History of depression – is she on any medication?' I'm glancing around the apartment as I speak, looking for anything that jumps out at me. The place is spotless though, not even a cushion out of place.

She shakes her head.

'He swears she'd never leave the dog unattended and off the lead. She loves it like a child apparently.'

See.

'Speaking of which, no kids?'

'Nope, "not yet" so he says, which suggests that may be on the cards.'

I nod; try and filter through the thousand thoughts that seem to rush me all at once, myriad possibilities and explanations as to where Darcie Bonneville could've got to. Statistically, most mispers leave of their own accord and turn up of their own volition, and I'm sincerely hoping Mrs Bonneville will be one of them. But right now, I have what can only be described as 'the wiggies'. Davis's right about something not being right.

'And he's called round family and friends, colleagues, hospitals... What about social media?'

'She doesn't have any social media apparently.'

'OK.'

'That doesn't strike you as a bit odd, gov? Someone her age who has no online presence whatsoever?'

'Perhaps...'

I'm cautious about making assumptions or jumping to conclusions at this stage, despite my intuition doing the samba inside me. 'Right,' I say, bracing myself. 'Best we get on with it then.'

'*We?*' She pulls her chin into her neck. 'But I thought you were on leave, gov? That you and Fiona and the kids were all going away together and—'

'I am. We are,' I repeat. 'OK, you and Parker stay here and do another search of the property. Check for any diaries, address books, letters... recce the cars – both of them – see if we can't find something that might give us a clue as to her whereabouts.'

Davis nods. 'Gov. And where are *you* going?'

'To check the woods. I'll take the husband with me – see if we can retrace her steps this morning. She could've had an accident, fallen; maybe she's incapacitated, smashed her phone in the fall...'

FIVE

'So, this is her usual route, is it – the one she took this morning?'
I ask Gabe Bonneville as we walk with purpose in a northerly
direction from his apartment.

'Yes, as far as I know anyway,' he replies. 'She would've
walked down this road, crossed over and then taken the
pathway that leads directly into the woods.' He takes his
phone from his coat pocket and makes a call, I assume to his
wife.

'Still ringing out?'

He nods, looking pensive as he replaces it in his pocket.

'You've lived here long? It's a beautiful place,' I remark,
admiring the impressive residences that sit either side of the
tree-lined avenue, their majestic stucco fronts and perfectly
manicured box trees screaming wealth and status.

'No, not really, not in the grand scheme of things,' he says.
'Five months or so – we moved late last summer... August. It
was such a hot day, the pair of us were a sweaty mess by the end
of it.' The memory makes him smile. 'Total contrast to now.' He
wraps his coat tightly around him as though to demonstrate.
'Something's happened to her, hasn't it? I know that's why

they've sent a DCI... You think something's happened to her, and frankly, so do I.'

'Let's just take one step at a time, OK?' I say diplomatically, not wishing to compound his fears. But it's patently obvious Gabe Bonneville isn't a fool. He's a doctor after all, a man of some regard, of professional status; a man who often deals with having to impart harsh realities himself I should imagine.

Doctors are generally considered trustworthy individuals by default. It goes with the territory: *Trust me, I'm a doctor.* I suppose the same could be said of my own profession, only I trust *no one.* Years on the job have taught me not to, whatever a person's status or profession. Doctors can – and do – commit crimes, as do coppers, judges, teachers, clergymen... No one is exempt from the dark side of human nature. Trusting someone on the merit of what they do for a living alone may be a natural inclination but an unwise one in my experience. And the reason we look at spouses first in a situation such as this is a valid one, statistically at least.

'She'll have been picked up by cameras,' I say in a bid to reassure him, noting that almost all the residences along Colville Terrace have them. 'She'll have been seen.'

He nods silently again, staring straight ahead.

'Try not to panic. In my experience, there's almost always a perfectly rational explanation, and she'll most likely turn up at some point, unharmed.' Statistically speaking again, this is also true, and yet as my words hit the ether, they seem to instantly evaporate, like they hold no weight whatsoever. 'I take it you have CCTV at your address?'

He nods. 'Yes. It was already installed when we – when she – bought the place.'

'Your wife... she bought the apartment?'

'Well, it's in our joint names, but yes, she bought it.' He pauses briefly, adding, 'With an inheritance she recently received.'

My ears prick up. 'A substantial amount of money?' I'm guessing so, if their show-home apartment is any benchmark.

'Yeah actually – it was a little shy of four million.'

Instinctively – and despite myself – I give a little whistle.

'Ah well, yes, that *is* pretty substantial. How long ago was that, when she inherited this money?'

'It was just before I met her I think, around three years ago. She didn't actually tell me about it until we were... well, until things got serious, although to be fair, they were always serious with me and Darc, right from the get-go.'

'I see...'

He turns to me then and exhales, his warm breath meeting the cold air like smoke.

'And before you think it, I wasn't with her for money. I was, am, financially secure myself. I was well established in my career when we met. I certainly didn't – don't – need her money.'

'I wasn't suggesting—'

He raises a hand as though to stop me. 'Please... it's fine. I'm sure it would cross most people's minds, to be fair. "What first attracted you to the millionaire Darcie Vernier?"' He flashes a thin, self-deprecating smile. 'But I had no idea about her financial situation at the time, not when we first met anyway. We both had our own homes and swung between the two for the first few months of dating. When we made the leap to move in together, she sold her place and we – she – bought the apartment on Colville Terrace – insisted on it. I sold my place a few months ago, and we're planning to use the proceeds to buy a holiday home in Italy together later this year. We've already started looking. Darc loves Italy. She spent some time there as a kid... learned the language. She speaks fluent French too – her mother was French – and her Spanish is also pretty good.'

'Her mother's dead – is that right?' I ask.

'Yes. Darcie...' He looks down at the ground as we walk. 'She, um... well, I think they were estranged.'

He *thinks* they were estranged? He doesn't *know*?

'Oh?'

I pose my answer as a question, but he doesn't bite, and I decide now isn't the best time to push, decide it's best to focus on trying to find her first and foremost before I start excavating through the family ruins, but I do know one thing: money is the biggest motivator in almost all major crimes – *crimes such as murder.*

There's still the lightest dusting of frost on the ground as we enter the woods, the edges of the leaves crunching underfoot as I let Gabe Bonneville show me the direction he believes his wife took on her walk this morning. I count two other dog walkers passing us as we continue along the path. A good sign – someone will have surely seen her.

'She – we – sometimes went a bit off-piste,' he says, 'off the beaten track so to speak.' He's forging ahead, pulling back branches with his hands as we navigate our way through. 'Purdy is quite the little explorer. The deeper in she goes, the more she likes it. This leads to a clearing I think,' he says, stopping momentarily and looking around to get his bearings. 'Just a little further.'

'Did you stay on the golf course all morning? You didn't come home for any reason, forget something, pop back to the apartment?'

He has his back to me, stops, turns around.

'No, I was at Dunstain Green golf course all morning. I left Matt, my colleague, around 10.50 a.m.'

'How long have you and Darcie been married?'

'Eighteen months next week,' he says proudly.

I smile; nod. That's what Archer told me. 'And you say you've been together for three years?'

'Yes... It's funny, but I knew she was the one the moment I

clapped eyes on her. Don't ask me how. I know it sounds corny, but I just knew, you know?'

Actually, I do. I felt exactly the same when I first met Rachel, my former fiancée, who was killed in a motorcycle accident – incidentally while carrying a tiny embryo inside her that I'd helped to make.

'Yes,' I say, deciding not to elaborate. Rachel is dead and I don't want to tell him that.

'Darcie – she doesn't work?' I don't suppose she needs to with a good few million in the bank.

He shakes his head. 'She says she loves being a stay-at-home wife – enjoys being a homemaker, for now at least. I know,' he says, as though he feels the need to explain, 'it's not exactly considered cool anymore is it, for a woman to want to devote her time to her husband and home, but she is actually – very cool I mean. She's the most incredible woman I've ever met...' His voice trails off thoughtfully as we approach a small clearing.

'You can actually get to this area via the long route,' he explains. 'The path does lead to it eventually, but we always took the cut-through across woodland. It's a bit tricky, as you've seen, but Purdy loves coming up this way, like I said...'

I look around me. It's not a particularly big clearing, and I can see the path that leads out of it to my right in the near distance. It's sheltered by trees, peaceful, quiet, and there's a small makeshift bench fashioned out of planks of gnarly old wood.

'And she definitely would've come this way?'

'Absolutely – every day practically. She knows these woods well.'

I look at the ground around me, my eyes searching for something, anything. I'm not yet sure what. 'And she would've taken that pathway out again?'

He nods. 'It leads back round, like a ring road – it takes you back up to the road on the other side eventually. It's about a fifteen–twenty-minute round trip from our apartment all told.'

'Call her phone,' I say. 'Try her again.'

He duly retrieves his phone from his pocket and presses it and... I hear something. My senses sharpened, I crouch down instinctively and edge forward, attempting to follow the direction of the sound's provenance.

'Oh my God!' he gasps. 'Her phone! It's ringing!'

I drop to my knees and start scrabbling around in the brush and leaves, following the sound until... I reach for it; take it in my hand carefully, mindful of contaminating any potential evidence – *a phone*. Inspecting it, I can see that the screen is cracked, though it's clearly still working, and there's something on it, splashes flecked across the shattered glass. I feel my heart plummet.

It looks like blood.

SIX

DARCIE – SIX MONTHS AGO

The young receptionist shoots me a formulaic smile as I tentatively approach the desk.

'You're a little early,' she says sniffily as she gestures for me to take a seat in one of the plush cream leather chairs. 'Dr Carmichael will see you as soon as she's able.'

It was Anita who'd given me Dr Elizabeth Carmichael's details, practically insisting I make an appointment to see her at her swanky clinic in Mayfair.

I'd recently made the grave error of casually mentioning to her over an oatmeal chai latte (hers; I had a regular flat white with full-fat milk, much to her dismay) that I suffer from claustrophobia, which had sparked a personal crusade for her – she'd insisted on getting me fixed via £250-an-hour therapy, even though I hadn't asked her to. It was the perfect example of why I like to keep people at a distance. Particularly when that person once slept with my husband – not that Anita and I have ever discussed this common denominator, despite it being an open secret.

I suppose part of me *is* curious to know all the 'gory' details of her and Gabe's historic 'romance' back when they were students, but I wouldn't want to come across as jealous or insecure, even if I am a little. Besides, I know what curiosity does to cats.

'I'm surprised you haven't been to see her already,' Anita said as she handed me a sleek black embossed business card with the name Dr Elizabeth Carmichael written on it in florid gold type. 'All the celebs go to her to get themselves fixed, and she's often on TV, on all those true-crime programmes, you know? Actually, now I think of it, I'm sure she mentioned... Haven't you two already met?'

'No,' I said quickly, concern lightly prickling my skin. *Can Anita tell just by looking at me that I'm a basket case who needs to get themselves 'fixed'?*

'Well, she's an absolute *miracle* worker – best therapist I've ever seen. She cured my social anxiety in one session,' she gushed, though I found it difficult to believe someone as gregarious as Anita could have ever suffered with such an impediment; after all, this is a woman who gave out 'wedding scent' as favours when she got married to Hugh – bespoke perfume in tiny bottles so that her guests could spray it and 'be reminded of our special day for the rest of their lives'.

I take a swig of the bottled water I've just helped myself to from the cooler, my left leg swinging manically over my right, and notice a man sitting on the cream couch opposite me. Unwittingly, I briefly make eye contact, which seems to give him the green light to start a conversation. *Brilliant.*

'You look nervous,' he says, cocking his head to the side. 'This your first time?'

'No,' I reply, 'I've been nervous plenty of times before.'

He blinks at me, my attempt at humour clearly lost on him. I hadn't meant to be facetious, but when I get nervous, I often overcompensate with lame jokes.

'You won't regret it.' He looks at me, leans forward conspiratorially and places his hands on his knees. I notice that his fingernails have a crescent of grime under them. 'That lady in there' – he points to a door behind me marked by a gold plaque that reads 'Dr Elizabeth Carmichael' with a string of letters following it – 'she saved my life.' He sits back in his seat, seemingly satisfied with having made such a dramatic claim. 'I've been coming here for years now – same day, same time every week. I don't know what, or where, I'd be without her...' He pauses thoughtfully, adding, 'Probably in prison actually – that or an institution somewhere.'

I give a little nervous laugh in response, but then I catch his (lack of) expression and it hits me that maybe he's not joking. I take another sip of water, and decide it's best to stay silent and not encourage him. I've never been one for small talk, but I can tell, as I pretend to read something on my phone, that he's still staring at me intently.

'I'm sure I've seen you somewhere before,' he pipes up after a moment, narrowing his eyes at me. 'You look really... familiar.'

'One of those faces.' I smile politely, go back to my pretend reading.

'No, you really do look familiar. I've *seen* you...' He practically leaps up from his seat. 'You're *her,* aren't you? The one on the news – the one who saved little Dolly from being hit by a car down on the high street a few weeks ago? Oh WOW! It's really you, isn't it?'

I feel myself deflate.

'You have a good memory for faces,' I say, smiling reluctantly. It's been a couple of months since that incident outside the pharmacy whereby my instinctive act of 'bravery' had grudgingly catapulted me into the media spotlight.

'Couldn't forget a face like yours,' he says, beaming, causing my heart to further plummet. If a perfect stranger can recognise me after a few seconds of some grainy teenager's uploaded phone footage then who else might've?

'I've watched that clip hundreds, maybe thousands of times,' he says, animated. 'Those few seconds when you think the car is going to hit Dolly and then you... You didn't hesitate, not even for a split second, just threw yourself right into the oncoming car.' He shakes his head in awe. 'So, *so* brave. No wonder Shannon publicly thanked you like she did – you saved her daughter's life. Dolly wouldn't be here today if it wasn't for you.'

Shannon Taylor – who I'd later learned was Dolly's mum – was, admittedly, and I suppose understandably, extremely grateful to me for my 'selfless' act that day and had gone on camera to say as much. She also hadn't left me alone. In tandem with the media, she'd continually contacted me in the weeks that had followed, requesting we give joint interviews to the press.

'*OK* magazine wanna do a shoot with all of us together, you, me and Dolls! OK *magazine*! Can you believe it? They said they'll pay us a grand – *each*!' she'd squealed down the phone, unable to contain her excitement. 'And they want us to go on breakfast telly with *Lorraine*! Like, *oh. My. God*! We'll be celebrities!' She could barely get the words out of her mouth through her excitement. 'I've already had one of them agents on the phone asking to represent me – *me*! He says we need to strike while the iron's hot and while it's fresh still on everyone's lips – reckons if we play our cards right, we could come out of this with all sorts: endorsements, hundreds of thousands of Insta followers... I could become one of them content creators, get loads of free stuff and holidays! Maybe I could end up on some reality TV show – how *insane* would that be?'

Well, she wasn't wrong about the last part – it was insane, and she was insane if she thought I'd go along with any of it. It was my idea of hell. *Not to mention potentially dangerous.* I'd thanked Shannon graciously, explained I wasn't interested in any kind of media attention, that I neither wanted nor needed the exposure or money, and that as glad as I was that Dolly was alive and unharmed, I just wanted to forget about it and move on. I suppose I'd felt a little guilty, refusing her requests, but I just couldn't risk drawing any more attention to myself. Shannon, however, wasn't taking no for an answer. She'd left countless messages begging me to reconsider. At first they'd been pleading, attempts at guilt-tripping me into acquiescing, but met with no response, they'd soon taken on a more forceful tone.

'This could be my chance of pulling myself out of the gutter, getting off Universal Credit and building a better life for me and Dolls... *You* might not need the money, living in that big house of yours with your fancy husband, but I'm a single mum, struggling on benefits, and her dad ain't paid me a penny in child maintenance since the day she were born... 'S'all right for the likes of you, ain't it?'

I'd been forced to block her number in the end, though I didn't feel good about it.

'I sent her a message, you know,' the man sitting opposite me says. 'Dolly's mum, Shannon. I wrote to her saying how happy I was that Dolly was unharmed, and how I sometimes see her on the high street, pushing her in her stroller,' he adds.

'That's nice,' I reply with another cursory smile as I look over at Dr Carmichael's office, willing my name to be called. This conversation is really causing my anxiety to double down.

Dr Elizabeth Carmichael is by all accounts a highly respected eminent psychologist, psychiatrist and hypnotherapist. Her slick website – which I'd duly googled – had read as an homage to her many accolades and professional successes, plus a detailed summary of her TV appearances and a nod to her notoriety in having assisted folk of the famous variety. Naïvely, it hadn't occurred to me until now that she might also work with people with serious mental-health issues, maybe even dangerous criminals – or that I may be sitting opposite one as I wait my turn to see her.

'I'm John by the way... John Evergreen – you know, like the Christmas tree?' He leans forward, offering me his hand, and I tentatively shake it, trying not to think about where it might've been.

'Nice to meet you, John.' I don't tell him my name and hope he won't ask.

'What time is your appointment with Dr Carmichael?'

'Eleven,' I say reluctantly. 'I'm a little early – wasn't quite sure how to find the place, so I–' I stop mid-sentence – I'm overexplaining myself.

'*My* appointment isn't until 1.30 p.m.'

Instinctively, I glance at the clock again. He's a little shy of being three hours early, which strikes me as somewhat odd.

'Oh?' I nod politely and think about picking up the glossy black-and-white coffee-table book in front of me and flicking through it to avoid having to continue the conversation but decide against it – it would be obvious, and besides, it looks a bit cumbersome.

'I just like to be *near* her, you see – Dr Carmichael. It makes me feel *safe*,' he says sagely.

Unsure of how to respond, I smile and sip my water. I'm nervous enough as it is without this off-key exchange on top of it.

'You'll understand what I mean once you've seen her,' he continues, gazing up at the door with the plaque on it. 'She's... Well, you'll see,' he says again.

'Mrs Bonneville? Darcie Bonneville?' The snotty receptionist finally calls my name.

'Yes!' I quickly stand, almost dropping my water with the haste.

'If you'd like to come this way...'

'Right. Thanks.' I take a deep breath. 'Nice to meet you, John,' I say out of politeness.

He nods at me, gives me a strange sort of knowing wink. 'TTFN, Darcie.'

SEVEN

DAN

'Who is Darcie Bonneville?' I address the team in front of me rhetorically. 'What do we know about her so far? Well, we know that she's a thirty-seven-year-old female who lives at 8 Colville Terrace with her husband, Gabriel Bonneville, a consultant cardiologist at St Catherine's Hospital, and that she went out this morning at around 7.30 a.m. to walk her dog in Ravens Wood' – I pause as I stand – 'and hasn't returned home.

'We also know that her concerned husband reported her missing at around midday after he returned home somewhere around 11.15 a.m. from playing a game of golf with a colleague to find the dog on the doorstep with no lead – and no sign of his wife – and there's been no contact since. Preliminary checks have thrown nothing up from local hospitals, and nothing as yet from any friends or family – of which I believe she doesn't have many – who may have heard from her or know where she is, though moving forward, this area will need to be investigated much more thoroughly.' I nod at Davis to continue.

'This is the most recent photo of Darcie,' she says, distributing photocopies out to our colleagues. 'It was taken about eighteen months ago, at her wedding.'

Interestingly, Gabe Bonneville had mentioned to me that his wife 'really disliked' having her picture taken. I'm not sure why this resonated with me. After all, I'm hardly a fan of a close-up myself, some might say for obvious reasons, but it's a fair observation that Darcie Bonneville is a strikingly attractive and photogenic woman. With long, almost black hair cascading past her shoulders in gentle waves, she has a slightly exotic look about her, a face you might not easily forget if you'd seen it. While she appears relaxed and happy in the photo, on the surface at least, I sense something behind her smile, something I can't quite put my finger on, a certain vulnerability perhaps.

'She's five foot two, weighs around 50kg – she's a tiny, petite woman. No tattoos, no distinguishing marks...'

Davis picks up seamlessly where I left off. 'And she was wearing black leggings and a black Nike running jacket with black Balenciaga trainers when she disappeared.'

'Gov?' Harding, one of my more vigilant DCs, raises a hand. 'How can we be sure she hasn't simply gone AWOL of her own accord?'

I take a much needed breath. The truth is, as yet, we can't be, not a hundred per cent anyway, but from the moment Archer mentioned this potential misper to me this morning, I had an intuitive gut reaction that something was – is – horribly wrong. And my intuition is something I've come to rely upon in my years of being a detective. If something doesn't feel right, it's usually because it isn't, and while my profession arguably makes you a more suspicious person, it also makes, or certainly should make, you a sound judge of your own judgement.

Given the circumstances – Darcie's supposedly out-of-character behaviour – and then finding her phone in the woods with what looked like bloodstains on it had only compounded those suspicions, ergo I'd immediately, and instinctively, called Archer and upgraded it to a code-red situation – a possible abduction – especially given what Gabe Bonneville had mentioned about her fairly recent and substantial inheritance. Better to suspect the worst and be surprised by the best rather than the other way round.

'It is possible,' I agree, because technically it is. 'But myself and Gabe Bonneville did a cursory search of the woods, of the route he claims his wife would've taken, and we discovered her phone, seemingly abandoned, with what looked like blood on it. It's with forensics now – we need clarity on those bloodstains, and who they may potentially have come from – and I've requested a fast track on it. But moreover, according to her husband, Darcie would absolutely never have left the dog alone or let him off the lead – he was adamant about this – and they were supposed to be going to lunch together today; he'd booked a table at her favourite restaurant, which she was by all accounts looking forward to, and, I'm sure you'll all agree, these don't appear to be the actions of someone who planned to go off-grid.'

'Well, unless she wanted it to look that way...' DC Mitchell, another tenacious member of my dynamic team throws some shade into the mix. 'Maybe he's lying, the husband – hey, it wouldn't be a first – and they've had a row and she's stormed off, or had an accident, hence the dog being off lead and making its own way home?'

Mitchell is right to play devil's advocate like this, to question everything and everyone, explore possible alternative scenarios, but I know I'm right about this one. *Something* has gone down. I can feel it as sure as there's calcium in my bones. And of course she's also right to suspect the husband, because statistically she'd be wrong not to. Yet, personally, witnessing Dr Bonneville's reactions as they unfolded in real time, I heard none of the usual alarm bells I've come to listen out for. Aside from his alibi, which we will of course thoroughly check, I got the genuine impression he was – is – as perplexed and concerned as anyone as to his wife's whereabouts. That or he's a very accomplished actor.

'It's possible, Mitchell,' I agree. 'But put together with the fact that she left her apartment with just a set of keys and her phone, wearing little to combat the cold – again, suggesting she had no intention of staying outside for any great length of time... Then there's the dog of course – him turning up alone on the doorstep – *and* the fact that there had, according to Gabe Bonneville, been no prior incident, no argument, no history of any mental-health issues or depression and nothing amiss. It's all cause for serious concern.' I pause again. 'I think we could be looking at foul play here, folks.'

'She,' Davis says. 'The dog is a *she*, gov.'

I grimace at her. She's nit-picking, but I guess I created the monster. I'm constantly reminding her that, 'It's always the little things.'

'Perhaps the dog identifies as a different gender?' an unexpected yet familiar voice pipes up from the back of the room, and my heart sinks like the *Titanic* when I raise my head to see who it's come from.

Martin Delaney. And so the day continues to give.

I've worked with Delaney on a couple of past homicide cases – the Goldilocks Murders being a memorable one – and he's one of those rare people I found myself taking an instant dislike to without really being able to explain why, although the fact I found him to be an arrogant, often unhelpful and uncompromising sort of person, who, while clearly a competent copper, made no secret of how highly he thought of himself, did nothing to help me warm to him. Incidentally, he also once had a fling with Davis – whose face, I notice, is now an absolute picture.

'DS Delaney!' I nod in his direction; force a cursory smile. 'Great to have you on board, Martin.'

'Good to be here, *Dan*,' he replies with cocksure familiarity. 'And it's DI now,' he adds.

Mildly irked as I am by his presence, now isn't the time to

allow personal feelings into the mix. I'll deal with Delaney as and when I need to. Right now, we have a missing woman to locate and this is the all-important golden period.

I return to addressing my team. 'Gabe Bonneville has informed us that his wife fairly recently received a hefty inheritance, somewhere in the region of four million.' Eyebrows are, unsurprisingly, raised when I impart this nugget of information. 'We could be dealing with a kidnapping, someone looking to extort her; extort both the Bonnevilles perhaps.'

'Four million...' DS Baylis says with a whistle. 'I mean, that's a lot of money by most people's standards, boss, but if you look at where she lives, some of those gaffs up there are worth five times that amount. You've got celebrities, oil tycoons, politicians... She's pretty much small fry in comparison to some of the other residents. So why her?'

Baylis has asked the million-pound question – or four million in this case – because she's absolutely right. The Bonnevilles, while I would hardly sniff at their kind of wealth, aren't the hardest financial hitters in the area they live, or even the street they live on. So, coming from the standpoint of a kidnapping for extortion, why indeed choose her?

I shrug. 'Opportunity? Small-time criminals on a maiden voyage? A personal vendetta? Someone stalking her, a disgruntled ex...?'

Truth is though, when it comes to money, even a relatively paltry amount, it no longer shocks me what lengths people will go to get their hands on it, even abducting and killing for it. I've seen what it does to people – how they're driven by greed, or sometimes need, to harm, scam, extort, steal, maim and even kill, just to gain financially. I've seen money turn husbands against wives, mothers against sons and literally every combination in between. I've seen it corrupt, destroy and drive good people to do heinous things, to abandon their morals and shed their integrity like skin. The power of money as motive cannot, and should not, be under-estimated.

'So,' I say, addressing the team's eager faces once more, 'SOCO and forensics are down at Ravens Wood as we speak. In the meantime, let's start digging into Darcie Bonneville's back-story – find out who she is, where she goes, who she's friends with, anything from her past of interest, anyone she might've upset – an ex-partner or colleague, a stalker... Similarly, we'll need to look into Dr Bonneville's affairs. A disgruntled patient, a family member of someone who died and has held him rightly or wrongly responsible perhaps... someone with a vendetta against her, him or even both. We need to find motive, a reason for her absence.' I'm talking so fast I almost run out of breath.

'If she doesn't show up imminently, then we'll conduct a proper search of the house, get forensics in there, get hold of her computer, check her socials, phone data, car...' I nod sagely at Mitchell, because this is her remit. DC Mitchell is a Rottweiler when it comes to intelligence. She was born to do the job she does and is an asset to this department in particular.

She nods back with her usual efficiency.

'CCTV, security cameras, Ring doorbells... it's full of it up that way for obvious reasons, and the Bonnevilles also have it, so let's get looking through it pronto. Similarly, we might want to run ANPR checks, see if there was anyone up that way this morning that could give us any potential cause for concern. Parker!'

'Boss!' He sits up to attention; stops scribbling in his notebook.

'You do door to door – find out if there were any sightings of her this morning, any witnesses, any neighbours who may have seen her or seen something: someone behaving suspiciously, someone they didn't recognise in the area, didn't like the look of, *anything*.'

He nods enthusiastically. Parker is in the relatively early

phase of his career on homicide where he hasn't had the crap bashed out of him and is still enthusiastic about everything. Ah, the exuberance of youth!

'And maybe we should speak to whoever else was at the house the night before she went missing too, gov?' he says.

'What do you mean, Parker, whoever else?'

'The table, boss.' He blinks at me. 'I noticed there were four place settings still on the table when Davis and I first arrived at the address. It looked to me like they'd had guests the previous evening.'

Funny. Gabe Bonneville didn't mention anything about having guests over to me. I make to open my mouth to speak again, but the sound of my phone ringing interrupts me.

Oh shit! It's Fiona.

Caught up in the moment, I have – *I know, I know* – unbelievably, momentarily forgotten where I'm supposed to be. I look at the clock and would physically flinch if I didn't have an audience. It's 3.38 p.m. We should be en route to Sandbanks, and all of a sudden, on top of this horror, I'm mortifyingly aware that I'm standing here, addressing everyone in my civvies, wearing a pair of old faded Billabong tracksuit bottoms that may – or perhaps not – have once been trendy somewhere back in the nineties.

'And what can *I* do, gov?' Davis asks expectantly.

I look down at my phone then up at her with my best pleading eyes.

'Answer that for me, will you?'

EIGHT

DARCIE – SIX MONTHS AGO

'Ah! Mrs Bonneville – Darcie. I can call you Darcie, can I? Come in. Sit down.'

Dr Carmichael's office looks more like a five-star hotel's lobby than I'd imagined a shrink's office would look, with large soft-looking squishy couches and cushions, a Persian rug and a sparklingly clean glass coffee table, replete with a vase of huge white hydrangeas, scented Jo Malone candles, books and...

A sudden chill runs through me as I spot it. There, sitting on a shelf next to some abstract artwork on the wall, its porcelain-white skin juxtaposed against its vacant black eyes... *a doll.* It seems incongruous somehow, so out of place with the rest of the decor. I stare at it, momentarily paralysed.

'Thank you,' I say, finally managing to avert my eyes from its creepy little face.

Dr Carmichael is as attractive in the flesh than she appears in the airbrushed photographs on her slick website. Her immaculately styled strawberry-blonde hair falls just at her shoulders, and she's wearing a soft pink silk blouse, the open buttons modestly stopping just short of displaying cleavage. The gold jewellery – a chunky necklace and ring (no wedding band I notice) – give off an air of understated wealth. I can smell her perfume too, floral with a bottom note of vanilla, distinctive and distinguished, a bit like her I suppose – anyway, I quite like it. I don't know why, but she feels oddly familiar somehow, like we've met before. Perhaps I have seen her on TV after all, although I try to avoid watching all those true-crime programmes that are popular these days – too many potential triggers.

'I hope I didn't keep you waiting too long?' she says, moving round from her desk.

'No, no – it's fine. I was a little early anyway.'

She takes a seat opposite on one of the couches, close but not close enough for her to reach out and touch me, and I wonder if she senses that I prefer to keep a safe distance from people.

'I met your biggest fan in the waiting room,' I remark, largely out of nervousness and something to say.

'Oh?' She smooths out her long pleated maxi skirt.

'Yes – John, I think he said his name was. He spoke incredibly highly of you.'

I may be imagining it, but I'm sure her smile wanes.

'Ah yes, don't mind John,' she says lightly. 'I'm afraid he can be a bit... *overzealous* at times, but he's totally harmless.'

My eyes involuntarily wander back to the doll on the shelf behind her, and I force myself to look away.

'So, Darcie...' She looks down at some notes in her lap. 'Claustrophobia. That's right, isn't it? That's the reason you're here?'

In truth, my claustrophobia is little more than a ruse as to why I'm *really* here, and probably the least of my concerns to be fair. I'd used it as a legitimate reason when I'd made the initial appointment with the snotty receptionist. For years I'd successfully kept my past, ironically, locked away in a box inside me, but ever since I'd met Gabe, I'd been plagued by the need to finally open it, let the truth out. I desperately wanted a clean slate, and I wondered if, perhaps, keeping it all hidden away was, somehow, what was standing between me and a successful pregnancy, my dreams of becoming a mother and having a child with the man I love.

'Yes, I... Well... I'm sorry.' I clear my throat. 'It's my first time in therapy and I'm a little...'

'Nervous? Apprehensive? Of course you are. Frankly, I'd be concerned if you weren't.' She flashes me a warm smile. 'The most important thing is for you to know what you hope to get from our time together and how you believe we might best work in achieving that.

'I like to develop a rapport with all of my clients,' she says, 'create a space in which you feel emotionally safe and confident to express yourself, to be your most authentic self. And for the record, it's a formality that I remind all my clients that every-thing – *everything* – you say within the confines of this room is completely confidential. This is a safe space, OK?'

I'm nodding like a dog.

'Trust is important, Darcie – *mutual* trust,' she states, her unblinking eyes still firmly fixed upon me. 'I need you to be as honest with me as possible; transparent, truthful... or else you'll be wasting your time – and mine.'

She holds my gaze for what feels like an eternity.

'OK,' she says eventually, the lightness in her tone return-ing. 'Well, now that's out of the way, maybe you can start by telling me why you're *really* here?'

The question blindsides me. Is it really that obvious? I'm unprepared for this, because to answer her honestly, like she's insisting, I'm going to have to do something I'm really good at not doing – tell the truth.

'I...' I open my mouth to speak again, but it's like I've devel-oped lockjaw.

'Maybe let me ask you some general questions first,' she

says, clearly sensing my discomfort, 'before we get to the nitty-gritty so to speak.' She glances down at my left hand. 'I see that you're married.'

'Yes!' I say, relieved to be able to talk about my favourite subject. She's right though; I'll need to overcome my reticence if I'm to relieve myself of all these stagnant emotions, the residue of my former life. I'm terrified that if I don't release them, then they'll destroy the only truly beautiful thing that's ever happened to me, ruin the only relationship I've ever really valued and cared about *not* ruining. 'A little over a year ago actually.'

'Ah! Newly-weds! How wonderful!'

I beam back at her. 'It's the best thing I've ever done.' This, at least, isn't a lie.

'My husband's a doctor himself actually – a cardiologist. Works at St Cat's. He's amazing. He saves people's lives.' I sound like I'm bragging and don't even care if I am. I'm proud of my husband.

'And you...?'

'Me?' I point to myself, feeling self-conscious. 'No, I don't save people's lives, although...'

I'm on the pavement, the metallic taste of blood on my tongue, faces peering down at me as I regain consciousness and I see him there too, among them, those dark eyes and that crooked smile...

The flashback of that day outside the pharmacy comes at me with such clarity that I'm forced to take a breath and, instinctively, my eyes are once again drawn to the doll on the shelf.

Dr Carmichael briefly turns behind her. 'Ah, I see you've spotted my little friend! A gift from a client,' she explains. 'One with pediophobia I successfully cured.'

I try and look away, but my eyes are locked upon it once more.

'A fear of dolls and mannequins,' she explains. 'Terribly common really... and I meant, what do *you* do for a living?'

'Oh yes...' I manage to suppress the burning urge to take my jacket off and throw it over the doll's face so I won't have to look at it.

'Actually, right now, nothing.'

'You're a stay-at-home wife – and mother?'

'Yes. No. Yes and no. In that order. Though we're hoping to start a family soon – trying...'

'I see...' She starts taking notes.

'I recently inherited some money,' I say in a bid to explain my current lack of employment.

She raises her finely arched brow ever so slightly.

'Quite a lot in fact – from a family member...'

She nods. 'I'm sorry to hear of their passing.'

I nod, my eyes dropping instinctively to my lap. 'Thanks.'

She stares at me inquisitively, her head slightly cocked. 'It was a difficult relationship...?'

I'm astounded by her observation skills. I'm usually very competent at hiding my emotions outwardly. I've had considerable practice after all.

'Fabienne... she was called Fabienne.' It feels unsettling to say her name aloud. I can't remember the last time I did.

'And yes, it was.' I quietly exhale. This is already proving harder than I thought.

Dr Carmichael continues to make notes. 'So who is – who *was* – she, this Fabienne that left you all this money?'

She blinks at me, expectantly.

She's right. I've just got to go for it.

'My mother,' I say. 'Fabienne was my biological mother.'

NINE

'Tell me about her – your mother...'

I hadn't expected to get onto the subject of Fabienne quite so quickly in my first therapy session with Dr Carmichael, but all roads lead back to her, and she is, partly at least, the reason I'm here.

'What do you want to know?'

Dr Carmichael smiles enigmatically. 'Do you generally do that?'

'Do what?'

'Answer a question with a question.'

'Do I?' I pull my chin into my chest, realising I have, embarrassingly, perfectly illustrated her point.

She smiles. 'But to answer *your* question... Whatever you want to tell me, Darcie.' She shrugs – waits for me to speak.

When I don't – can't – she says, 'OK, let's start with why you refer to your mother by her first name perhaps?'

Well, that's an easy one to answer at least.

'She said the word made her feel "*mal fagoté*" – it's French for "frumpy",' I explain, hoping I don't sound condescending – this woman's got half the alphabet after her name after all. 'Fabienne was French, as you've probably guessed. Technically speaking, so am I, in as much as I was born in Paris. Fabienne always told people that she was Parisian, but she was actually from a small village in Marseille. She thought it made her sound more chic by saying she was Parisian.'

'To who?'

'The second-biggest love in her life – men.'

'The *second* biggest?' Dr Carmichael looks intrigued. 'What was the first?'

'Money,' I say without hesitation. 'Fabienne never had relationships with anyone she couldn't or wouldn't benefit from in some fiscal capacity.'

'Including your father?'

This feels like it's all happening way too quickly, and I begin pulling at strands of my hair, another nasty little habit born of anxiety.

Dr Carmichael must be able to read my expression though because she says, 'Fabienne never told you who your father was?'

'Yes actually,' I say, 'often. Sometimes he was a painter, at other times an actor or an academic... On another day he could be a writer, maybe a soldier, or an aristocrat... Oh, and he was even a famous stuntman at one time, if I recall.' Suddenly, I find myself wanting to burst out laughing – it sounds so absurd. 'I think Fabienne was incapable of telling the truth about anything, even to herself.' My head suddenly drops into my hands before I can stop it. 'Perhaps *la pomme ne tombe pas loin de l'arbre* after all...'

Dr Carmichael's left eyebrow twitches slightly. 'The apple doesn't fall far from the tree? You're concerned that you're like your mother?'

I swallow the emotion I feel rising inside me; try to force it back down my oesophagus. I shake my head, only I'm not being entirely truthful when I do because I *am* worried that part – or parts – of me are like her. And it terrifies me.

'Fabienne was ostensibly a con woman and a thief. She started her criminal career as a pickpocket and shoplifter, and she was exceptionally skilled at it. As a young child, I don't recall her ever paying for all the lovely clothes and jewellery she used to wear – and dressed me in too.'

I wait for Dr Carmichael to say something in response to this, but she doesn't.

'She had this innate ability to sniff out men with money and instinctively sense a person's vulnerabilities. Honestly,' I say, gathering rhythm, 'it was a real talent, some might say a gift even, and it was quite something to watch up close. She was a master manipulator.'

I audibly exhale, try to get my breathing back on track – it's sped up a little. 'Fabienne's currency was her looks, and she traded on them heavily, used them to get whatever it was she wanted at that given moment. She was exceptionally smart, well read, entertaining and devastatingly beautiful. As a child, she told me that she could've been a model in Paris if she'd wanted to, but instead...'

It strikes me that although I've been here in Dr Carmichael's office for less than a few minutes, it's probably the most I've *ever* spoken about Fabienne to *anyone*, at least so candidly. Maybe Anita is right and Dr Carmichael *will* change my life.

'Instead...?' Dr Carmichael prompts me.

'Instead she chose to drag me around from place to place and "Papa" to "Papa". As a child, I had no real home, no real roots and no real friends.'

The compulsion to start pulling my hair out again is so strong I feel I may have to sit on my hands to get them to behave.

Dr Carmichael looks up from her notebook, and I watch as

she slides her fingers up and down the gold pen she's holding, turning it upside down then repeating the process as she fixes her eyes upon me.

'She was just eighteen when I was born. I think I was probably a mistake that couldn't be erased in time,' I say. 'So, like many people's mistakes, I was brushed under the carpet.'

'And is this also what you do with your own mistakes, Darcie – brush them under the carpet?' She stares at me, unblinking. 'We learn by example after all, though we often have to learn the hard way.'

Dr Carmichael's comment triggers me, reminding me of something *he* said...

'You'll have to learn the hard way, Darcie.'

I feel my pulse immediately quicken, and my eyes find that horrible doll on the shelf behind her again. I screw them shut; look away.

'Are you OK, Darcie?' Dr Carmichael cocks her head to the side. 'I can see how difficult this is for you to talk about...'

I will the flashback to pass and try to reroute myself back on topic.

'Fabienne had been married – and divorced – three times before I'd reached my twelfth birthday.' I gather myself a little. 'By this time, we'd lived in many different countries – France of course, all over the UK and Europe, Dubai... We even spent time in Russia for a bit. God' – I snort – 'it almost sounds impressive when I reel it off like that.'

'And was it?' she asks. 'Impressive?'

'No.' My laughter seems to be getting louder, a touch manic perhaps. 'No, it was miserable actually. We were never really anywhere long enough for me to make lasting friendships, and I learned pretty fast how painful it would be for me to say goodbye if I did.'

'That must've been tough on you as a child, a lonely exis-

tence I should imagine?' Dr Carmichael's voice softens at the
edges.

She doesn't know the half of it. I blink back tears. Pity
always undoes me.

'Fabienne deliberately targeted rich men,' I continue, 'and
she left most of them devastated in her wake, be it financially or
emotionally, usually both. She conned people into loving her –
not that it was especially hard – she was exceptionally charming
when it suited, seductive, a chameleon who changed her colours
to fit. I feel as if I never really knew who she truly was. Maybe
she didn't know herself.'

I glance at Dr Carmichael, but her expression is unreadable.
Maybe my dysfunctional childhood isn't particularly shocking
to her at the end of the day. *Only I haven't even scratched the
surface yet.*

'None of them worked out, these relationships that your
mother pursued with rich men?'

I shrug. 'Some stories lasted longer than others, but the
endings were always the same. Fabienne would seek out another
sucker and work her magic. The grooming would begin; the
romance would become intense very quickly. We would move to
be with them, wherever that may be in the country, the world
even, and things would be great, in the beginning at least. Each
time I hoped that this time would be different and that we'd have
the opportunity to lay down some roots, build a life and family,
have normal friendships, stay in a school for more than one term.
"You don't need to go to school to be clever in life, Darcie."
That's what she'd say to me whenever I would object to being
pulled out of yet another place of education just as I was finding
my feet, always trying so hard to fit in, forever the new girl. But
Fabienne didn't care about that, about the impact any of it had
on me. We just went wherever the men – and the money – was.'

I cross my legs at the ankles in a bid to stop them vibrating.

'Of course, not everyone was powerless to her charms. Some didn't want to know her because she had a young child, and she resented me for this, for standing in the way of her goals. *"You're* the reason he doesn't want to be with me. If it wasn't for *you,* I'd probably be a rich countess by now."' I can hear the bitterness in my own inflection.

Dr Carmichael doesn't break eye contact for a second. 'This must've been very distressing for you as a child, Darcie,' she says, her smooth dulcet voice soothing, almost like a lullaby. 'You must've felt extremely... *invisible.'*

'Somehow I knew the way that Maman—' I stop myself. I haven't referred to Fabienne that way in so long that it sounds strange; catches me off guard. 'The way that *Fabienne* conducted herself would somehow lead to trouble and that one day it would all go bad – *really* bad. When I think about it, there really was only one way it could ever go.'

Dr Carmichael is watching my knees jiggle. I try and still them, but it appears they have their own agenda.

'And did it all go bad?'

I can't stop myself now; I've said too much. The horse has bolted. It's all going to come out whether I want it to or not.

'Because I assume,' she continues, 'from the healthy inheritance Fabienne bequeathed you, that perhaps she was successful in her quest to die a wealthy woman?'

I look at the clock on the wall. I've been talking for what feels like hours yet I've barely started.

'I suppose she must've.'

'You don't know?' Dr Carmichael seems a touch surprised.

'Before she died, I hadn't seen her in over twenty years.'

'Why was that? Did something happen? Something bad, like you predicted?'

I pause. The air feels suddenly thick and heavy around me, harder to inhale. I know I have to tell her. I want to tell her; to tell *someone* anyway. I've been pretty successful at keeping my secrets all these years, of hiding all the dark things that happened back then. But since I met Gabe, I've been plagued by the need to tell the truth – and that's the reason I'm here, sitting in front of a stranger and paying her a king's ransom to listen to me.

Falling in love for the first and only time in my life has changed me. It's changed *everything*. The events that took place all those years ago forced me into becoming a liar, and quite an accomplished one too, because the truth is just so ugly, and I fear that if I ever were to tell my husband it – all of it – he'd stop looking at me the way he does, in that way I'll never tire of, and yet something within me burns and yearns to be honest with the man I love.

'We were happy at the time I suppose, Fabienne and I, or as happy as I felt I ever could be anyway, living in Prague. We'd been there for the best part of eighteen months. Fabienne would spend her days wafting through her lover's incredible apartment, listening to classical music, watching old black-and-white movies, drinking champagne cocktails and ordering in exquisite food that she never ate. Her lover at the time, Carter Jackson, was an American banker who worked in the financial sector and travelled around the world. He was one of her few conquests who I actually quite liked – an intelligent, gentle man really, no match for Fabienne...' My voice trails off slightly.

'What happened?'

'Fabienne tired of men shockingly easily, though she never tired of spending their money. It was like a black hole inside her that could never be filled. Nothing and no one was ever enough... When I returned home from school one afternoon, she announced that we were leaving, that we were going to do a *"vol au clair de lune"* that night. I knew just by looking at her that she'd found her next victim.'

I swallow noisily. 'She told me his name was Alastor and that he was richer than even she could've hoped for. She said he had a huge mansion, land and status and was highly respected in his field of work – and so we moved to Scotland to be with him.'

My eyes are once again instinctively drawn to that horrible porcelain doll on Dr Carmichael's shelf, its beady black eyes almost mocking me.

'That's when it all started.'

TEN

DAN

As predicted, the vultures have already started to congregate outside 8 Colville Terrace with their vans and cameras as I pull up outside, and I'm still dressed in my civvies, looking like a nineties reject. *Brilliant.* It's a palpable relief to get inside the Bonnevilles' apartment and shut the door behind me. And then I see Delaney. *Today just keeps on giving.*

'What's *he* doing here, gov?' Davis whispers at me from the corner of her mouth. 'I thought you asked him to...'

'I did.' I shoot her one of my looks, the silent kind that only Davis seems to be able to translate accurately, perhaps with the exception of my wife. If I still have one of those, that is.

'Seven days, Daniel Riley,' Fiona had said to me after Davis had – quite rightly – refused to do my dirty work for me and answer my phone. 'You've got seven days to sort this out and get your arse out to Sandbanks and spend some time with your family – otherwise, I'll be straight down to Kingfisher's and Co on the high street for a decree nisi the second we're back.'

It was no less than I deserved. Anyway, the clock's ticking, for both Darcie Bonneville *and* myself it seems.

Gabe Bonneville jumps up from where he's sitting on the

couch the moment he sees me. 'Dan! You have some news?' His
face is the colour of chalk as he runs a hand through his curly
hair, the anxiety coming off him in waves. 'Have you found
her?'

I shake my head.

He curses and begins pacing up and down, his eyes wide
with disbelief. 'Where in the name of God is she? How can she
have just disappeared off the face of the earth like this?' Even
the curls on his head seem to be vibrating with anxiety. 'Something's happened to her. It must've... She wouldn't... She would
never just go off like this. It doesn't make sense. None of it
makes any sense!'

'Gabe, let's sit down, shall we? I know this is tough, but we
need you to stay calm, OK?' My tone is gentle but firm. I need
him to be rational, to think rationally, like a doctor would. Only
he's not just a doctor; he's a husband too – and a human being.

And I wish Delaney would just *piss off*. His presence alone
seems to bring a less than favourable dynamic to what's already
an emotionally charged situation.

Gabe sighs. 'Sorry. I'm sorry.' He holds his hands up. 'It's
just madness that's all... complete madness.'

'Tea.' I turn to Delaney, smile brightly at him to do the
honours then take a seat on the couch. Nod at the space next to
me for Gabe to sit.

'I'm a husband and father myself, and this must be your
worst nightmare come true, but we need to work together, OK?'

'Yes, yeah, of course. I just want to find her.'

He looks up at me, his piercing blue eyes filled with a thousand emotions. I suspect Dr Bonneville knows all about
imparting upsetting news. But that doesn't make it any easier,
I'm sure. Because it's only when things happen to *you* do you
ever truly understand the gravity of the emotions that follow in
times of extreme crisis.

'Forensics are down at Ravens Wood now.' I begin by telling

him what we do know, and what we're doing in a bid to give him some peace of mind. 'Uniformed officers are searching the immediate area, and we're collating CCTV footage and making door-to-door enquiries, checking with the neighbours in case anyone has seen her, and the phone is with forensics too, OK? We've put a fast track on it, so hopefully that will give us something.'

He nods intently.

'Regrettably, the press has already got wind of the situation, and I feel I must warn you...'

'They'll think I'm responsible,' he says for me. 'It's always the husband, isn't it?'

'Statistically,' I say gently. 'But we've already checked your alibi out. You understand why we have to do—'

'Yes,' he interjects, 'of course I do. Just do whatever you have to do to eliminate me and we can get on with finding her.'

'Look, as yet,' I say, 'we don't know what, or if anything, has happened to Darcie.'

'Well, quite clearly *something* has!' He's getting animated again. 'I should've gone out to look for her,' he berates himself. 'I shouldn't have waited.' His foot is tapping against the wooden floor, anxiety leaking through him. 'I knew – *I knew* – something had happened to her.' He bangs his chest with a fist.

Delaney places a black tea down onto the low LED-lit coffee table.

'Did you two have a row, Gabe?' he asks. 'This morning, before she left?'

I know, professionally, he's right to ask this question because it's entirely possible that Dr Gabriel Bonneville and his wife could've had a real humdinger, for whatever reason, and he killed her before, or after, his game of golf. It's also entirely possible that a hundred other things took place – random, weird, unexpected, surreal, unimaginable, unthinkable things – that he could never have foreseen or predicted.

'DS – sorry, *DI* – Delaney, if you don't mind, I'd really like to talk to Dr Bonneville alone for a few moments.' I dismiss him with as little offence as I can force myself to while making it clear that I'm in charge. Momentarily, it feels good, but then almost instantly I feel as if I've sunk to his level. *Great.* What a holiday this is turning out to be! 'What we *need* to talk about – who we need to talk about – is Darcie.'

'Of course.' Gabe's head drops. 'What do you want to know?'

Purdy, the little chocolate sausage dog, bowls towards him then jumps up and positions herself next to him on the couch. He tickles the top of her head.

'It's been over nine hours now and... it all just feels so surreal, like a bad dream.'

Instinctively, I reach out and briefly place a hand on his knee. He doesn't seem to object.

'Tell me a little about Darcie, Gabe – as much general stuff as you can think of.'

He scratches the back of his head; blows heavily from his lips. 'Well... where do I start? She's very beautiful obviously; you've seen her photograph – not that she likes having her picture taken, as I mentioned before. She's been camera-shy ever since I've known her.'

I nod and smile.

'And she's funny and kind' – he glances sideways at me; smiles – 'and even though she's only tiny... well, you know how the Shakespeare quote goes.' His voice dissipates into a whisper. 'She hasn't got a bad bone in her; she likes helping others. She's a real-life hero actually.'

'Oh?'

'It's quite a story,' he says. 'She saved a little girl's life a few months back, on the high street – pushed her out of the way of an oncoming car. Could've been killed herself. It made the news – some kids uploaded the incident on social media, and the press got hold of it. The little girl's mum wanted her to give all these interviews, TV and magazines and all of that, but she turned it all down – didn't want to draw attention to herself. She was quite persistent, the girl's mum – kept calling and leaving Darcie messages; wouldn't take no for an answer. Saw a few pounds to be made out of it, I suppose.'

'How long ago was this incident, Gabe?'

He shakes his head a little as though to rearrange the jumbled thoughts in his head. 'About six, seven months ago now – not long after we moved here.'

'Do you remember the woman's name – the name of the child's mother?'

He audibly exhales; shakes his head. 'Dolly... The little girl she saved, her name was Dolly, but I can't remember the mother's name. I'm sorry.'

I scribble the name into my notebook and put a question mark next to it.

'Gov!' Davis suddenly beckons me over to where she's standing. 'Quick word.'

Gabe nods as I excuse myself.

'Darcie had an appointment, a doctor's appointment, scheduled for this morning with a Dr Morcombe – her gynaecologist – and she didn't show apparently.'

'I see. Keep looking around the apartment. There may be something here that will shed some light.'

Davis nods.

'Gabe...' I return to him on the couch. 'Were you aware that Darcie had an appointment this morning with a Dr Morcombe – a gynaecologist?'

His eyes widen in surprise then fill with confusion.

'An appointment...?' He gasps; stands abruptly. 'No... Oh no...'

'Gabe?'

'I think... I think she may be... pregnant!' He starts pacing. 'I knew it! I knew something was up! She was keeping something from me – I could sense it.'

'You didn't know about the appointment?'

'No – no I didn't, but...' Tears have started to form in his eyes, glistening, like they're ready to burst free. 'She probably didn't want to get my hopes up again. We've already been through some disappointment, you see – she's had a couple of miscarriages,' he explains. 'But we kept going – kept trying. We desperately want a family. Maybe she wanted to be sure first before she told me... That's the only reason I can think why she didn't mention it.'

Delaney hovers in the background behind Gabe, watching him carefully.

'Actually, maybe that's why she wasn't drinking last night, now I come to think of it. Damn!' He slams his fist down on the arm of the sofa, causing Davis to look over. 'I should've known – should've guessed!'

'Last night?'

He comes back to the moment. 'Um, yes. We entertained – had some friends over for dinner.'

So it seems Parker's perceptiveness was correct. I blink at him, but he doesn't elaborate further; looks distracted by his thoughts.

'Can you tell me who they are – these friends you had over?'

He appears a little awkward all of a sudden. 'Er, yeah. The Abberlines – Hugh Abberline and his wife, Anita. Hugh's also a doctor, a neurosurgeon at St Cat's, where I work. We went to med school together.'

He's *definitely* awkward; he's shifting in his seat and drops eye contact for a moment. I write the names down in my notebook.

'I'll need a contact number for them, if that's OK. It's

possible Darcie may have mentioned something in conversation. Is she particularly close to Anita – are they friends?'

'I... I suppose so,' he says, somewhat evasive. 'They do a yoga class together sometimes – the studio down on the high street.'

It strikes me as a touch odd that he's only just mentioned the dinner party. It could simply be an oversight though, all things considered.

'Has anything strange happened recently – anything unusual that you can think of, something out of the ordinary... What about last night – anything that struck you as odd?'

He shakes his head. 'No, nothing. We had a nice evening. Darc cooked a beautiful meal, and we got a bit merry, although...' His expression suddenly switches.

'You've thought of something?'

'No. It was nothing – just junk mail, she said.'

'Junk mail?'

'The dog started barking – something came through the door late last night... I remember because Hugh remarked about it being a bit late in the day for the postman, or words to that effect.'

'What time was that, Gabe?'

Davis suddenly reappears holding something in her hand, though I can't see what it is from here.

'Gov?' She mouths the word silently; I nod and raise a finger, signalling for her to hold tight.

'I couldn't say for sure – 9 p.m., maybe 9.30 p.m. I know it was late though, because as I say, Hugh commented on it. I suppose it was a bit odd now I think of it.'

'Do you know what it was – what came through the door?'

'Like I say, just junk mail. Actually, I think she may have put it in the bin, the one by the front door.'

I go over to the rattan bin, look into it and see a screwed-up piece of paper and what looks like an envelope at the bottom.

I'm getting unsettling vibes as I put on some gloves and fish it out.

The front of the cream envelope is addressed simply: 'Darcie', written in black ink. My sense of unease increasing, I unscrew the ball of paper, hear the sound of my own breathing in my ears.

FOUND YOU!

'What is it?' Gabe asks urgently. 'What does it say?'

I hold it up to show him. 'Does this mean anything to you?'

He looks at it, puzzled. '*"Found you"*? What the... What does *that* mean? Who's found her?'

His confusion mirrors my own.

'You've no idea who could've sent this? Darcie didn't mention it to you last night?'

'No! No, she didn't say a word. She told me it was junk. I... I...' He looks on the verge of tears again, his face a mask of fear and confusion. 'What does it even mean?'

'She never said anything to you about a stalker, any unwanted attention, an admirer perhaps?'

'No nothing – nothing whatsoever.'

'Gov!' Davis's eyes are like saucers as she waggles whatever she's holding in her hand. I duly go over to her.

'What you got, Davis?'

As a father of two 'surprises', I recognise it instantly. It's a pregnancy test.

'I found it upstairs, in Darcie's lingerie drawer. It's positive, gov,' she says gravely.

I stare at the visible blue lines, slowly close my eyes and look up to the ceiling. So now it seems our misper is very likely a *pregnant* misper and even more vulnerable than we thought. I hand Davis the note, and she places it inside a ziplock bag to protect.

'It was in the wastepaper basket by the front door. Bonneville says it was delivered last night, around nineish.'

Davis stares at it as I rake my hands through my ever-thinning hair.

'I think we're going to have to get the helicopters out.'

ELEVEN

DARCIE – AGED FIFTEEN

I pull a face as we made the final ascent up the hill towards the sprawling mansion. 'I don't like it – it looks creepy,' I say.

'How can you say that, *chéri*?' Fabienne says, briefly glancing sideways at me, her eyes alight. 'Look at it! It's so... grand! I will be *dame du manoir*!'

'Among other things,' I mutter under my breath.

'What was that you said?' But she's too distracted by the view to be fully invested in anything I have to say. '*Mon Dieu*, it's enormous,' she gushes. 'The view, the grounds... You'll be able to ride horses, *chéri*, and think of the garden parties in summer!'

I half expect her to start jumping up and down on the spot.

She clasps her hands together, unable to take her eyes from the house. 'We've hit the jackpot!'

'You said that last time,' I say flatly, the strap of the heavy holdall I'm carrying painfully digging into my shoulder. 'Anyway, I *liked* our last place. I liked Prague, and I liked Carter. Why do we always have to move all the time? I'd just got settled in school and—'

Fabienne turns sharply to me, her dark hair swishing with

the momentum. 'You don't speak like this in front of Alastor – do you understand? You say nothing, not a word about Prague or about Carter, about anything or *anyone* from our past. You nod, and you smile, and you answer any questions politely – do I make myself clear?'

I exhale loudly.

'Do I make myself clear, Darcie?'

I roll my eyes. '*D'accord, d'accord.*'

'You will *not* ruin this one for me – for us,' she adds, her tone softening a touch. 'I plan to marry Alastor and live in this house – for a while at least – the three of us, together. We'll find you a school to attend...'

My mood gently lifts upon the mention of school, though the thought of being the new girl for the thousandth time somewhat dampens it.

'Alastor likes children,' Fabienne says, still unable to take her eyes off the prize. 'His former wife left him some years ago and took their daughter with her. She was of a similar age to you apparently, so he's very much looking forward to meeting you.'

My heart sinks like my shoes in the damp earth beneath me. The feeling wasn't mutual, but there was no point in saying as much. I could scream my objections from here to Timbuktu and they would fall on deaf ears.

Damp and uncomfortable from the boat crossing to the small remote island, I'm looking forward to changing into some dry clothes as I stare up at the imposing residence. Hazy through the light evening mist surrounding it, it appears almost dreamlike, like something from a film. There's no doubt about its size – it's huge – with a grand stained-glass entrance, and I count ten, twelve, fourteen windows from the front, the fading light of the early evening gently reflecting off the surface of the glass.

Instinctively, my eye is drawn to a window right at the top. It's small and round, like a porthole, different to the others, which are bigger and square. I glance up at it, and for a moment I think I see something – a shadow in the reflection perhaps? I stop for a second; squint.

'He lives here alone, this Alistair?'

'Of course,' Fabienne says. 'And it's *Alastor*.'

'What kind of name is that anyway?'

'The name of your new papa,' she quickly responds. 'Just remember everything I've told you about who we are and what our background is. Your father died in a car accident, and we've been living in Paris with my mother for the past few years.'

I shake my head. I never got to meet my grandmother. She died when Fabienne was a child, or so she says. I don't even know where she's buried, though I suspect that wherever her grave is, she's probably turning in it.

'It looks like *un putain de musée*,' I say, loud enough for her to have heard me, though part of me hopes she hasn't. Fabienne has a fierce side sometimes, one you don't much care to be on should you find yourself there.

'*Nous sommes la!*' she says as we finally reach the front porch. 'We're here.'

TWELVE

Admittedly, and somewhat begrudgingly, my initial assumptions about the foreboding-looking house on the hill – and about Alastor – were perhaps a little premature, or so I thought. My vast bedroom, one Alastor told me he'd had decorated especially for my arrival, was a teenage girl's dream come true, complete with a huge four-poster bed strewn with colourful fluffy cushions and muslin drapes, squishy beanbags and chenille rugs that felt butter soft underfoot. It even had a walk-in closet filled with beautiful clothes; clothes I might even have chosen for myself – combat pants and cropped T-shirts, soft hoodies and sweaters and cute summer dresses that I'd spent that first week trying on in front of the full-length mirror, parading around like a catwalk model. It was the perfect room for sleepovers too, something I looked forward to hosting when I finally found a school to go to and made some friends.

There had been something strange though. I'd noticed it as soon as I'd walked into what was to be my new room – a doll. It was positioned on the bed, sitting up against one of the cushions, one of those horrible old-fashioned-looking ones with a porcelain face. I'd stared at its dead black eyes, its painted red mouth and frilly little antique dress. It looked so out of place in among the rest of the modern furnishings, like it didn't belong there.

'Eww,' I'd grimaced, immediately removing it from the bed and hiding it behind some boxes on a shelf inside the walk-in closet. It gave me the creeps.

'I *told* you you'd like it here, didn't I?' Fabienne says to me one morning during our first week at the house as she breezes into the enormous kitchen wearing fancy floral-print silk pyjamas. 'All that whinging over nothing...'

I shrug. 'It's OK, I suppose.'

'*Just* OK?'

Alastor enters the kitchen then and clearly overhears me. Fabienne shoots me a hard look, and I feel my cheeks redden. He ruffles the top of my hair as he moves past me and gives me a crooked smile, one that turns up slightly at one corner of his mouth. It makes him look off balance somehow.

'Did you girls sleep well?'

'I slept like a log, darling,' Fabienne says.

I brace myself for what I know is coming next.

'And when I woke up, I was in the fireplace!'

I inwardly cringe as she makes the same lame joke I've heard her make a hundred times over to as many different men. *So embarrassing.* Alastor laughs along with her, his dark eyes staring lovingly into hers.

'And you, Darcie?' His eyes find mine. 'Eventually I mean.'

'Eventually?' Fabienne turns to him, then to me, expectantly.

'Yes, thank you.' I nod as I help myself to some French toast from the large kitchen table. It wasn't an entirely truthful answer though.

We'd only been living in the old mansion for a few days when I was first awoken in the night by strange noises – noises I could neither identify nor determine the provenance of. They'd started off as small, scratching sounds – a bit, I imagined, like mice foraging for food – but then I heard what sounded like footsteps above me, the tentative creak of floorboards, as though someone were tiptoeing across them.

I opened my eyes, lay statue still in my bed and listened. And then a sudden thud caused me to sit bolt upright. 'Hello?' I called out instinctively. 'Is someone there?'

Pulling back the covers, I slipped form my bed and padded barefoot to the door, flicking the light switch. Only it didn't turn on. *Great, the bulb must've blown*, I thought as I turned the door handle to open it – only it wouldn't move.

I took a breath, tried again, turned it from one side to the other, pulled at it, but nothing. It wouldn't budge.

The first flutters of panic prickled the surface of my skin as I continued to rattle the handle, turning it from left to right and back again, pulling as hard as I could in the dark.

'Hello! Hello!' I called out. 'The door is stuck! Hello! Can someone let me out? I'm locked in!'

I could hear the panic rising in my voice as I cried out. The noise would wake someone up surely? My bedroom wasn't even on the same floor as Fabienne's and Alastor's though – it was on the floor above them, so I started to stamp my foot against the floor while continuing to twist the handle in an attempt to alert someone to my predicament.

After a while, I became frantic, my hands slipping against the brass as my palms grew clammy, making it even harder to maintain any purchase on the door handle. There was a lock on the door, just as there was in every other one in the house, but I'd never seen a key in any of them, though I supposed they must exist. *Had someone locked me inside?*

'Fabienne! Maman!' For the first time since I could remember, Fabienne had requested that I address her as Maman. 'Alastor prefers it,' she'd announced a day or so after our arrival. 'He doesn't think it's right that you call me by my

first name. So from now on, you'll address me as Maman,
d'accord?'

I'd rolled my eyes.

'Whatever... *Fabienne,*' I'd said, turning away from her, but
she'd gripped me by my shoulders, preventing me from doing so.

'Listen here – you'll do as I tell you, young lady,' she'd said
so sharply I'd felt her words almost cut into me. 'I realise you're
getting older now, finding your voice, but you're still only
fifteen, and all the time I'm responsible for you, you'll do as I say
without question, *vous comprenez?*'

I'd squirmed from her tight embrace. Her fingernails had
been digging into my flesh.

'And what if I don't?' I'd snapped.

She was right, I *was* getting older, and braver I suppose, my
teenage hormones making me more inclined to vocalise my
objections than my younger self had ever felt safe to. And as
nice as my bedroom might've been, the clothes and shoes and all
of that, I didn't want to be here, isolated with Fabienne and her
latest lover, in the middle of nowhere where the nearest town
was miles away and could only be reached by car or boat. I
wanted to go to school, make friends, meet boys and *be normal.* I
wanted to attend sleepovers and parties, experiment with alcohol, kiss someone for the first time, hang around parks and go to
the cinema and fast-food restaurants like other teenagers did.
But instead, here I was, stuck in this mausoleum which, though
it looked impressive on the surface, was actually quite dilapidated on closer inspection, crumbling and in desperate need of
renovation.

'Do not test me, Darcie.' Fabienne's steely gaze had fallen
upon me. 'Alastor has gone to a lot of effort to make you feel
welcome, so don't even think about causing trouble.'

'I want to go to school,' I'd spat at her. 'I want to do things
that other girls my age do, not rattle around this stupid old
house playing gooseberry to you and your latest victim. And

how long will this one even last anyway – a month, three, five – before you cart me off to live with someone else, someone richer, someone "better", and I have to leave everything, and everyone, behind *again?*'

The slap had blindsided me, causing me to take a sharp intake of breath, my hand instinctively rushing up to my face to deaden the sting. As selfish and thoughtless as Fabienne was, she'd rarely, if ever, struck me.

'We'll be here for a long as *I* say – and you'll do *exactly* as you're told. If you think for a moment that you can start speaking to me with disrespect, then there'll be no school for you, no friends, no sleepovers and parties. Do I make myself clear?'

I'd rubbed my face, fighting back that tears that had pricked the backs of my eyes and started to blur my vision. In that moment, I'd truly hated her.

'Fabienne! Hello! Maman! Maman! I'm locked in... I can't get out! *Maman!*'

My cries were accelerating, growing louder and more urgent as I yanked at the handle, now frenzied with panic, banging against the wood with my fists until they started to throb. 'LET. ME. OUT!'

After a few more frantic, futile moments, I gave up, exhausted, and slid my back down the doorframe, tears stinging my cheeks, confusion and frustration swishing through me.

After a moment or two, I felt something give behind me, the sound of the lock mechanism turning as the door opened.

'What's all this racket then?' Alastor stood in the doorway, his eyes running the length of my body as I faced him, wearing only a pair of light cotton bed shorts and a bralette that barely covered my small breasts.

Instinctively, I crossed my arms over my chest.

'You'll wake the entire house up, banging and screaming like that.'

'I thought I heard someone,' I croaked, my voice still tight with panic. 'I heard footsteps... and I tried to open the door, but it wouldn't open. It was locked.'

He'd flicked the light switch on, instantly illuminating the room as his eyes continued to scan my body.

'But it didn't work when I tried it. I thought the bulb must've blown!'

He blinked at me as he turned it off and on again in demonstration then began twisting the door handle, the catch moving in and out with ease. I stared at it, dumbfounded and confused.

'Seems to be working perfectly fine to me,' he said with a light shrug. And it was probably just the wind... This house is incredibly old, Darcie – you can hear all sorts after dark. The sound of the floorboards swelling and shrinking with the change in temperature...'

I swallowed dryly; willed my accelerated heart rate to settle. 'But... but I heard someone. Footsteps, scratching noises... And the door – it was locked, I'm sure of it. It wouldn't budge. I...'

'It's probably just a bit sticky is all. I'll get some WD-40 on it, loosen it up a bit.' He paused for a moment, his gaze still fixed on me. 'There's no one else here, Darcie – it's just you and me,' he said. 'And your mother of course.'

A slow, crooked smile formed on his lips, and I felt a shiver vibrate through me.

'Let's get you all tucked back up in bed, shall we?' He moved towards me, but instinctively I took a sharp step backward.

'It's fine,' I said, a little too loudly and quickly. 'It was my mistake. I'll go back to bed now. Sorry I woke you.'

A few days pass before the same thing happens again and I hear what sounds like scratching and floorboards creaking above me. And once again, when I rise to investigate, I find the door won't open. When it happens a third time, I feel compelled to say something to Fabienne, who promptly dismisses my claims as 'attention-seeking nonsense'.

'Your door is working fine,' she informs me with an exasperated sigh. 'I've tried it myself and there's nothing wrong with it.'

'But I thought I heard someone moving about in the room above me. It sounded so much like footsteps... And I'm telling you, the door was locked!'

She shoots me a sharp look. 'You will stop this, Darcie – do you hear me?'

I know it's pointless to argue – she won't believe me, no matter how much I try to convince her.

Two more strange incidents occur in the weeks that follow.

I go to bed one evening following another monotonous day of solitude and another day of empty promises from Fabienne about finding me a school place.

'Alastor thinks you should be homeschooled,' she informed me. 'He says the journey there and back to the nearest one on the mainland will be too much day to day. He has experience in teaching,' she said, 'and has offered to be your personal tutor.'

Horrified, I threw a complete strop, screaming my objections loudly until Fabienne threatened to take away my Walkman and magazines if I didn't stop crying. I stomped off to my bedroom, distraught, my thoughts of making new friends and kissing boys rapidly evaporating along with any hope I had for a normal existence. I couldn't bear the idea of being stuck in this sinister house round the clock with my mother's weird boyfriend playing teacher. I'd rather have been dead.

I see it the moment I tear open the door to my room, tears streaking my angry red face. There, on the bed, in the exact same position it had been the night we'd first arrived – that horrible doll. I stop dead in my tracks and stare at it. Had Alastor found where I'd discarded it, behind some boxes on the shelf in the closet, and replaced it?

The hairs on my arms immediately stand to attention. He must've been in here, in my room, looking through my things... I want to tell Fabienne about it. I even turn around to go back downstairs and ask her to come and see for herself there and then, but then I think of my Walkman and my books and magazines and how my life will be even more miserable without them.

In a rage, I snatch the doll from the bed and make to throw it out of the window, only it won't open, won't even budge an inch, which only serves to further enrage me. On closer inspection, I see that it's been nailed shut.

'Does anything ever open in this hellhole?' I scream to no one.

Holding the doll by its horrible synthetic hair, I begin smashing it against the wooden floor instead, attempting to break its face into pieces, only it takes some doing. I have to put some real force behind it before I finally hear the crack of the porcelain.

Afterwards, I gather up the pieces and place them inside a pillowcase before tossing it back into the closet and slamming the door behind me.

Something isn't right about this place – I sense it like an impending storm.

At night I feel a strange presence, like there's something or someone else in the house. The noises, though inconsistent, always sporadically return, and there's something off about Alastor too, the way I often catch him looking at me, his eyes lingering on me for longer than I somehow know that they should, than I feel comfortable with.

But as unsettled as these collective incidents have made me feel, it's *nothing* compared to what was to come.

THIRTEEN

DARCIE – SIX MONTHS AGO

I was genuinely looking forward to my second session with Dr Carmichael. Even though I'd only really scratched the surface during our initial meeting the previous week, I'd come away from it feeling lighter somehow – and more positive. It was cathartic to tell someone some of the things that had happened.

'Back again I see?' A voice behind me causes me to swing round. 'I knew you would be.' He flashes me a knowing smile. It's that same man I met last week: John somebody or other – Dr Carmichael's biggest fan.

'Hello.' I smile at him as I take the seat furthest away in the plush waiting area and pretend to look at something on my phone. This simple acknowledgement is all the encouragement he needs though – he gets up and plonks himself down directly next to me, his knee almost touching my own.

'Do you remember me?' He grins; points to himself. 'It's me, John – John Evergreen. We met last week, remember?'

'Of course I remember you. It's nice to see you again.' It was just a figure of speech, but it makes me think how much we all lie on a daily basis. Little white lies upon lies. He seems thrilled by my recognition though, almost childlike, and instantly I feel a bit guilty, remembering what Dr Carmichael said about him being harmless enough.

'I *said* you wouldn't be able to stay away, didn't I, eh?' He leans in closer. 'She's a little bit magic, isn't she, the lovely Dr Carmichael?'

I begin fiddling with my hair, coiling a piece of it around my forefinger. 'Yes, she seems... great.'

He chuckles, omitting a fleck of spittle from his mouth, and I surreptitiously lean further back into my seat in a bid to create more distance between us.

'I'm glad we've met again,' he continues with exuberance. 'I was only just talking about you to Shannon the other day – you know, Dolly's mum? I told her how our paths had crossed, how I'd met you here, in this waiting room. I mean, what are the chances of that happening, eh?'

He chuckles some more, and I shrink away from him. Shannon Taylor, Dolly's mum, whose persistent calls and requests for me to do joint press interviews had forced me to eventually block her. Now, thanks to John's unlikely connection to her, she knows that I'm visiting a therapist – which is more than my own husband does. Great!

'She says you stopped taking her calls – says she didn't understand it, what with you saving little Dolly's life and all...'

I shake my head, feel silently aggrieved that I'm being forced to explain myself. 'I'm not keen on being in the spotlight really,' I say thinly. 'It's nothing personal.'

He eyes me strangely. 'Well, I'm sure we'll be seeing much more of each other from now on, you and me. You can never have too many friends, can you?'

Well, that was debatable, or at least as far as I was concerned. But I flash him a polite smile anyway; feel a touch sorry for him. I get the impression he's something of a lonely soul really. Sometimes I wonder if people think the same about me – or at least did before I met Gabe anyway.

I feel another sudden stab of guilt in my solar plexus. *Il mio caro marito* doesn't even know I'm here today. He'd naturally want to know my reasons for wanting to see a therapist, and I don't want to lie to him directly – which is, ironically, ostensibly the purpose of my coming here in the first place. *Should I confess my past to my husband – tell him all my sordid sins and secrets and risk falling from the lofty pedestal he's put me on?*

I know I have to tell *someone*. I'm hoping Dr Carmichael may give me the answer to this nagging question though, one which has gradually moved towards all-consuming as it slowly erodes my conscience. I need Dr Carmichael's professional judgement, her guidance. Do I come clean and confide the truth to Gabe, or is it all best left where I've kept it these past two decades – unsaid and in the past, locked away in the dusty vaults of my sketchy memory? After all, I've lived with my secrets for this long, but then again, until I met my husband, I hadn't really been living at all – or so I've realised. So, erring on the side of caution, once again, I've said nothing to him, because not saying anything isn't exactly the same thing as actually lying – or at least that's how I've justified it to myself.

I can feel John's eyes upon me as I notice the snotty receptionist raising her hand at me in my peripheral vision.

'This is me then, John,' I say, standing.

I can feel him still watching me as I turn away from him.

'TTFN, Darcie,' he says cheerfully.

I'm almost bursting at the seams as I take a seat on Dr Carmichael's comfy cream couch, the herby scent of Jo Malone's Lime Basil & Mandarin alive in my nostrils. The wheels have been set in motion now, and the compulsion to open up and confess everything to her has suddenly become almost unnervingly urgent. Perhaps John was right after all and she is a little bit magic.

'You seem in good spirits, Darcie.' She smiles at me professionally as I admire the pale blue silky wrap dress she's wearing and her impeccably styled strawberry-blonde hair. There is definitely something about Dr Carmichael – I feel myself drawn to her in ways I don't usually find with other people.

'I trust you found our first session last week helpful?'

'Yes.' I nod enthusiastically. 'More than I could've hoped in fact.' My eye instinctively wanders to the shelf behind her, but the doll that was there last week is gone.

'That's wonderful to hear.' She takes the position opposite me; begins clicking the top of her shiny gold pen in quick succession. 'Shall we pick up where we left off? You were starting to tell me about having to move to an old house in Scotland, to live with your mother's— sorry, with *Fabienne's* new boyfriend, Alastor.'

I'm impressed by the clarity of Dr Carmichael's memory for detail, but then I remember that she was taking notes during our last session and has probably gone back through them to refresh.

I watch as she continues to click the top of her pen. The click-click-clicking sound almost mesmerises me into a trance.

'Something really terrible happened at that house,' I say weakly. 'And I've kept it a secret for twenty years – never told another living soul.'

'I see,' she says gently, 'but now you'd like to – tell another living soul?'

The pause that ensues would make most people feel uncomfortable – it makes *me* uncomfortable – but Dr Carmichael simply stares at me, her blank expression unchanging as she click-clicks her pen. After a short while longer, the silence becomes too unbearable for me not to fill it.

'I thought he was odd.' My voice sounds strained, my mouth dry as I speak, and Dr Carmichael hands me a bottle of water from the table without breaking eye contact with me for a second. 'Alastor I mean.'

My stomach lurches as I think of my fifteen-year-old self greeting Alastor for the first time. I want to cry for her, to reach out to her and put my arm through hers – *and run!* She could never have predicted what would happen; no one could've really.

'But then again, I was only fifteen – what did I know?' I hear the resentment in my voice. 'Anyway, he was just another one of Fabienne's scam victims to me – at least at first – but as soon as she saw that house, those grounds, the size of it... I knew she'd be hell-bent on getting her hands on it all, and that's why she wouldn't believe me when I told her about the weird things that kept happening.'

'Explain what you mean by weird things?'

'Do you know,' I say, going slightly off track, 'I don't even actually know where it was, that horrible old house – can you believe that? I know it was somewhere in Scotland, but the exact location...' I shrug away my own incredulity, almost forgetting for a moment that Dr Carmichael is in the room.

'Why didn't you like the house, Darcie? What happened to make you describe it as "horrible"?'

I begin picking at my hair – almost slap my own hands to try and stop myself.

'It was a huge house and very old. I suppose some people might have thought it was beautiful, at least once upon a time. I wish I could've been one of them. Anyway, a week or so after arriving, I started to hear noises.'

'What sort of noises?'

I explain to Dr Carmichael about the strange scratching sounds, the creaking of the floorboards above me and about the light switch not working, the door to my bedroom, how it wouldn't open and then, '... suddenly the door opened and the light goes on and... he's standing there!'

'Alastor? He came to your room in the night?'

My head dips.

Dr Carmichael leans into me a touch. 'Were you scared of him, Darcie?'

'Freaked out more than scared I think, at first anyway.'

'That sounds truly awful,' she says, her tone perfectly balanced.

'And it happened again – twice, maybe three times more. I know now that it must have been him who was locking my bedroom door from the outside and messing with the electrics. Who else could it have been?'

Dr Carmichael looks hesitant for a second. 'What about the noises you mentioned – from the room above? Do you think there could really have been someone up there?'

I lower my eyes and shrug. Even I can admit that it sounds a bit far-fetched – the workings of an overactive and hormone-fuelled teenage mind.

'You never went to check – to see for yourself if you'd heard what you thought you had?'

'No,' I say, suddenly regretful. 'I was too scared. I was scared full stop. Alastor was always watching me somehow. I'd catch him sometimes – often, as I was absentmindedly going about my monotonous day – always staring, his eyes lingering on me, following me everywhere.' I shudder at the recollection. 'He gave me the creeps, and I didn't want to be there, stuck in that strange, isolated house with him – or Fabienne for that matter. I was a fifteen-year-old teenager. I wanted a life. I wanted friends and experiences. I *wanted* to leave.' I can hear myself becoming emotional and take a deep breath.

'You don't need to justify yourself, Darcie – not to anybody. You have every right to be aggrieved – to be upset about the things that have happened to you.'

Dr Carmichael smiles gently, and, grateful, I force myself to return it.

'The initial shine of being in a new house wore off very quickly for me – in a matter of days really. I was lonely and bored and I desperately wanted to go to school. I honestly can't tell you how many schools I'd been to by the time I'd reached fifteen, but I had always *gone* to school. Fabienne made sure of it, even if she dragged me out of it again a few weeks later. It got me out of her hair for a few hours a day, so she could plot and scheme in peace, no doubt – and I got to be away from her too.' I'm relieved to be able to expunge some of the poison I feel about Fabienne. I've always wanted so much to hate her, but even now I still can't quite manage it. 'But she told me in no uncertain terms that it wasn't going to happen and that, instead, Alastor was going to be my personal tutor.'

Dr Carmichael's eyes align with my own, and for the briefest second, strangely, I feel a flash of fear, though it passes quickly. *Click-click-click...*

'I was distraught – incensed! There was *no way* that was happening – and Fabienne and I had a dreadful fight about it.'

My eyes begin searching Dr Carmichael's office for that doll again, and I have to stop myself from asking her where it is.

'I did try to tell her how uncomfortable I felt around Alastor. As a mother she should've seen it herself; she maybe even did and turned a blind eye. It wouldn't have surprised me,' I spit. 'She had a single goal – to get her hands on his money – and nothing was ever going to get in the way of that.'

'She sounds like a very selfish woman,' Dr Carmichael says – observantly in my opinion.

'She was. And I didn't trust him. Fabienne told me that Alastor was "an eminent doctor" or something, a professor of some sort, well educated – the house did have a library full of books – and that he came from good stock and was, of course, very rich. But there was something off about him, something sinister beneath that crooked smile...' My voice tapers off. 'Fabienne should never have trusted him either. He shouldn't have trusted her! She didn't even *know* him; didn't know most of the men she dragged me around the world to be with to be fair, so I knew the odds would turn against her – and me – eventually.'

'And did they?'

I nod. I can feel my emotions churning over in my stomach. I need to remember why I'm here, to purge it all, let it go and decide if I should tell Gabe everything. How I wish none of it had ever happened and worry if he'll ever feel the same about me.

'One night I woke up to find him sitting on the end of my bed.' The words seem to drop from my mouth like bricks as I focus on the clicking sound of Dr Carmichael's pen once more. 'I'd felt this presence, even in my sleep. I must've, because it woke me up.'

Dr Carmichael pauses; leans in a touch closer. 'Did he touch you, Darcie?' she asks carefully.

'No. He was just sitting there, at the end of my bed, watching me sleep.'

I can feel the tears coming; will them back.

'Did you ask him what he was doing?'

'He told me he was just checking on me. But I knew he'd been there for some time. *I felt it.* And that's when I made the decision to run away.'

FOURTEEN

DAN

'Who in the world would ever want to abduct Darcie?'

Anita Abberline is sitting, legs crossed, in the vast kitchen diner of her impressively stylish home as she lights a cigarette with, I notice, lightly shaking fingers.

'For goodness' sake, don't tell the old man,' she says, forcibly blowing smoke from her plump lips and looking down at the cigarette a little guiltily. 'I don't really smoke,' she says. 'Only in times of stress anyway.'

'We can't yet say for sure that she's been abducted,' I reply, without much confidence, because as time is ticking on, I'm more and more convinced that this is exactly what's happened to Darcie – someone has taken her, though currently I'm no closer to finding out who – or why.

'Do you think it was a random stranger?' Anita asks as a bit of ash falls from her cigarette and onto the pristine glass table in front of her. 'That she's been snatched by some lunatic on the loose?'

'It's very rare,' I say honestly, 'though at this stage we can't rule anything out. Statistically, if she has been abducted, it's more likely to have been by someone she's familiar with.'

'Good God, I'm not sure if that makes it better or worse.' She drops her head; shakes it. 'It's all so... frightening. I mean, poor Darcie, poor *Gabe*. How can something like this be happening to people like them?'

'People like them?' Davis interjects.

'You know, good people? We were only at their place last night. They threw a little soiree, just the four of us. Darcie made a beautiful meal, and we all had such a giggle. It just seems so... so unbelievable that something like this has happened – that it could've happened to her.'

'So nothing was off last night? Something Darcie or anyone may have said perhaps; anything unusual? Did she seem worried to you or confide in you about anything?' I think about the pregnancy test Davis located in Darcie's lingerie drawer, about the blue lines running through it.

Her brow furrows. 'No. Nothing, nothing at all, but then again, Darcie is a bit of a dark horse – she probably wouldn't tell me even if there was anything bothering her.'

'A dark horse?'

'You know, a bit of a closed book. When Hugh and I moved out this way a few months back, when he got a position at St Cat's, Darcie and I started doing yoga together, on Tuesdays. We sometimes go for a coffee afterwards, although actually...' She pauses thoughtfully. 'I do know she was seeing a therapist for a while – fairly recently in fact.'

'Oh?' My antenna twitches. 'Did she say who – or why?'

'I introduced them – I gave Darcie her card. Dr Carmichael – Elizabeth Carmichael. You may have heard of her? She's a forensic psychologist, a psychiatrist and hypnotherapist, ridiculously clever, a real favourite with all the celebrities. She's even a bit of one herself I suppose; been on the TV – those crime documentaries that everyone watches,' she muses. 'Anyway, she's brilliant. She worked wonders for my social anxiety.'

I attempt to hide my surprise. Anita doesn't particularly

strike me as the socially anxious type, but then again, looks can be deceiving.

'Darcie told me she suffered from claustrophobia, so I suggested she go and see her, although I thought they may have already met.'

I write the name 'Elizabeth Carmichael' in my notebook.

'And did she go and see her, do you know?'

'I believe so, though we never spoke about it directly. Like I say, she was— sorry, she *is* quite a closed book.' She looks up, apologetic. 'I still don't know an awful lot about her – family history, that sort of thing. From what little she's ever told me, she was an only child who moved around a lot. But don't get me wrong, Darcie has always been perfectly nice to me, easy to get along with, if a touch guarded perhaps, and she is of course' – she rolls her eyes a touch – 'terribly beautiful, but it didn't go unmentioned, when Gabe married her.'

'What didn't go unmentioned?'

'Hmm,' she muses. 'How it was all a bit soon, or words to that effect. What is it they say – "marry in haste and repent at leisure"? Anyway, he told me he'd never felt that way about anyone before, that he was truly in love with her and couldn't wait to marry her.'

I'm pretty sure I'm not imagining it when I detect a slight hint of bitterness in Anita's voice. She flicks her blonde hair from her face; extinguishes her half-smoked cigarette in a mug on the table. It makes a hissing sound as it meets the remnants of the liquid inside.

'I've only known Darcie since she met Gabe. But I've known Gabe since forever. We were in sixth form together – that's how we met originally. Gabe and Hugh were at med school together too. In fact, it was Gabe who first introduced me to Hugh ironically.'

'Ironically?' I'm careful to keep my tone soft, but something in her demeanour is beginning to feel slightly off to me.

'Yes.' She looks up pensively; reaches for another cigarette from the soft packet on the table but thinks better of it. 'I thought perhaps Gabriel might've already mentioned it?'

'Mentioned what?' I say, my senses pricked.

Anita sighs. 'Just that he and I used to be an item. I'm talking many, many years ago now though,' she quickly adds. 'We dated for some time, on and off, when we were students.'

'I see.' Now this could be interesting. 'So it was serious between the two of you?'

'Oh gosh, yes,' she tinkles with laughter, like it's an absurd question. 'We were *madly* in love at the time...' Her voice trails off slightly. 'But we were very young of course, and, well, I guess I wasn't the one for him in the end.'

There's undoubtedly a tinge of regret to her tone, and clearly I'm not the only one to pick up on it as Davis throws me a shifty sideways glance.

'Did Darcie know about your relationship with Gabe?'

'Yes, of course. It was never a secret. It was all a lifetime ago now.' She waves her hand dismissively and yet unconvincingly somehow.

'When did the relationship end between you and Gabe?' Davis probes.

Anita rakes a hand through her blonde highlighted hair, displaying a handful of tasteful gold jewellery and manicured nails, and inhales deeply. 'Like I said, a lifetime ago. We've always remained friends though, even after we broke up. In fact, we were better as friends,' she adds, though it sounds slightly disingenuous to me, like an afterthought she feels obliged to say. 'We called it a day, finally, during his first year at med school. That's when he introduced me to Hugh, and things went on from there... and, well, here we all are!'

Anita pauses, her left shoulder raising slightly. 'I was very happy for him when he finally met someone though – when he met Darcie. I never thought he would...'

'Meet someone you mean?' My intrigue is blooming now.

'Oh no!' She laughs again. 'I knew he'd meet someone else of course – I mean, look at him! He's an extremely attractive man, clever, charismatic, talented, dynamic, interesting, kind...'

I glance over at Davis again, and her eyes widen a touch.

'Women adored him – sometimes to his detriment – all those student nurses fawning over him... He had a few false starts before he met "the one" though.' She uses her fingers to illustrate the inverted commas. 'I never thought he'd marry her though and certainly not as rapidly as he did – I mean, he hardly knew her; none of us did. He always said to me that he never wanted to get married anyway, back then at least, but I think it was all that terrible business that put him off.'

'What terrible business was that?'

Anita covers her mouth with her hand and shakes her head. 'I've said too much, haven't I?'

'I don't know, Anita, have you?' I give her a small smile so as not to discourage her from continuing. 'Any background information you can tell us could prove useful, however unrelated you might think it is.'

'Well, I know for a fact that Gabriel has nothing to do with Darcie going missing. He really loves her,' she says, her eyes lowering. 'I can tell. Plus he's one of the most altruistic men God put on this earth. He *lives* for helping others.'

'You said something about some kind of terrible business...?' I prompt her again.

'Oh yes! Well, it all turned out to be complete nonsense of course, but at the time, there was this young student nurse who worked at the hospital where Gabe was undertaking an apprenticeship as a junior house officer, and she made up some elaborate claim about him behaving inappropriately towards her – you know, sexual harassment or some such crap.' She waves the words away contemptuously. 'He was completely exonerated of course. No truth to any of it whatsoever – just some infatuated nurse whose affection for him wasn't reciprocal in any way, a fantasist. It caused Gabe the most horrible stress at the time though – she almost finished his career before it even got started because of her lies. It sent him completely off the rails for a while afterwards.'

She appears to be on a roll now, her earlier concern of having said too much already a distant memory.

'He was devastated by those claims. I mean, mud sticks, doesn't it? And it all had to be thoroughly investigated by the powers that be. He hit a bit of a depression afterwards, even when it transpired there was nothing to account for, started drinking a little too much, gambling...'

'Gambling?'

Anita's eyes widen as my ears prick up. 'Yes, well, now I *really* have said too much I think.'

Davis and I make eye contact again.

'Did he get into some financial difficulty back then, with the gambling perhaps?'

We're already looking into the Bonnevilles' financial matters, but if it transpires that Gabe Bonneville had – or has – a gambling addiction, then that would indeed give him something in the way of motive to stage his rich wife's abduction. Gabe told me he had no knowledge of Darcie's inheritance when they met. Had he lied?

She shrugs. 'Not that I was aware of. Gabe comes from a wealthy family, and from what I recall, he put all that terrible business behind him years ago, and as you can see, he's gone on to achieve enormous success in his career – he's ridiculously talented.'

She looks at Davis and I simultaneously, her nervousness leaking through her eyes. 'All this is historic,' she reiterates, mildly panicked now. 'Happened years ago.' Her eyes continue to dart between ours. 'You don't think... Gabe would never, ever do anything to harm Darcie. I want it noted down on record that I've said that as well.' She looks really spooked now.

'Do you remember the woman's name – this nurse who made false allegations against Gabe?'

She shakes her head. 'It was over fifteen years ago now. No, I really couldn't say... Caroline somebody or other maybe. You'll have to ask Gabe.'

Why hadn't Gabe mentioned any of this to us? Why hadn't he spoken of his former relationship with Anita or the allegations that almost put paid to his promising career as a young doctor? Did he just not think it was relevant, or is it because he's hiding something?

'Don't worry' – I turn to Anita – 'we will.'

FIFTEEN

I hear the unmistakable whir of the chopper, buzzing like a giant wasp, as it hovers almost menacingly above us as I take a right turn down Colville Terrace. The whole area has been sealed off while uniform and the dogs search the immediate area and allow SOCO access to find and collate as much evidence as possible – something, *anything* that might give some indication as to what's happened to Darcie. Both Ravens Wood and the Bonnevilles' apartment are being treated as potential crime scenes, particularly given the sinister fact that what appeared to me to be a small amount of blood was found on Darcie's mobile phone. A phone which, incidentally, has so far produced sweet FA – to use the technical term – in terms of solid forensic evidence. All we've really got at the moment is that note.

'Well, that was a bit of an eye-opener, wasn't it?' Davis says. 'Don't know about you, gov, but I got the impression Anita still holds a bit of a torch for Gabe Bonneville. I mean, you wouldn't want Fiona talking like that about an ex-partner, would you?'

'Right now, I probably wouldn't blame her if she did,' I say miserably. 'But yes, it certainly raises a few questions,' I remark as I spot a group of press, congregated at the bottom of Colville Terrace, mooching around behind lines of blue tape in their little gangs, dressed in hats and scarves, clutching Starbucks coffee cups with fingerless gloves in a bid to combat the bitter cold. Uniform has been instructed to keep them well away from Gabe Bonneville, who, by now, I'm pretty sure has already been cast as the baddie in this unfolding story, whether that transpires to be accurate or not.

This kind of incident has got it all going on in terms of sensationalism, whipping up the perfect media storm: a beautiful, wealthy wife vanishes into thin air on a dog walk and a distraught, handsome, talented surgeon husband – at least on the surface. They'll dig for dirt on Gabe because that's what they do, and it'll no doubt all come out, what Anita's just told us about the nurse's historic accusations against him, adding fuel to the fire and casting further suspicions on his character. Like Anita rightly said, mud sticks. Nowadays, it's all trial by media anyway, everyone a keyboard juror and amateur sleuth, and I've no doubt already that Gabe Bonneville's every move, every word, his reactions, body language and any skeletons in his closet are being exposed, discussed, dissected and judged on various social-media platforms in microscopic detail. The press – and the public – creates their own narrative to fit around the story. It's all about clickbait – the truth, in truth, is largely secondary.

'Much as I don't like to say it, I think Archer's right. We need to make a public appeal as soon as possible. Any news from forensics yet on that note?'

'Nothing yet, gov. They're aware we need a rush on it.'

I tap the steering wheel impatiently. 'We need witnesses to come forward... dash-cam footage, sightings. Someone saw something – someone always does.' And I'm relying on the public's help, because so far we've very little to go on, and the clock is ticking so loudly it's giving me tinnitus.

'Where are we with CCTV from the neighbours? The Ring doorbell?' I briefly turn to Davis.

She shakes her head. 'Delaney's at the Bonnevilles' going through it now, and Mitchell's heading up CCTV. A witness did come forward earlier and said she saw Darcie out walking the dog around 7.40 this morning though, and that they exchanged a few pleasantries before Darcie headed off into the woods.'

'Good. We need a start point... she'll definitely have been picked up on camera along Colville Terrace, and moreover, so might whoever delivered that note yesterday evening if the doorbell doesn't give us much to go on. We need to find the route she took – in and out.'

On cue, Davis's phone rings, and she places it on loud-speaker. It's Delaney.

'Hey, Luce,' he says familiarly when she answers.

'Martin...' she says, glancing sideways at me. 'You're on loudspeaker.' I don't know why she's felt the need to tell him this, but clearly she did. 'What you got for us?'

'It's bingo on the Ringo,' he says, pleased, I imagine, with his own wit.

I mentally fist-pump. 'Go on...'

'Well, we've got a suspect going up to the door of the Bonnevilles' last night – an unidentified male, stocky build, around six foot, wearing black clothing, his face concealed by a hood.'

My imaginary fist pump evaporates. 'Nothing of the face?'

'Nope,' Delaney says. 'It was covered, and he placed a hand – a gloved hand – over the camera as well. The Ring doorbell detected motion at around 9.27 p.m., and the husband got an alert on his phone – one he didn't see at the time – which we've now got in our possession, as well as both his and Darcie's laptops.'

'Just remember, Gabe Bonneville is currently a witness.' I

keep my voice at its usual pitch, but Davis gives me a small sideways glance. 'And I'd ask you to be respectful of that.'

There's a silence on the line.

'Sure. I was just— Anyway, Darcie's picked up on the doorcam this morning, 7.32 a.m., with the dog... and again, we get Gabe Bonneville returning home at 11.17 a.m. After that, zero. SOCO has the clothes he was wearing, and forensics are combing the place now.'

'Waste of time,' I find myself saying. 'There's nothing in that house.'

'Apartment you mean,' he corrects me, seemingly determined to give me as many reasons to be irritated by him as he can. 'And how can you be so sure, Dan?'

I have to silently count to five before I can answer him.

'Because he's got nothing to do with her disappearance, *Martin*. Everything he's said so far checks out – the alibi, timings, dozens of witnesses from the golf club and now this.'

I'm going out on a bit of a limb with this statement because of course an alibi alone isn't rock-solid evidence of his innocence. We can't exonerate Gabe Bonneville entirely at this stage, but my intuition has never failed me.

'He could've followed her down to the woods,' Delaney hypothesises. 'Gone round the back of the apartment and avoided the cameras – there are none there. He reckons they were planning on putting some in but never got round to it.'

He's clutching, though annoyingly, while it's not *probable*, I suppose it is *possible*, and I mustn't allow my personal feelings to cloud my professional judgement.

'I want you to see if you can corroborate Anita and Hugh Abberline's alibis for this morning,' I say. 'Apparently they were both at home nursing hangovers when Darcie was taken and ordered a McDonald's breakfast from Uber Eats.'

'Healthy choice for a doctor,' Delaney remarks. 'Doesn't take a *brain surgeon* to work out that they're not good for you.'

He starts to chuckle but stops when I deliberately don't join in.

'And let's focus on the unidentified male who delivered the note,' I instruct him sharply. 'See if we can get anything from forensics – prints, fibres, DNA... and I want *all* the CCTV available from Colville Terrace and surrounding areas gone through. Our masked man will have been picked up elsewhere – I'm sure of it.'

It'll be hours and hours of painstaking work, going through that lot, but that's the job.

'Where are you two going?' Delaney asks. 'Have you been to see the—'

I lean over and cancel the call on Davis's phone abruptly.

'Gov!' Her mouth has formed a perfect 'O' shape.

I shake my head; I don't want to open my mouth for fear of what might come out of it.

Once my irritation levels have resumed to a normal baseline, I turn to Davis. 'Someone was watching her, stalking her – they knew her movements. It was premeditated.'

Davis sighs heavily but doesn't disagree. 'You think we're looking at a kidnapping situation and that there'll be a ransom, or do you think there's another motive – a sexual predator maybe?'

'It's someone she knows.'

Davis raises her eyebrows. 'Yeah, but this is the problem, gov. Because from what we've got so far, she doesn't seem to actually really *know* many people. She has no family apart from the hubby, and no real close girlfriends either it seems, and she's not even on social media.'

'"Seems" being the operative word. You should know by now that things aren't always what they *seem* on the surface.' Except for maybe the likes of Martin Delaney. Like the old man used to say, "If it looks like a duck, walks like a duck and quacks like a duck, then it's a duck." Replace the word duck with 'schmuck' and, well, you get the picture.

'Why do you think she's not on any social media; doesn't even have a Facebook account? How is that even possible for someone her age in today's society? Do you think it could be at Gabe's request? Maybe he's the jealous, controlling type – doesn't want her putting herself out there because she's an attractive woman?'

'It's a possibility,' I reply, but I'm unconvinced. I just don't get that vibe from him, not even remotely. 'The note,' I say. 'It said "found you", right?'

'Right?'

'It suggests that whoever sent it was actively looking for her.'

'Riiight.'

'What would a person do if they didn't want to be found?'

Davis shrugs. 'Hide?'

'We'll make a DCI out of you yet,' I tease her. 'If you don't want to be found, then you don't plaster yourself all over social media, do you?'

'I guess not.'

'And Gabe mentioned how Darcie hadn't wanted any media attention when she rescued the little girl from getting run over on the high street, and that the little girl's mum, what was her name...?'

'Shannon,' Davis says, starting to flick through her notebook. 'Shannon Taylor.'

'He said that Shannon was quite persistent – that she put pressure on Darcie to agree to give press interviews and all of that. In fact, didn't Mitchell say her number had been blocked on Darcie's phone?'

'You think Dolly's mum might have something to do with this, gov?'

'Maybe she took umbrage when Darcie refused to do any publicity – publicity that could've been quite lucrative for her?

Or perhaps she discovered that Darcie is a rich woman and staged a kidnapping, wants to try and extort her? We can't rule it out.'

But even as I surmise the possibility aloud, I can't help feeling that there's something else I'm missing.

'I wonder if Darcie knew about the nurse,' Davis muses, 'about the accusations and his subsequent breakdown, the gambling and drinking, or if Gabe kept it secret from her?'

'Well, DI Davis,' I say, 'there's only one way to find out.'

SIXTEEN

DARCIE – AGED FIFTEEN

I'd been dreaming about how I might leave for weeks before the opportunity presented itself. I *had* to get out of this house. I was old enough now; I'd seen kids younger than me with their friends on the streets of Paris, and I was perfectly capable of looking after myself. Certainly more than Fabienne ever could. My 'lessons' with Alastor are due to begin in just a few days, and the idea of being alone with him fills me with dread.

At breakfast, Alastor announces that he's going to make the journey to the mainland to purchase some stationery, books and items that he's planning to use for my imminent lessons.

'I think I'll make the drive,' he says. There's a small bridge linking us to the mainland, though it's miles away on a road that's seen better days – taking the boat is usually quicker. And it looks like rain today.'

My ears prick up. Alastor has never left Fabienne and me alone in the house since our arrival, and I'd started to wonder if it was deliberate on his part, though Fabienne appeared oblivious to it, just as she has everything else I've attempted to bring to her attention, like the windows.

'Why are all of them nailed shut?' I demanded. 'The one in

my bedroom, both of the living-room ones, even the bathroom –
not one of the windows opens in this whole house! It's weird.'

Fabienne brushed it off. 'It's to stop them from rattling in
the wind, Darcie,' she explained. 'It's very draughty in this
house, and these windows are centuries old.'

'But when it gets hotter, we won't be able to open them, let
the air in... And what if there was a fire? We wouldn't be able to
get out.'

She rolled her eyes and cast me one of her 'looks' that
instantly silenced me. There really was no point trying to
reach her.

Now, Fabienne turns to face Alastor in the kitchen. 'Oh,
darling, I was planning to go into town myself today. I need to
pick up a few things. What perfect timing!'

Alastor's expression drops slightly. 'But what about Darcie?
We can't leave her here on her own.'

I have to think quickly.

'Actually, I'm really not feeling well this morning,' I
announce. 'I have terrible stomach pains – they kept me awake
most of the night. I think I might go back to bed.'

Fabienne narrows her eyes at me. She assumes I'm only
saying this in a bid to scupper her plans to accompany Alastor
into town. But she couldn't be more wrong. I *want* her to go
with him so I can be alone for the first time since we arrived.

'Well, you can't leave her, not if she's feeling unwell.' Alastor's tone is measured but still amenable. 'I'll only be a couple of
hours or so at most. I'll take us all into town together soon, once
Darcie's feeling better.' He smiles his crooked smile at her.

Fabienne is silent. She isn't used to hearing the word 'no'.

'I'll pick us up something from the deli while I'm there,
some of that French cheese you like. And some red wine – a
vintage bottle.'

I can tell he's trying to appease her with promises of gifts so
that she'll stay here, with me. Does he suspect my plan, or is it

that he doesn't want me to go nosing about the place in their absence, maybe find something I shouldn't, whatever that might be?

'Really, it's OK,' I say casually. 'I'm going back to bed. I don't feel myself. You two go into town together. I'll be fine. I'm not a child; I can be left alone for five minutes,' I say, running myself a glass of water from the tap.

Fabienne approaches me and places a hand on my forehead. 'Perhaps you're sickening for something, *chéri*,' she says, doing a stellar job at pretending to show concern. 'But only if you're sure?'

Alastor is watching me closely. 'No. You stay here, with Darcie. She looks peaky,' he says. 'I'll pick up some medicine for her while I'm in town.'

He whispers something to Fabienne then, but I can't make out what – they're too far over the other side of the kitchen for me to hear.

A huge grin erupts across her face. 'Oooh, *mon Dieu*, how exciting! Of course, of course.' Fabienne clasps her hands together and starts making little clapping noises. 'I'll stay here then, darling.'

I don't know what he's said to her that's caused her about-turn but she seems pleased by it.

'Right, that's settled then,' Alastor says. 'I'll get my coat.'

He hurries out of the kitchen.

Fabienne turns to me. 'Nice try, *chéri*.' Her voice has a menacing edge. 'I know you're faking sickness for attention, trying to ruin my day, but Alastor has just told me he's going into town to buy me an engagement ring!'

Me, the fake attention seeker? That's rich coming from her! I close my eyes; inwardly roll them.

'How nice,' I reply. 'Another one to add to the collection.'

She narrows her eyes at me.

Ignoring her, I run myself another glass of water from the

tap and take a few gulps. I have more important things to do than to get into an argument with Fabienne. I never win anyway – she's impossible.

'I'm going back to bed,' I say, hearing the satisfying crunch of tyres upon gravel, signalling Alastor's departure. I intend to go ahead with my plan, even if Fabienne is going to be in the house.

I rush upstairs to my bedroom and begin stuffing various items of clothing inside the holdall I brought with me that first night. I need to act fast. I'll write Fabienne a note – place it underneath her pillow so she won't find it until she goes to bed.

Locating a piece of paper and a pen on the table on the landing, next to the old-fashioned phone that never rings, I quickly start to write.

Fabienne, I cannot stay in this house a moment longer – it's not safe. For fifteen years I've been dragged all over the world in your quest to find men with the fortune you value over your own daughter's happiness, but now I want to be free of you forever, of Alastor and of this horrible old house. Do *not* try to find me or tell the police. If you do, I'll tell them all the horrible things you've done, and Alastor won't want to marry you. I hope you'll be very happy together, but somehow I doubt it. I wish you *bon chance, Maman.*

Ta fille, Darcie. X

I could write her an essay with all the things I want to say to her, but I'm conscious of time so this will have to do.

I take the stairs two at a time then place the note underneath the silk pillow in her bedroom. I know she won't risk showing it to Alastor. How would she explain it?

As I close the bedroom door behind me, I look up at the ceiling and think about the room above mine, the one right at the top with the porthole window, the room I'm sure I've heard footsteps coming from on more than one occasion. I think about taking the small separate staircase that leads to it, but when I try, the external door is locked. I stand with my ear against it, listening for a second, my heart beating loudly in my ears as adrenalin pumped through me. But there's nothing but silence.

I can hear Fabienne playing classical music loudly in the kitchen as I creep back down the stairs and see her fixing herself a mid-morning cocktail through the partially opened door. 'It takes the edge off,' she's always said, though the edge of what I have no idea.

I tiptoe through the house barefoot, my holdall over my shoulder, carrying my shoes in my hand. For the first time, I notice just how truly dilapidated this old house is – paint and wallpaper peeling from the crumbling walls, the vast chandelier that hangs in the hallway virtually entombed with cobwebs and dust. Not that Fabienne would ever consider cleaning it. She never gets her own hands dirty.

I don't know why I'm so surprised when the front door won't open.

'*Merde!*' I say crossly as I jangle the lock, wincing as the bolts squeak and object as I attempt to slide them open. It must be locked from the outside, just like my bedroom door was.

Undeterred, I creep into the drawing room at the front of the house and glance around for something I might use to carefully break one of the windows.

Spying a paperweight on the desk – a large glass one with colourful swirls inside it – I take a T-shirt from my holdall, wrap it around the paperweight and over my hand to protect it then take a breath, hoping, praying, that the noise won't alert Fabienne back in the kitchen.

I grimace and flinch as it makes contact with the glass, which finally breaks on the third attempt with a sharp crack.

I stand still. Wait.

When I think it's safe, I throw my holdall through the window, the glass scratching my arm as I crawl through it. Wincing, I press my fingers on the cut then lick them. The blood tastes metallic on my tongue.

'Yes!' I cry triumphantly as I hit the grass below with a dull thud, snatching up my holdall, my body awash with endorphins. I have no money and no idea where I'm going – not even which direction to take. All I know is that I have to get away from this strange, sinister house and its owner, before something terrible happens to me.

When I look out towards the water, there's no boat. I scan the small jetty where it's usually moored, but oddly, it's gone.

I drop my holdall in dismay and force myself not to burst into tears. After a few seconds, I gather myself together. Forget the boat – I'll make my way on foot, walk a thousand miles if I have to.

Bracing myself, I briefly turn back to look at the house. I can still just about hear Fabienne's music emanating from the kitchen. Ironically, she's playing Beethoven's Symphony No. 5 – the finale.

And then I start to walk away.

SEVENTEEN

DAN

'If these walls could talk, eh, boss?' Davis remarks as we sit inside Dr Elizabeth Carmichael's pristine, plush office on what can only be described as a quintessential shrink's couch, albeit an exceptionally comfortable and expensive-looking one.

'Dr Carmichael is on her way,' the confident young receptionist informed us upon arrival. 'She knows you're here and has asked you to wait for her inside her office. She won't be long, traffic permitting.'

'I can only imagine,' I say to Davis, my foot tapping manically against the polished wooden floor. I'm not altogether overjoyed at being kept waiting, not when I've got a vulnerable, pregnant woman still missing, but any information Dr Carmichael may be able to share with us could prove vital.

It's now been over twenty-four hours with no sign of Darcie – or a ransom – which is rapidly and reluctantly forcing me to fear the worst. Working on a high-risk misper case is perhaps even more emotionally challenging than a murder. There's something final about finding a body. While it's tragically the end of the line, there is, at least, some small consolation – a modicum of comfort if you will – for those left behind in that they're able to bury their loved one and begin the arduous process of grieving. In cases like this, there's the added frustration of ambiguity, the agony of not knowing. There's no ambiguity about time however, because it's running out fast, and finding traces of what's almost certainly Darcie's blood on her phone certainly suggests the worst. The longer our girl stays gone, the more likely it is that we'll be looking for a cadaver instead of a living breathing human being. And I can't allow that to happen – not on my watch.

'There's more holes in her backstory than a pair of fishnets, gov,' Mitchell said during this morning's briefing. 'Darcie Vernier, as we know she was before she married, is something of an enigma. She's listed as attending various schools at different locations throughout the country in the late 1990s, early 2000s, though these enrolments aren't consecutive, and were, by all accounts, for relatively short periods. There's times, years in fact, where there are no public records for her whatsoever.'

'Nothing?'

'Zip. Nothing from the educational authority; nothing from the NHS or social services... There's a couple of old addresses from the electoral register, namely where she was living prior to becoming Mrs Bonneville, but there are large gaps of time when she appears to have gone completely off-grid.'

'Didn't Gabe say something about her having lived abroad when she was younger? What about former places of employment, further education...?'

Mitchell nodded. 'We're looking into it now, gov. There's still nothing in terms of her online footprint, except for when she comes up following that incident on the high street with the little girl.'

Mitchell played the shaky amateur video clip of Darcie's heroic act to the team. It showed her sitting on a kerb, her head buried in her hands, as onlookers surrounded her. There was blood on her face, and it was patently clear, as she turned her head away, that she wasn't exactly keen for her image to be caught on camera.

What is it about this woman that's given her the desire to remain anonymous? I wondered.

'It took her late mother's solicitor, the firm dealing with her will and probate, over sixteen months to eventually track Darcie down,' Mitchell said. 'Her mother had been dead for almost two years by then, and incidentally, her solicitor passed away himself before he could execute her will. It had to be passed on to a colleague.'

I nodded. 'I see. Thanks, Mitchell – good work.'

It's actually pretty tricky for a person to go missing these days, not without leaving some kind of footprint, thanks in part to social media – which Darcie seems to have deliberately eschewed. Someone was looking for her, and I suspect they let her know in the form of that anonymous note, which, poor Harding had the misfortune of telling me, has produced no forensic evidence whatsoever – no prints, fibres or DNA, nada.

'The paper and envelope used are made by a company called Smythson of Bond Street,' Harding said, giving me a compensatory look. 'It's 115gsm watermarked laid writing paper, expensive stuff, widely available online, and most big department stores sell it, as well as the flagship store in Bond Street. Interestingly, though, the ink used is seriously high grade and again, expensive – black, 200g, possibly produced by Kobaien, a Japanese company.'

The lack of DNA is a real downer, but Harding's finding did tell me something about the provenance. The paper and ink used to write the note isn't your common or garden kind. It's top-of-the-range stuff, suggesting the user may have been a professional, someone with money perhaps, and if that's the case, then the idea of kidnapping for ransom seems increasingly less likely, unless someone used it to purposefully throw us off the scent – Darcie's husband, or Anita Abberline, for example.

The other question nagging me is why didn't Darcie tell anyone about the note? Why didn't she mention it to her husband the night she received it; call the police even? Was it because she didn't take it seriously? Why do I feel that whoever sent it must've been fairly certain that she wasn't going to alert the authorities? Is she an innocent victim in all of this, or is there something in her past that prevented her from coming forward, something that might cast her in a bad light perhaps?

I brought this up in the team meeting.

'We're working on the assumption that whoever abducted Darcie – potentially Doorcam Man, but let's keep an open mind at this stage – knows her and that they forewarned her by sending her the note,' I said, pointing to the blown-up photocopy of it on the board. 'The question is why? Why would you forewarn someone you'd found them if you were planning to abduct them? She could've come straight to us with it, so why didn't she?'

'There's nothing in any background checks to suggest she had any enemies, gov,' Parker said, which reminded me of Dolly's mum, Shannon. It's clear from Darcie's phone records that she contacted her on quite a few occasions, though it seems Darcie deleted any text communication between them before she blocked her.

'Equally, she didn't have many friends either, not close ones, although everyone we've spoken to so far doesn't have a bad word to say about her. She's a private person by all accounts, and it appears she was happy just to be a stay-at-home wife, although I suspect she may be hiding something from her husband.'

'A wife, hiding something from her husband?' Delaney snorted. 'Well, that would be a first, wouldn't it?' He turned to look at Davis then, and I might've imagined it, but I swear he winked at her.

'I think we need to speak to Bonneville again,' Delaney continued. 'Get him in informally – at this stage anyway. He must know more than he's letting on.'

I hated to admit it, but he was right. We haven't yet discussed with Gabe what we learned from Anita, and we need an informal chat before today's appeal in front of the hungry media – if we ever make it that far.

Dr Carmichael's tardiness is holding us up, and it's beginning to test my patience. I need to go home and change before I go in front of the cameras. Not that what I wear has any bearing on what I'm going to say. However you dress it – or me – up, the message will be the same, although I'm pretty sure Archer would have a small fit if I turned up in the current nineties-boyband-reject holiday get-up I'm *still* wearing.

Restless, I start to mooch around Dr Carmichael's swanky office; pick up a glass paperweight on her slick designer desk. There's a Post-it note underneath it, I assume from her PA/receptionist, that reads: 'John Evergreen called FIVE TIMES – says it's extremely urgent and can you call him back as soon as you return.'

John Evergreen... It could just be wishful thinking, but I'm sure I recognise that name from somewhere.

I replace the paperweight and start pacing up and down, checking my watch. In the corner of the room is an old leather tub chair, and there's a doll sitting on it, one of those old-fashioned porcelain-type ones, dressed in vintage clothing. I feel compelled to pick it up. Clearly it's been repaired at some point because I see visible cracks on its face, fine spidery lines where it's been carefully glued back together.

'They give me the bloody creeps those things.' Davis pulls a face and shudders. 'Look at it – those horrible vacant eyes...'

'They're more popular than you think, Lucy,' I say. 'Some people actually collect them.'

She snorts. 'Yeah, weirdos.'

'Weirdos and criminal psychologists by all accounts. Come on,' I say, 'let's get out of here and come back later. We haven't got time to be kept waiting – the press briefing is at 3 p.m., and I need to go home and get changed.'

Davis raises an eyebrow as she gives me the once-over. 'No shi—'

'Wooooo!' I waggle the doll in front of her face childishly.

'Stop it, gov!' She pushes it away, grimacing. 'It's horrible. Gives me the bloody willies it does.'

And then the door opens.

EIGHTEEN

I feel my face flush red with embarrassment as I place the doll back down on the chair in haste. There's nothing remotely amusing about the circumstances of our visit, but sometimes the need to inject a little lightness into proceedings is imperative just to stay sane in this job. We're only human ourselves after all.

'I must apologise for keeping you waiting – the traffic was especially busy this morning.' Dr Elizabeth Carmichael eyes me curiously as she breezes into the room with a perfumed flourish and removes her smart trench coat. 'Alicia called me and told me you were here, though she didn't say why exactly.'

I shake her hand with some degree of purpose in a bid to claw back some professional dignity.

'DCI Riley – Dan Riley,' I say. 'And this is my colleague, DS Lucy Davis.'

'An absolute pleasure to meet you both.' She smiles affably. 'And please, call me Elizabeth.' She gestures to the sofa. 'Take a seat. Then you can tell me what this is all about.'

We duly sit, though I'm reluctant to in case I can't get back up again.

'I see you found my friend?' She smiles wryly at me as she nods in the doll's direction.

'Ah yes,' I say, my tone apologetic. 'My colleague here isn't a big fan of dolls.'

'Well, she's not alone, Detective Riley. Pediophobia is really quite common. An irrational fear of dolls and mannequins,' she adds.

I'd guessed as much but I suspect she already has me down as some sort of buffoon who needs educating.

'She was a gift actually, from a client,' she explains. 'One of many gifts in fact. I've had some very generous clients over the years.'

'Very thoughtful,' I say, staring down at the doll, 'though I see that she's been broken at some point.'

'Ah, well, haven't we all in some way, Detective? I'd be out of a job if none of us ever were.'

I give a wry smile.

'Actually, we're here to talk to you about someone who may or may not have been a client of yours, Dr Carmichael,' Davis says, cutting to the chase. 'Darcie Bonneville?'

She picks up a gold pen from the table and begins clicking the top of it as she reclines in her seat. I notice that she reads the Post-it note from her PA about returning John Evergreen's urgent calls before disposing of it in the bin under her desk.

Evergreen... Where have I heard that name before?

'Darcie... Darcie Bonneville... Oh yes!' she says after a moment. 'Darcie! Of course. That was quite some months ago now though.' She looks at us expectantly.

'I take it you haven't watched the news in the past twenty-four hours?'

'No,' she says, 'I'm afraid I haven't. I've been shooting a new serial-killer documentary for Netflix these past few days, and, well, it's been a rather demanding schedule. Why, has something happened?'

'She's missing,' I say flatly.

'Missing?' Surprise registers on her even features.

'Yes, since yesterday morning,' Davis continues. 'She went out to walk her dog in the woods near her home, and she hasn't been seen since.'

'We have reason to believe that she may have been abducted,' I add.

Dr Carmichael straightens up in her seat. 'Abducted?' She pulls her chin into her neck, her green eyes widening. 'Oh gosh, how awful! What makes you think that?'

'We found her phone, abandoned, down in the woods and traces of her blood; her dog, returning home without her after its walk; lack of communication with her husband or friends since she left yesterday morning; and a rather foreboding note that was hand delivered to her address the evening before she vanished...'

'A note?' Her eyes widen some more. 'Like a *ransom* you mean?'

'No,' I say, 'more of a... warning.'

'That's interesting.' She pauses thoughtfully. 'What did it say?'

I don't want to divulge the contents of the note to anyone just yet. It may yet turn out to be the secret weapon in our arsenal. In this game, it's often what you don't say as much as what you do that can be telling. Knowing what to reveal and, more importantly, when is paramount. Like most things in this life, timing is everything.

'I'm afraid I can't divulge that information at this stage,' I politely inform her, 'but we know Darcie was a client of yours and that she's been to these premises, perhaps more than once, so we were hoping you might be able to give us some information, anything at all that you feel may be pertinent to our enquiries.'

She shakes her head; looks thoughtful. 'Gosh, well, like I say, I met her some months ago now, just a couple of times...'

'But you keep records, appointment times, and could find them if requested?'

She doesn't take her moss-green eyes from mine. 'If requested, yes, of course. Who told you she was a client of mine?'

'A friend... an associate of Darcie's mentioned that she'd been to see you and that she'd recommended you to her.'

'Really? Ah well, it's always nice to come recommended.' Her affable smile returns. 'Do you know who it was who recommended me?' she asks, adding, 'Just out of interest?'

Davis is about to reply, but something instinctively tells me not to let her.

'And why was Darcie here, Dr Carmichael?' I quickly interject. 'You don't have to give us exact details of the conversations verbatim, just an idea... Was something troubling Darcie? Did she mention anything of note that could potentially be linked to her disappearance? Were you concerned for her mental wellbeing? Did you prescribe her any medication? Did she mention being stalked, being afraid of anything, of anyone...?'

Dr Carmichael takes an audible deep breath. 'Well, as I'm sure you already know, DCI Riley, I'm bound somewhat by client confidentiality as to what I can and can't tell you.'

I sit forward in my seat slightly. 'I suspect that Darcie's been taken from her family, Dr Carmichael, abducted in broad daylight, and we believe that her life may be in danger. If you have *any* information, then I urge you to impart it, because it could make all the difference, and while I respect your professional integrity, I must politely inform you that you also have a duty of care to your client to tell us anything you know that may prove useful to our investigation.'

She holds my gaze for a micro second.

'Of course, of course,' she says after a beat. 'If I can help in any way, I will.' She pauses. 'From what I can remember, she came to me with a phobia she wanted to deal with, something very common, and our sessions were largely successful.'

'A phobia?' I glance sideways at the doll on chair.

'And no' – she smiles – 'it wasn't pediophobia; it was something even more common than that actually. Nothing life-threatening though; nothing to cause me any due concern about her state of mind or mental well-being, at least not at the time.'

'So you didn't diagnose her with depression or any other kind of psychological affliction?'

Dr Carmichael shakes her head vehemently. 'I treat a wide variety of patients and clients, Mr Riley, with problems ranging across a whole spectrum of issues, and of varying degrees, although I treat everyone's concerns equally as seriously of course. If my memory serves me correctly, I found Darcie to be eloquent and personable with no serious psychological issues.'

'Did you take notes from the sessions you had together?' Davis enquires.

'Oh gosh,' she says again, placing a hand briefly on her forehead. 'I'm sure I must've, it's standard practice...'

'There may be a clue, clues plural even, in something she said, something she mentioned... something you may not have picked up on at the time but could prove to be relevant now.'

'Possibly, but I really can't recall offhand,' she replies.

'It could certainly be useful to us if you went through your notes. It may help refresh your memory.'

She looks up at me with a smile. 'The memory is an unreliable witness, Mr Riley. Memories are simply interpretations of what one believes they have seen and experienced. Sometimes, like old paint, it's not always best to stir them.'

She's absolutely right of course, about the former at least. One person's recollection of something can vastly differ from another's, even those who may have experienced the exact same thing at the exact same time. This is why there's often discrepancies in witness statements – no two people's account of anything will ever be a precise match.

'We know her mother died a couple of years ago and left her quite a substantial inheritance. Did she talk to you about that, Dr Carmichael? Did she talk about her mother; about her past?'

She exhales. 'She may well have done, but I see an average of around five patients a day, five days a week, Detective Riley, and sadly I'm not in possession of a photographic memory, though perhaps she did mention her mother, now I come to think of it... and her husband. They'd not long been married if I recall.'

'Did she raise any issues she may have had with her husband, or any issues with anyone in general?' Davis pushes her.

'Hmm, she may have mentioned some unresolved issues with her mother before she died.' She shrugs. 'But like I said, she came to me to cure a phobia ostensibly. Claustrophobia I think it was,' she says. 'It's a very common form of psychological anxiety that anyone can be afflicted by. Anxiety can manifest in myriad ways, through phobias, obsessive thoughts and behaviour, panic attacks... I'm afraid that's as much as I can remember offhand.'

I glance at Davis. 'Darcie has no presence on any social-media platforms and never has done. Were you aware of this, Dr Carmichael? Did she ever mention it, or mention why that might be?'

'No.' She shakes her head; appears baffled. 'I wasn't even aware of it.'

'Don't you find that odd?' I say. 'That someone of Darcie's age had no social-media presence at all?'

'Define odd, Detective?'

She's put me on the spot.

'Unusual, against the norm, peculiar, different, strange, irreg—'

'Perhaps,' she interjects, 'but I was unaware of it. I don't believe it ever came up in any of our sessions together. The potential harm of online activity awareness is becoming much more prevalent though these days, Detective Riley. I have other clients who eschew social media for these very reasons; Darcie may well have been one of them.'

'You're something of a celebrity I hear,' I say, changing the subject. 'Apparently you're a regular on our TV screens, evaluating criminal behaviour, giving an insight into the minds of murders and psychopaths and the like for various crime documentaries?'

She smiles coyly, though I suspect her bashfulness is somewhat disingenuous.

'For my sins.' She blushes slightly. 'I specialise in criminal and forensic psychology and behaviour. In fact, I have and often do work with the police and the justice system. I find the criminal mind fascinating.' Her green – and somewhat seductive – eyes meet mine directly. 'Like your good self I should imagine.'

'Well, that would be one description for it. Actually, while we're here, perhaps you'd be good enough to give us your professional insight into what kind of perpetrator we could be dealing with here – a psychological profile on the type of person who may have abducted her?'

'I'd be delighted to,' she says, her smile still firmly fixed. 'You can contact my agent directly; schedule an interview.' She picks up her pen, scribbles a name and number on a piece of paper and hands it to me. 'I'm sure she'll be happy to set something up.' She stands then, the gesture making it clear our time is up.

'I'm terribly sorry,' she apologises with a head shake, 'but my next client is waiting... and I'm sorry I can't be of more help to you. If I think of anything else, I will of course let you know. I sincerely hope Darcie's found soon. I'm sure she will be,' she says with much more confidence than I'm currently feeling. 'From what I remember of her, she was nothing if not one of life's survivors.'

NINETEEN

DARCIE – AGED FIFTEEN

My feet, numb from hours of walking, feel like they've been amputated. I must've covered acres of distance since leaving the house, vast expanses of space that seem to endlessly stretch out before me. I've no clue where I am or which direction I'm headed. I've seen no landmarks or signposts, no phone or post boxes, nothing but 360-degree blanket green space for miles and rough, rugged terrain that the trainers I'm wearing clearly weren't designed to navigate.

The nearest town can't be too far away; I just need to find the road that leads to it, only there's not even a footpath in sight. My calf muscles burn like they're on fire as I continue to forge ahead on autopilot. I can't turn back now though, even if I have to walk for ten days solid. The more distance I put between myself and that awful house – and its owner – the safer I'll feel.

The light is rapidly disappearing now, the sky a soft, cashmere grey, smattered with contrasting charcoal-coloured clouds that suggest rain. *Great.* I stuff my hands into the pockets of my fleeced hoodie, pull my arms in tight to my body to conserve heat and turn the volume up on my personal stereo. I've allowed myself ten-minute listening slots with breaks in between. I have no idea how long it'll take to reach the town, and I don't want the batteries to die. It's desolate here, and without my music to distract me, I'll be completely alone. Soon the temperature will plummet and the light will disappear, and, stupidly, I realise I haven't even packed a coat. There wasn't time, and besides, I genuinely expected to have reached my destination by now.

As I amble down yet another decline over the terrain, I think about Fabienne and wonder if she's discovered my note yet. Alastor will have long since returned home by now – complete with promised engagement ring no doubt. What will she tell him? How will she explain my absence? Whatever she says, I suspect it won't be the truth. Fabienne is a consummate liar. It's in her DNA somehow, as automatic as breathing.

The sense of her betrayal feels palpable as I continue putting one foot in front of the other. If only she'd listened to me; heard what I was trying to tell her and taken my feelings into consideration for once in her life, then I wouldn't have been forced to take such drastic action.

Sadness overwhelms me. I'd always thought, hoped, that Fabienne would change – and that I'd never have to leave her. Despite everything, she's still my mother, and she's all I have. But Fabienne only sees what she wants to see, and faced with a choice between me and the pot of gold at the end of the rainbow she's forever chasing, I know I wasn't even in the running.

I couldn't tell you which direction I'm headed – north, south, west or east. I'm just following my gut, which is, incidentally, starting to make strange noises. My last meal was yesterday evening – I avoided eating at breakfast to sell the lie about my stomach pains. I haven't even brought any snacks for the journey, though thankfully I did manage to grab some bottled water from my bedside table and stuff it into my holdall before making my exit.

An overwhelming urge to burst into tears suddenly comes over me as I turn in circles, and the sheer hopelessness of my situation hits me. Nightfall is imminent, and if I don't reach the town, I'm not sure what I'll do. It's freezing, and I'm starving.

The light has all but disappeared now. It could take another ten or so hours of crossing uneven terrain to get back to the house if I turn around, and I'm not sure I have the physical strength left to do that. Plus, I can only imagine the punishment Fabienne would mete out if I did. She'd probably smash my stereo to pieces, burn my books and magazines and—

Suddenly something catches my eye in the near distance. I stop, a little breathless, and stare out into the abyss. I haven't even brought a torch with me – how stupid is that? I feel a rush of self-loathing mushroom through me. *Idiot!* I hadn't thought any of this through properly. I hadn't thought at all.

I think I can detect a soft change in the light ahead. It's some distance below me, but I head in its direction, the steep decline I meet forcing me to gather pace until I have no choice but to break into a run.

Moving closer, I make out what looks like a narrow country lane. It's not lit, but the newly appearing moonlight reflecting off the tarmac gives it a gentle illumination.

'Yes! *Yessss!*' I'm half laughing, half crying as I reach the verge, my chest heaving like it's ready to burst open. It's all I can do to stop myself dropping to my knees and kissing the tarmac beneath me. *The road to town!*

I feel a fat droplet of water splash onto my neck then, quickly followed by a few more, until the sky bursts open like a faulty pipe. It's started to rain, as I'd predicted. But I don't care. *I'm free.* All I need to do now is follow the road ahead. But which way do I take – left or right?

I stand in the middle of the road, acutely aware of the potential consequences of taking the wrong turn and—

There's no time to react as I see the headlights of a car speeding towards me, only realising what's about to happen a second before the vehicle careens into me.

. . .

The first thing I feel when I open my eyes is relief, closely followed by pain. I'm in a bed, though it doesn't feel familiar. I try to move, to sit up, but when I do, a sharp sensation splinters through my ribcage, causing me to cry out. Once it subsides slightly, I glance around the room from my horizontal position.

It's a tiny space – I estimate no more than six foot by four – and it's empty, save for a small chair in the corner, one of those old-fashioned ones you see in primary schools – metal and wood. There's something on it, though the lack of light makes it difficult for me to determine what.

I blink; allow my vision to try to adjust to the near darkness.

A thin outline of light escapes around the edges of the boarded-up window, telling me it must be daytime. I attempt to move again; shuffle downwards on the bed, but the pain shoots up through me like an arrow, and I wince in agony. *What happened to me? Where am I?*

As the pale yellow dots and splashes in front of my eyes begin to dissipate, I realise what it is, on the chair. *A doll.* It's pale porcelain face glows through the inky darkness, the sliver of light from the window gently highlighting its synthetic hair and—

A bomb suddenly detonates inside me, exploding through my internal organs. *The window... the doll...*

'Hello?' I call out, the shaky vibration of my voice sending shockwaves of pain through my chest. I'm hurt, but I'm not sure how badly, or how I've become that way. 'Is anyone there?' The last thing I remember is walking down a hillside towards the road and...

'Hello, Darcie.'

The voice startles me, and I turn my head to try to locate it. A tall, shadow figure moves towards me through the darkness.

'Alastor?' My voice is a shaky warble. 'Is that you?'

TWENTY

'Fabienne! Maman! Maman!' I cry out, despite the pain it causes me. 'Where is she? Where is Fabienne? I want to see my mother!'

'Now, Darcie, calm yourself,' Alastor says. His tone is even, but there's something about it that immediately unsettles me.

'Fabienne! *Fabienne!*' I attempt to pull myself up into a seated position, yelping through the agony.

'Shout all you want, but she'll not hear you,' he says, almost apologetically. 'This room is completely soundproofed.' He bangs the wall with his fist as though to demonstrate. 'I installed it myself – walls and floor. Mass-loaded vinyl and plywood.' He surveys it, seemingly pleased with his handiwork. 'Very dense.'

I have no idea what he's talking about.

'Soundproofed? Why? What for?' A deep sense of unease is multiplying like bacteria in my gut and slowly morphing into stone-cold fear. 'What happened to me?' I grip the sheets on the bed. 'I'm in pain.'

'Yes, I'm sure you are, but not to worry – I'll give you something for that. I'll make sure you're comfortable.' He smiles crookedly. 'I'm going to look after you, Darcie, I promise.'

'Where's my mother? I want to see her,' I demand.

He sighs gently and sits down on the edge of the bed. I shrink away from him.

'You had an accident,' he says.

'What kind of accident?' I feel groggy, like I've woken from a hundred-year sleep, but split-second flashes of memory are starting to fire up inside my brain.

The monotonous left, right of my unsuitable trainers marching over hilly terrain... The sound of Destiny's Child playing on my personal stereo...

'When Fabienne told me you'd left, I knew you couldn't have got too far, although I was quite impressed by the distance you managed to cover, I must say – and then suddenly, BOOM!' The sharp clap of his hands causes me to flinch. 'You stepped right out in front of me! There was no time for me to brake.'

The country lane... The road that led to the town... Headlights.

'Here, have some water.' He brings a bottle up to my lips; tilts it. 'That's it, drink up. There's a good girl.'

He watches me as I gulp it back greedily. My mouth feels tacky and dry, like straw.

'I think you may have broken a rib or two, and you have some bruising, but nothing life-threatening.'

'You... you hit me, with your *car*?' My instincts are telling me it was no accident, though I try to push the thought away, ignore it. 'Shouldn't I be in the hospital?'

It's only then I realise, when I look down at myself, that I'm wearing what appears to be an old-fashioned nightgown, long and gauzy, like something a grandmother might own. Did he undress me while I was unconscious? Nausea rises through my belly.

'No need for that,' he says, almost jovial. 'They'll not do anything for you that I can't. Anyway, how do you like your new room?' he asks. 'I realise it's something of a step down from your former residence – one you decided was no longer good enough for you – but this one even has its own en suite, look!' He makes the few small steps it takes to reach the bathroom door and opens it. 'Ta-da! Your own sink and toilet. No shower I'm afraid, but in time you may earn the right to take one, under strict supervision of course.'

What does he mean 'earn the right' and 'under strict supervision'? I try to swallow back the fire of fear that's igniting in the pit of my stomach.

'I... I want to see Fabienne,' I repeat, but I drop the attitude down a notch. 'Does she know that I'm here – that I'm hurt?'

His head cocks to the side, his small, dark eyes narrowing as he looks at me. 'I'm afraid not, Darcie. Your mother told me that you'd gone back to Paris, to be with your sick grandmother. She said you left her a note, that it was all rather sudden... So this' – he gestures around the room with his hands theatrically – 'this is your new home now, the *forever* home you've always longed for.'

Forever home? Fear and nausea collides within me, but a surge of rage suddenly ameliorates the feeling inside me, pushing right past it and up into my throat.

'What are you talking about, you freak? I want my mother! I want Fabienne... You can't stop me from seeing her! You can't keep me in this room! LET ME OUT!'

I attempt to swing my legs over the edge of the bed, to stand, but the pain in my ribs rips through me, disabling me. I flop back down onto it, clutching my diaphragm.

He shoots me a look of exasperated pity. 'You really are quite the spirited little thing, aren't you?' He smiles that crooked smile again; appears amused. 'But you see, Darcie, sometimes we all have to learn the hard way...'

'What do you mean?' I protest, my voice cracking. 'Just let

me see my mother! I want to see Fabienne.' I start to cry; I can't help it.

'I'm afraid that's not possible, Darcie. Anyway, Fabienne is busy with our wedding plans. We have just a couple of days to organise everything. It's a shame you won't be able to attend. Perhaps, if you're a good girl, I'll bring you a slice of wedding cake as a special treat.'

I attempt to roll away from him. I don't want him to see the tears that have started to leak down my cheeks.

'There, there, Darcie – don't upset yourself,' he says as he begins stroking my hair, brushing strands of it from my face almost lovingly.

I push his hand away, but he continues, 'Beautiful...' His voice is a trailing whisper as he fixes me with a glazed expression. 'Like a living doll...

'Oh! Speaking of which.' He goes over to the chair, takes the doll from it and places it next to me on the bed. 'There,' he says. 'I managed to repair her after you broke her. Poor Tabitha.' He touches the doll's face with gentle fingers. 'What did she ever do to you to deserve that kind of treatment, eh? *You* wouldn't want someone smashing *your* pretty little face in now, would you, Darcie?'

It sounds like a thinly veiled threat and I silently shake my head.

'I'll bring you something to eat,' he says, smacking his knees with his hands in that way people do when they're about to stand with purpose. 'Don't worry, I'll not starve you. There'll be three meals a day – breakfast, lunch and supper. And, depending on your conduct, there'll be opportunities to earn yourself snacks and treats, maybe even some privileges, like your personal stereo for example.'

I screw my eyes tightly shut, paralysed by pain and confusion and fear.

He removes a set of keys from his inside jacket pocket. 'I'm going to lock the door now, Darcie. Keep you nice and safe. Papa will get you all better soon, so he will.'

'Please, Alastor,' I beg him, 'don't lock me in here. Let me see Fab— let me see *Maman*. She'll be worried about me; I know she will. I promise I'll not run away again, ever, just please... please don't lock me in.'

His head is still cocked to one side as he watches me plead, a crooked smile on his face.

'Rest up now, Darcie,' he says. 'I'll be back soon.'

TWENTY-ONE

DARCIE – SIX MONTHS AGO

'Twenty-seven days.' I glance up at Dr Carmichael. 'That's how long he kept me locked inside that tiny, airless room. Twenty-seven desolate days of a despair I'd never felt before – and never *ever* want to feel again.'

I suppose I'm expecting some kind of reaction from Dr Carmichael as I impart this all to her – shock or pity – but there isn't so much as a slight widening of her eyes; her face is almost unnervingly blank, making me wonder if it's a deliberate tactic psychologists use to encourage their clients to keep talking. Not that I needed much of that; not now that the touchpaper has been lit.

I've come to look forward to my weekly sessions with Elizabeth Carmichael. Opening up to her seems to have kick-started a process whereby I'm finally beginning to release all the bad memories – and the myriad emotions attached to them. Such catharsis had imbued me with a sense of well-being that's difficult to describe, like the gratitude you feel after recovering from a particularly nasty illness and your health returns. Anyway, whatever it is that Dr Carmichael's doing, it seems to be working. Even Gabe has picked up on my next-level good vibes.

'You seem especially chipper today, gorgeous,' he noted as I readied myself for my appointment this morning, checking my hair in the mirror by the door and spritzing myself with perfume.

I suppose I've started to feel slightly less guilty about concealing my weekly visits to Dr Carmichael from my husband on the premise that it's going some distance in helping me to unpick and unpack my troubled and traumatic past, which will ultimately be good for our relationship.

'Chipper?' I ribbed him, tickled by such an old-fashioned choice of word.

He approached me, pulled me close into his body and started making small animal noises as he nuzzled and nibbled at my neck affectionately. I giggled like a giddy schoolgirl. That's how my husband makes me feel, like I can just forget myself and simply be happy in the moment.

'Yeah, you seem, I don't know... full of beans.'

Our bodies began to do a little jig together before I eventually retreated from him, conscious of time.

'And you *smell* gorgeous.'

I kissed him full on the mouth then snatched my handbag from the console table. Perhaps all I'd ever really needed to do was just to tell *somebody* about it.

'Each day was the same as the next,' I duly continue to Dr Carmichael, 'nights seamlessly blending into endless days and vice versa. I would try to gauge the time of day by the change in the thin outline of light that slipped through the boarded-up window, but it wasn't always easy to tell. At first I used mealtimes as an indicator – breakfast, lunch and "supper" as he called it, though I've always disliked that word for some reason... Anyway, he soon cottoned onto this and started deliberately mixing it up just to mess with my head, bringing me breakfast at suppertime, lunch in the morning... He wanted to keep me off balance.'

'Tell me, if you had no real concept of time, as you say, then how do you know you spent twenty-seven days locked away inside that room?' Dr Carmichael appears genuinely intrigued as she clicks the top of her pen up and down in quick succession. I try not to focus on it; it's distracting, irritating even.

'I used my hair.' I take a strand between my fingers, pull it out from the root and hold it up to her. 'I'd pluck a strand out for each day I was locked up, placed each one carefully between a concertinaed sheet of toilet paper. That's how I knew – how I counted the days.'

'How imaginative of you.' Her brows rise with a small, bordering-on-wry smile.

That first night, locked inside that tiny cell, I battered my fists blue against the door in an attempt to alert Fabienne of my presence. I screamed and shouted until my voice was hoarse. My throat felt like it was bleeding as I cried and hollered through the pain in my ribs until I exhausted myself to sleep, beginning the process over again once I woke. Eventually, after a few days of repeating this ritual, I was forced to concede that Alastor was right – no one was coming.

I was alone.

As much as I couldn't put anything past Fabienne, I didn't want to believe that she'd willingly allow such a thing to happen to me, to her own flesh and blood. She may have been cruel in that she was greedy and selfish and narcissistic, but she wasn't a sadist. And I'd unwittingly shot myself in the foot in writing her that goodbye note. She knew I'd run away of my own volition, and I'd promised that Alastor would discover her true motives if she told him as much. So she probably wasn't searching for me, especially after spinning him that story about me returning to Paris, to be with a sick grandmother I'd never met and was also, according to Fabienne, long dead. I wondered if Alastor believed her. But I knew Fabienne: she could tell you black was white and you wouldn't even think to question it – she really was that skilful a liar.

I knew that once Fabienne had achieved her goal and married Alastor, she would almost immediately begin planning her exit, and that terrified me. What would Alastor do once he realised the woman he'd married in good faith had tricked him to get her hands on half his fortune? Would he punish *me* for her deceptions, and if so, *how*? Stuck inside that cell alone, with nothing but silence and darkness around me – and that horrible doll for company – my imagination travelled to the darkest places.

'During those first few days of my captivity, I clung on to blind hope that I'd be found somehow. But as the hours turned into days, and those days turned into weeks, that blind hope gradually ebbed away until it ceased to exist at all.' I feel an ache in my chest as feelings of raw and utter despair resurrect within me.

Dr Carmichael can see I'm struggling.

'Try to feel through those difficult memories, Darcie,' she encourages me gently.

'Silence has a sound all of its own,' I continue, willing my heart rate to slow. Just talking about it catapults me back there. 'I became hyper aware of every tiny noise, the almost musical sound of the wind as it whipped against the window, the crunch of the bed sheets as I tossed and turned among them, the algorithm of my own breathing... Night-times were the worst.'

'Yes.' Dr Carmichael's eyes soften. 'I understand.'

Only I'm not quite sure that she does, or that she, or anyone else, ever could unless they'd been where I was.

'You must've been very frightened.'

'Sometimes I heard scratching, that same scratching noise as before, and the creaking of wood above me. One night there was a soft tapping sound, like fingers playing out the chords of a song against the floorboards.'

'What did you think was making those sounds, Darcie?'

I suck in a deep lungful of air. 'Not what,' I say, 'but who.'

I check Dr Carmichael's face to gauge her reaction. She probably thinks I'm a little bit tapped to be fair.

'You thought it was a person you heard in the room at the top of the house?'

I feel a sharp shift in my energy, like a dark cloud has moved over me. Suddenly I don't want to talk about it anymore.

'Anyway' – I briefly look up at her – 'I was half deranged by then; I think I was starting to go crazy through fear and despair. I was hearing things, imagining things; my mind went to such awful places, and—'

My breath catches in my throat, and Dr Carmichael's hand shoots to my knee where she gently rests it for a moment until my heart rate settles.

'I was in a perpetual state of heightened anxiety, always waiting for that key to turn in the lock, not knowing if today would be the day that Alastor...'

'The day that Alastor what, Darcie?'

'I don't know.' I try to shake the words out of me. Just remembering it all is so re-traumatising. 'Attacked me, tortured me, raped me, forced me to do inhuman things... *killed me?*'

'And with the obvious exception of the latter, did he do any of those things to you?'

I pause for a moment; wipe the rims of my eyes with a finger.

'No.'

She removes her hand from my knee, and I instantly miss it.

'I had fantasies of overpowering him of course, but I was no physical match for him at all. I was fifteen and weighed about 40kg at the time, and Alastor was at least six foot' – surreptitiously, I see that Dr Carmichael has written down the words 'six foot two' in her notebook and circled them – 'and he probably weighed almost three times what I did. Overpowering him remained nothing more than obsessive and indulgent wishful thinking. But by then my fear was ever so gradually rolling into something else – a fight for survival. I didn't want to die in that room never having lived. I *had* to get out somehow.

'I'd thought of hiding behind the door and smashing him over the head with the small metal chair when he came to bring me food, only it was screwed tightly to the floor. The cutlery he gave me to eat the bland, unappetising food he brought daily were made of plastic, utterly useless as weapons, and he always took them away with the plastic plate he served my meals on. Every evening – or perhaps morning; I could never be sure which was which – he brought me a plastic beaker of milk to drink.

'"Drink it all up – there's a good girl, Darcie. Calcium – it's good for the bones!"'

The memory of his voice makes me shudder.

'After a while, I suspected he was drugging me, slipping something into the milk, trying to keep me docile and compliant. So I'd stick my fingers down my throat and throw it back up in the toilet once he left.'

I glance up at the clock on the wall. I hear it ticking, something I hadn't noticed until now. I've been talking so much I hadn't realised that our session should've ended ten minutes ago.

'Don't worry about the time,' Dr Carmichael says with a reassuring nod, catching me. 'It's important that we continue. So,' she says, edging a little closer to me, almost conspiratorially, 'tell me how you did it, Darcie. How exactly *did* you escape?'

TWENTY-TWO

DAN

I'm sitting opposite Gabe Bonneville in a small holding room ahead of the public appeal we're about to give to a packed room full of eager hacks. Understandably, he looks like half the man I met yesterday, like he's somehow lost a few inches with worry. He rakes a hand through his enviably thick mop of curly hair.

'I honestly didn't think it was relevant,' he says flatly when I ask him about the business Anita mentioned with the nurse. 'It didn't even cross my mind to tell you about it – why would it? It was something that happened years ago, and there was absolutely no truth to it whatsoever.' His voice sounds strained at the edges. He drops his head into his hands for a split second before gathering his composure.

'I wasn't the first doctor she'd made false allegations against either. There were two others whose lives and reputations she almost ruined.' He pauses, looking pained at having to resurrect the clearly unpleasant memory. 'She wasn't a well woman,' he adds.

'I'm sorry I've had to bring it up,' I say with genuine remorse. 'No one wants to cause you any more distress, Gabe, I assure you, but these things always have to be looked into.'

He exhales loudly. 'Well, if you think she's got anything to do with Darcie's disappearance, then I can assure you that's not possible.'

I tilt my head towards him.

'She committed suicide about two years after I was exonerated. Like I say, she wasn't a well person.'

He links his hands together, placing them on top of his head as he stands then starts pacing. 'The press are going to have a field day with this, aren't they? They'll make me out to look like some kind of sex pest – someone who's capable of killing his wife.'

'No one mentioned killing anyone,' Martin Delaney, who until now has been sitting silently to my left, suddenly pipes up.

Gabe shoots him a withering expression. 'This is insane!' he says.

'OK.' I nod. 'OK.' The poor man looks on the verge of collapse.

'It was bad enough dealing with it at the time, trust me, let alone having it all raked up again now on top of everything. I know how people will think, even though all the allegations were proven to be false. Mud tends to stick,' he says resignedly.

'Actually, that's exactly what Anita said,' I say.

'It was Anita? She told you about Caroline Bradley?' He emits a soft snort of laughter, though there's no real humour to it. 'Never could keep a secret that one.'

'She mentioned that you two were once an item, you and Anita.'

He flops back down in the chair. 'Anita and I dated on and off for a couple of years when we were kids – just *kids*. It wasn't anything serious.'

'She claims you were both "madly in love" with each other.' I feel my eyebrows rise a touch.

He sighs heavily. 'Yeah, well, Anita does like to embellish our historic romance a little, make out we were some sort of modern-day Romeo and Juliet, when in truth, it was little more than a student relationship that was never going to go the distance, for me at least.'

'Do you think she might be jealous?' I put the question to him coolly but candidly. 'Of you and Darcie's relationship? The two of you have remained friends...'

He blows air through his nostrils. 'Don't get me wrong, Detective Riley. I like Anita – always have. But she wasn't the one for me.' He leans forward in his seat. 'It was over twenty years ago now... I was the one who introduced her to her husband, Hugh. We're good friends – and colleagues. If Anita's jealous of my relationship with Darcie, then she hides it pretty well, at least to our faces. It's not a secret that we once dated, but we don't discuss it, and it's never been a problem as far as I know, not for any of us.' He looks up at me. 'We're all adult about it.'

'She, Anita, told me that you'd suffered something of a breakdown after the accusations were made against you and that you started gambling, drinking...'

He snorts derisively. 'Really? I'm surprised she didn't tell you my inside-leg measurements!'

I lean towards him. 'Look, I realise this all must be awkward and unpleasant for you. I assure you that I'm not here to judge; that's not my job, but finding your wife *is*. We've all got skeletons in our closet – things we'd rather others didn't know about. But you must understand why I—'

'Yes, yeah of course,' he sighs. 'I suppose I did go a bit wonky for a while after all that business – partying too much; the occasional night in a casino to blow off steam – but that's all it ever was. I never found myself on the wrong side of it, if that's what you're getting at. I knew it was a mug's game; knocked it on the head after a while and got my act together. I wasn't going to allow myself to be a victim and lose everything I'd worked so hard to achieve.'

'I'm glad to hear that, Gabe,' I say.

Delaney clears his throat loudly; leans back in his chair. 'Did you know that Darcie had been seeing a psychiatrist, Gabe – someone by the name of Dr Elizabeth Carmichael?'

He glances over at Delaney then back at me.

'No,' he says. The surprise seems genuine. 'Recently you mean?'

I nod.

'About six months ago, she attended therapy sessions with someone called Dr Elizabeth Carmichael.'

'Never heard of her. Darcie never mentioned it to me.'

'Did Darcie ever talk to you about her mother; about her childhood in general?'

I strongly sense that something in Darcie's past is the missing link in all of this, though what that something is I've no idea.

Gabe drags his palms down his face. Frankly, I think it's testament to the man's character that he hasn't already buckled under the strain of everything. I feel a stab of admiration for him as he reaches for the plastic cup of water on the Formica table.

'Like I've already told you, not much. I knew her mother's name was Fabienne and that they were estranged when she died; hadn't seen each other in twenty-odd years or thereabouts I think. And that obviously she left her a fortune when she passed.'

He opens his palms. 'They moved around a lot when Darcie was a child, and I think she resented her mother for it. I could tell she was uncomfortable talking about her, so I never really pushed it. Maybe that's why she went to see someone – talk to a professional?'

Delaney's cage suddenly rattles. 'So you *didn't* know that Darcie was pregnant, you *didn't* know she was seeing a psychiatrist, you *don't* really know exactly why she and her mother – who left her shy of four million when she died – became estranged, and you also can't explain why she's never had any presence on social media? Please don't get me wrong, Gabe, but you don't seem to know an awful lot about your wife, do you?'

There's a pause, then Gabe looks up from the table. 'Well, I know *one* thing.' He meets Delaney's eye. 'I know that I *love* my wife, love her deeply, and that I want – hope – to spend the rest of my life with her and watch our child, maybe even children, grow up together.'

Delaney has the good grace to stay silent. I'm not a fan of his interview approach. I'm not a fan full stop. He possesses all the balance of a truck on a tight rope, and right now, on top of everything, I'm unenviably tasked with having to tell Gabe that we've upgraded the investigation to a suspected homicide.

Archer called me into her office earlier. 'There's been no sign of her, no ransom...' She looked at me gravely. 'We're going to send in the cadaver dogs; start searching for a body.'

My eyes dropped down to my embarrassing trainers. A body? I wasn't so sure.

'I want you to reassure the public in today's appeal that we're still doing everything in our powers to find her, and that her safety is paramount. Seriously, Dan,' she sighed, pushing her glasses a touch further up her nose so that they sat precisely on the bridge, 'what's your gut telling you on this?'

'I think she's still alive, ma'am,' I said.

'Wishful thinking perhaps?'

'Intuition.' I shrugged, awaiting some kind of barbed response from her about facts and evidence, but it didn't come. 'I think she's still out there.'

'Yes, but *where*, Riley, and *why*?' Her voice rose an octave. 'And what's all this about the husband? Did I hear noises about sexual harassment allegations made against him by some nurse?'

I nodded. 'Historic allegations, and I believe he was exonerated completely, but we're checking whether there might be a link. Someone holding a grudge.'

'What about the girl's mum – the little girl Darcie saved on the high street that time? Didn't the husband say she'd become something of a pest?'

'We'll be speaking to Shannon Taylor later today, ma'am. She has a couple of arrests for shoplifting on file but no convictions. The only motive I can see for her being involved would be money, and without a ransom demand...'

'Bloody hell!' Archer slammed her hand down onto her desk, sending her pens scattering across it. It was tricky to tell what she was most upset about – our lack of progress or the pens.

'Listen, Gabe.' I broach the subject softly. 'I'm sorry to have to tell you this, but after due consideration, the investigation is now being treated as a potential homicide.'

'Oh Jesus.' He drops his forehead against the small table, and I glance at Delaney's expressionless face.

'I thought I should tell you before we greet the baying mob in there. Look,' I say, 'with no ransom forthcoming, the evidence we have so far of the note and the CCTV footage of a man delivering it, we don't have much choice, *but—*'

'No... not my Darc – not my Darcie,' he says, sitting up straight. 'She's alive – I know she is. I'd feel it if she wasn't; I'd feel it here.' He bangs his chest with a fist, and it makes a hollow noise against his ribs.

'Listen, we haven't found a body, and there's evidence to suggest she may have been taken but nothing yet to indicate that she's been murdered, OK? I haven't given up hope, Gabe, so please, don't you.'

'This can't be happening,' he says, pressing his eyes with a thumb and forefinger. 'You think my wife – my most likely *pregnant wife* – and my child are dead!'

I squeeze his shoulder in reassurance as he opens the collar on his shirt, which incidentally is notably slicker than my own.

I'd rushed back home to my apartment earlier with Davis in tow to finally change out of my nineties-boyband-reject 'leisurewear' only to discover that Fiona had, for some reason, taken my two best – my two *only* – suits, plus most of my clothes, which incidentally isn't many – for the holiday I'm supposed to be on.

'There's a charity shop down the road,' Davis said in a light-bulb moment as we both stared at the back of my empty old wardrobe. 'I'll run down there now – see what they've got.'

She returned less than half an hour later holding something grey and shiny on a hanger.

'The seventies called,' I said, staring at it in horror. 'They want their suit back.'

I'd thrown it on anyway in the absence of options. I just hoped no one had died in it.

I just hope no one has died full stop.

TWENTY-THREE

My late father, God rest his soul, was a big fan of an adage.

'Never judge a book by its cover, Danny Boy!'

'A leopard never changes his spots, son!'

'Strike while the iron is hot.'

Well, you get the idea.

One of my least favourite sayings was, 'Things could always be worse,' a line he'd deploy whenever I confided a gripe or problem I might've had to him. I've always felt that the phrase somehow minimised the problem and thus invalidated the person with it.

Oddly though, this is the exact phrase that comes to mind as Davis and I pull up outside Brownstone Estate, a particularly aesthetically displeasing concrete tower block monstrosity, so high it almost disappears into the clouds.

'This place is *so* depressing,' Davis remarks as she pushes the burned-out button to call the lift to take us to the thirteenth floor. *Unlucky for some.* 'Look at it – they should've pulled it down years ago.'

I don't disagree with her. Brownstone Estate is notorious for all the wrong reasons. Poverty is rife here; and ergo it follows

that crime is too. One rarely exists without the other. That isn't
to say that everyone who resides here is of an unsavoury nature
of course – families call it home too, decent folk as well as a few
dregs. Still, you wouldn't want to walk through it on your own
late at night.

'Come *ooon*.' Davis pushes the button in quick succession
impatiently. 'There's only one bloody lift working in the whole
place,' she says, just as the door finally opens with a hiss and
we're hit by the pungent smell of urine.

'Ew, it stinks.' She pulls a face as I tentatively step inside the
lift, careful to check where I'm treading.

'Well, Davis' – I turn to her – 'things could always be
worse.'

We're met by a cacophony of human noise as we take the
walkway along to number 118 on the thirteenth floor: TVs blar-
ing, mothers shrieking at unruly kids, the deep repetitive thud
of techno music... I press the buzzer. Wait. Press it again.

'Who is it?' a young woman's voice finally echoes from the
intercom.

'Shannon? Shannon Taylor?'

'Who's this?' I can hear a child in the background – the
squeaky high-pitched voice of a little girl.

'Detective Chief Inspector Dan Riley,' I reply, 'and my
colleague, DS Lucy Davis. Can we come in?'

There's a pause.

'Why?'

Davis rolls her eyes and sighs. It's no more than we
expected. Coppers and Brownstone, like the proverbial oil and
water, just don't mix.

'We'd like to talk to you. It won't take a few minutes.'

'What about?' she asks cautiously.

'Just let us in, Shannon, and we'll tell you,' Davis interjects
irritably. I suspect, like me, she's suffering from fatigue and is
feeling ratty. We've been on the go for a day and half now.

'Got a warrant, 'ave ya?'

'Do we need to get one?' Davis asks. 'Because we can, Shannon, if we have to.'

Another pause.

'All right, all right.' She tuts, opens the catch to the door then turns her back on us as she slinks back up the hallway.

The apartment is certainly compact, which is a diplomatic way of saying you couldn't swing a cat in it – incidentally, another saying favoured by the old man, but it's clean and tidy.

'Hello there.' I spot Dolly on the floor by the TV, playing with a naked biro-covered doll and a small squishy-looking giraffe. An ache forms inside my chest as I watch her happily chatting away to herself in a language I'm pretty sure only she understands. She's a similar age to Juno, to my Pip, and I feel a stab of guilt, like a jab to my ribs. I should be with my daughter now, with my wife and my baby son and Leo and Mimi. We should be enjoying a rare family vacation together, playing board games and enjoying long chilly beach walks and making memories... But instead I'm here, and as yet no closer to locating Darcie, to bringing her home, safe and unharmed.

'What you got there?' I crouch down next to her, and she looks up at me with a pair of wide, inquisitive brown eyes.

'Geruf,' she says, handing me the squishy-looking soft toy.

'Ah... giraffe!' I say. 'Look at his *loooooooong* neck!'

A smile explodes onto her small, chubby face, and I run a hand over the top of her soft brown curls.

'Don't be fooled by the butter-wouldn't-melt looks,' Shannon remarks, watching me. 'She can be a right little cow when she wants to be.'

I smile. 'I've got one of my own like this – similar age.'

She shoots me a backward glance as she resumes folding clothes on the small kitchen table. 'Lucky you. So, what's this about then? If you're looking for him, he ain't 'ere; ain't been here pretty much since she was born.'

'He?'

Shannon continues folding the washing without looking up. 'Her dad, Jason. That's why you're 'ere, ain't it – for him? That's why you lot are always ere, and I tell you the same fing every time. I ain't seen him, and I don't want to.'

I straighten up; leave Dolly to her toys. 'Actually, we're here to talk to you, Shannon.'

She flashes me a brief sideways glance. 'This ain't about the tab down the corner shop, is it? That miserable old bastard Mr Ahmed? I told him I was gonna settle up as soon as my Universal Credit came through.'

I glance at Davis.

'Actually, we wanted to ask you about Darcie Bonneville,' she says.

Shannon stops folding the washing for a second but doesn't look up.

'Oh... *her.*' I detect a slight hint of bitterness in her tone. 'What about her?'

She takes a roll-up from the ashtray on the table; lights it.

'You do know that she's missing?'

'Missing?'

I can tell by her response that it's come as a surprise to her.

'You haven't watched the news lately, Shannon?' Davis enquires.

She shrugs again. 'Same old crap about rich politicians and that... I prefer a bit of *Love Island* meself.'

'We believe that Darcie was abducted from Ravens Wood yesterday morning, and that she may have come to harm.'

She pulls her chin into her neck. 'What? Like... snatched, you mean? You're kiddin' me, right?'

She blinks at Davis and me; appears genuinely shocked.

'I only wish we were. How well do you know Darcie?'

'Me? Not very... In fact, I didn't really know her at all.'

'But you kept in contact with her, following the incident on the high street when she saved Dolly?'

She glances at Davis and I simultaneously; flicks her long hair from her pretty face.

'Well, yeah... I mean, I text her a few times after and that, thanking her, you know.'

'Do you still have those texts on your phone, Shannon? We'd really like to see them.'

She looks nervous all of a sudden. 'I dunno. Maybe. Probably.'

'We'd be grateful if you would check,' I say, flashing her an amenable smile. 'You see, your number was blocked from contacting Darcie. Have you any idea why?'

She lowers her eyes back to the washing on the table; starts balling up small pairs of socks and pink glittery tights.

'Am I in some kind of trouble?' she asks cautiously.

'We just want to find out about the exchanges that took place between you both,' Davis reassures her.

She visibly swallows. 'After it happened, you know, her saving Dolls and that, the media picked up on the story. Some kids had posted it on YouTube and Insta, and they wanted me to give interviews, only they wanted us both to do 'em, together like – was gonna pay us and everything.' She looks over at us. 'Well, I weren't gonna look a gift horse in the mouth, was I? Why shouldn't I make some money out of it? It's not like I couldn't do with it, is it?' she says miserably, glancing around the pokey flat.

'And Darcie?' Davis asks. 'Did she agree? Was she up for doing any publicity?'

Shannon sniffs. 'Nah, she weren't. She didn't want anyfink to do with it; told me to piss off – well, in so many words.'

'And you weren't happy?'

Her demeanour feels defensive suddenly. 'Well, I weren't exactly over the moon was I? I suppose I... Well, maybe I bugged her about it a bit, sent a few too many texts. And then she blocked me, didn't she? So that was that. It's like what I was saying to John – the magazines and TV shows weren't interested in the story unless she was part of it. It was all right for her; I read in the papers that she's some rich housewife, married to a doctor or something, lives in some big posh house – basically loaded. I mean, all she had to do was give 'em a couple of interviews, pose for a few photos! Not exactly a hard day's work, but she was having none of it.'

'John? Who's John, Shannon?'

Dolly wanders into the small kitchenette area then, looks up at Davis and shows her the doll.

'Where are her clothes?' Davis crouches down to meet her eyes. 'She's naked!'

Dolly starts giggling. 'Bum-bum!' she says.

'Go in there, Dolly,' Shannon snaps at her, shooing her away.

'I dunno really, just some weirdo I see on the high street sometimes,' she continues. 'He saw the clips on YouTube; recognised us from them – started acting like we was famous or something; kept trying to talk to us. He's a bit odd, but he's all right I suppose. He bought Dolly some sweets last time we saw him. I told him about how she, Darcie, didn't want to do no publicity and that I was a bit pissed off about it, about losing out on making some extra cash for me and her.' She nods in her daughter's direction.

'When was that?'

'I dunno,' she says, looking slightly bewildered. 'A couple of weeks ago maybe... He agreed with me though; said it was selfish of her to say no, specially with all her money.' She holds up a small pair of denim dungarees. 'I mean look at 'em – second-hand from the charity shop. Everything we own is second-hand.'

I wander over to the small, grubby sofa, take a seat on it

without asking permission and surreptitiously slip a twenty-pound note from my pocket down the side of it.

'And what's John's surname, Shannon? Did he ever tell you?'

She takes another long drag on the roll-up before extinguishing it in the ashtray. 'Yeah,' she says, eyeing me up disdainfully as she blows smoke from her lips, 'funnily enough I do. Like the Christmas tree – that's what he said; that's why I remember it – John Evergreen.'

TWENTY-FOUR

DARCIE – AGED FIFTEEN

This morning – or perhaps it's afternoon; I can never tell – he brings me my usual plastic bowl of porridge that's been mixed with water, made only barely edible by the bruised banana that sometimes accompanies it. He locks the door behind him after he enters, as he always does, places the tray down on the small chair in the corner of the room and put the keys back into the inside pocket of his corduroy jacket.

'Breakfast is served,' he says with a majestic flourish.

I glance over at the bowl of unappetising grey slop and turn away from him on the bed. Having long since given up on begging and pleading, on trying to reason with him, I can't bear to look at him.

'I'm not hungry,' I lie, trying not to think about the warm, flaky *pain au chocolat* pastries that Fabienne and I often used to enjoy of a morning with a foamy coffee, or the soft, sweet pancakes with crispy bacon topped with a drizzle of maple syrup, the sensual mouthfuls of oily, crunchy French toast... My mouth begins to water at the thought of them, and I wonder, miserably, if I'll ever get to taste such things again.

'Come on now, Darcie, don't be like that,' he says. 'You've got to eat something.'

I don't answer. I've run out of things to say to him. I've tried every tactic I could think of to convince him to let me go. I'd been nice, attempted to sweet-talk him. I'd been confrontational, cursing at him angrily, calling him a string of less-than-flattering names – which I soon learned resulted in the punishment of having my banana taken away and therefore quickly gave up on.

I'd made promise after promise, given him my word that I'd never so much as think of running away ever again if he'd just unlock the door to my prison cell. I needed to stretch my legs so badly that I felt like I was turning to wood.

'I promise I'll never try and leave again; I swear it to you, Alastor – you have my word. Never.'

'Ah, but you *will*, Darcie,' he replied with a sigh. 'They all do. They all try and leave in the end.'

I had no idea who 'they' were, but it strongly suggested there had been others before me. I wondered what might've happened to them? Had they somehow managed to escape? I thought of asking him, but in truth, I was too scared of what the answer might be.

'So now it's just thee and me!' he said triumphantly. 'Just the two of us – or three if you include Tabitha!'

Over those next few days, Alastor's resolve to keep me prisoner, locked up like a caged animal, remained unwaveringly strong.

'Your mother has taken a trip to Paris,' he announces this morning, making conversation, like this is all perfectly normal. 'She's visiting with your grandmother. I suppose she'll be expecting to see you when she gets there.'

I feel my empty stomach lurch. I know what this means. Now that Fabienne and Alastor are married, she's going to do what she always does and pull a disappearing act with his money, leaving me behind, here, with this sick, twisted maniac, unwittingly or otherwise. Momentarily, I wonder if I'll ever see her again, and panic sweeps through me, though with my back still to him, he can't witness my expression of sheer dread.

'I'm not sure what she'll do when she arrives to discover that you're not there,' he says, an edge of concern in his voice. 'You'll have to write her a letter – tell her that you're safe and well and that you decided to stay elsewhere.'

He actually believes Fabienne really is visiting her sick mother, a mother she claims died when she was a child herself, and that she'll return. Only I know better. He thinks he's clever, but Fabienne has tricked him, just like all the other gullible fools before him.

The piece of porcelain feels warm in my palm where I've kept it all night, or perhaps day. My ribs still feel a little sore from the 'accident', my body still bruised, but having heard this news about Fabienne, I decide it's now or never. I have to get out of this room, this house, because I don't want to be here when Alastor realises that Fabienne isn't coming back and that he's been duped. He'll surely kill me – or worse, keep me here forever, a thought that sends shockwaves of raw despair and terror ripping through me.

I'd weighed up the idea of trying to steal the keys from him. I knew I was capable of it. Thanks to Fabienne's example – she was an exemplary shoplifter – I'd become an accomplished pickpocket and thief myself over the years. Effortlessly slipping my nimble fingers into bags and pockets had become second nature, all under Fabienne's instruction of course. But she'd taught me well, had even said I was 'a natural'. Receiving any kind of praise from Fabienne was a rarity, and although I didn't want to admit it, it had made me feel good.

The only stumbling block was how to disarm him once I'd taken the keys. I'd spent days – weeks – trying to fathom a way to disable him so I could steal the keys and unlock the door to

my prison, but having long since established that I was no physical match for him, I needed to think outside the box. Finally,
though, it came to me: *the doll*.

Each night (or whatever the real time of day was) Alastor
would come to 'tuck me in', pulling the blanket up around me
and placing that horrible, ugly doll in the bed next to me before
kissing the top of our foreheads respectively.

'Goodnight, Darcie. Goodnight, Tabitha. Don't have nightmares now...'

He'd check the doll again when he came to wake me with
my bland breakfast the next day then place her back onto the
chair.

It had proven much easier this time round, breaking
Tabitha's face open. After all, I'd done it before. This time
however, I took more care in it. I needed a decent-sized piece of
porcelain to use. Now, I feel the sharpness between my palm as
I poise myself.

'I'll bring you something to write with, a pen and some
paper... Now, where's Tabitha? I haven't seen...'

I leap from the bed, the shard of porcelain between my
fingers, and aim for his neck, bringing it down as hard as I can
into his flesh.

I gasp as he screams out in pain, his eyes widening in shock
as his hands automatically reach for his neck and the piece of
porcelain that's sticking out of it. I gasp again as the blood starts
to flow from the wound, momentarily paralysed before I
remember – the keys!

He staggers away from the bed, clutching his neck as he
stumbles backward against the door. I seize my chance and
swipe the keys from his inside pocket, my skin crawling as my
fingers touch his body through the formal shirt he's wearing, one
which is gradually becoming soaked in his own blood.

'What... what have you done?' His voice is a stuttering

gurgle, barely comprehensible. 'You... you stupid girl... what... have you... done?'

A balloon of adrenalin bursts inside my stomach, and I can almost feel the redirection of blood from my heart as it flows down into my legs, preparing them to run. The keys feel slippery in my bloodstained fingers as I attempt to put them in the lock, and I curse as I drop them, continually glancing at him as I vibrate with adrenalin.

He's half slumped on the floor now, one arm outstretched against the wall in a bid to keep himself upright, the other cupped against his neck, attempting to stem the blood from the wound I've inflicted on him. He looks outraged, saliva foaming from his crooked mouth as he tries to remain conscious.

I finally feel the key give in the lock. *It's open.*

He's starting to pull himself upright now though, attempting to get to his feet. *No!* Have I done enough damage to prevent him from coming after me? The amount of blood on his shirt and spilling out onto the wooden floor would suggest so, but he's pulling himself up into a standing position.

The door handle slips as I try to twist it, my bloodstained fingers making it tricky to maintain any purchase. *Come on... Come on!*

The second it opens, I'm through it. My legs feel like springs as I sprint from the room and down the stairs, stumbling over the final few in my terrified haste.

'Darcie! *Daaarcieeeeee!*'

I hear the door to my cell as it creaks open; the sound of him stumbling out onto the landing. I should've stabbed him harder. *I should've killed him!*

I tear barefoot through the house – I suspected I'd been held prisoner here all along – heading for the front door, praying aloud that it will open; that I can make it open and escape.

Relief floods my veins as I hear the satisfying clunk of the bolts sliding. I'm outside!

Daylight is fading as I gulp the air greedily, welcoming its beautiful coldness against my skin as I sprint towards the lake, heading for the rowing boat, my feet slipping and sliding beneath me in the damp grass as I check for him over my shoulder.

'Darcie... Darcie, come back. Come back here now!'

I fall onto my knees as I reach the rowing boat, the thin gauzy nightgown I'm wearing sticking to my skin, to the mud beneath me. I hear him approaching as I throw myself into the boat.

It rocks so violently with the momentum that I'm convinced it'll capsize.

Panting heavily, my heart galloping so fast inside my chest that I'm fearful of passing out, I pull myself into a seated position and start to row.

I watch as he staggers down towards the lake, still clutching his neck with one hand, waving manically with the other. He's still standing, still conscious. *I missed the jugular vein.*

A surge of almost superhuman strength comes over me as I pull the oars forward and backward, desperately trying to create distance between us, but he's almost at the jetty now. *Faster – row faster...*

I hear the splash of the water as he enters it; begins to wade through it then breaks into a swim. But he can't keep up – he's wounded, and I'm too far away now. I've outrun him; *out rowed him.*

I start to cry as I watch his futile attempts to get to me. 'Screw you, you freak!' I scream, deranged with a sense of triumphant joy I'd never before experienced, my entire body awash and alive with endorphins. I did it! I did it! *I'm free!*

I stare up at the house as it gradually starts to shrink away from me, and him with it, the light disappearing with each passing second, and I think I see a shadow, there in the window, the round porthole at the very top, as though someone just walked past it. I blink; look again, but there's nothing there, and I figure it's just the light reflecting off the glass.

I look out across the water, watching gleefully as he waves his arms in the air in the ever-increasing distance.

'I will find you, Darcie!' His sinister voice echoes across the lake as he shrinks away. 'If it takes me a lifetime, I WILL FIND YOU.'

TWENTY-FIVE

DARCIE – SIX MONTHS AGO

'I never saw either Alastor or Fabienne again after that night.'

Dr Carmichael closes her notebook; places her gold pen down on top of it.

'It's an incredible story, Darcie,' she says after a moment, her green eyes meeting mine. 'Thank you for trusting me enough to confide in me, especially since I'm the first person who's ever heard it.'

I nod. Though I'm not entirely sure that's true. It's possible I may have told Gina about what happened to me all those years ago, only I can't quite remember, because what followed after I escaped that house of horror was perhaps equally, albeit in a different way, as traumatising as being locked up inside it.

'But that can't be the end of the story. What happened to you after you escaped from the house – from Alastor?'

She's right of course – it wasn't.

'I ended up sleeping rough in Edinburgh,' I say.

'You were homeless?'

I nod. 'Throughout my childhood, Fabienne told me horror story after horror story of what life would be like if I were ever to be placed in care. I don't know why I always took everything she said at face value, given that I knew what an accomplished liar she was. Perhaps it wouldn't have been so bad...'

'Do you think Fabienne herself may have been in care at some point?' Dr Carmichael throws the question out there. 'Perhaps she never wanted to admit it to you, and the fear she instilled in you was really her own born of first-hand experiences?'

I shrug. 'It's a theory. Anyway, whatever her reasons, she'd done such a good number on me that I didn't even consider it an option at the time. I feared going to the police or the authorities. Perhaps even more crazy was the fact that I still felt the instinct to protect her, even then. I didn't want to be the one to expose Fabienne's scams and possibly get her into trouble. Despite everything' – I lower my eyes – 'she was still my mother...'

A lump like a stone has suddenly formed in my throat, and I swallow it back and continue. 'I stole clothes from washing lines, a pair of old trainers from someone's back door. I slept in a park; begged and stole for the first few nights... And then I met Gina.'

'Gina?' Dr Carmichael reopens her notebook; resumes clicking the top of her pen in quick succession. I really wish she wouldn't do it. It's like a fly buzzing in the room.

'She was a drug addict who lived in a trap house in a run-down area of Edinburgh.'

Gina. At twenty years old, she wasn't much older than I was at the time, only years of crack addiction had put another ten years on her, so she looked more like thirty.

'Ye'll catch yer death oot here on yer own, hen. Look at you... I seen more meat on a butcher's dog.'

I hear her thick treacle-like accent in my head – I'd always liked it – as if she's here in the room with me; can see her mop of unwashed greasy hair hanging like curtains around her thin but once pretty face. *'It isnae safe for a lassie your age t'be oot here on yer own...'*

'She took me back to the squat, the trap house, where she lived. It was a real hole: dirty mattresses on the floor, dishes in the sink, filth and squalor everywhere... but it had running hot water and the basics needed to survive. Moreover, it wasn't *that house*. But...'

'But what, Darcie?'

Oddly, perhaps this is the part of my story I find the most difficult to talk about, to *think* about. 'But in a strange kind of way, I substituted one prison cell for another.'

Dr Carmichael cocks her head to one side, a gesture I've come to learn means she wants me to elaborate further.

'Drugs.' I almost swallow the word as I say it; feel the shame beginning to creep over me like a shroud.

'You started taking drugs?'

I nod. 'Drugs and... alcohol. All of it really. I'm not proud of it.' My voice sounds like someone else's, which is ironic because I struggle to relate to the person I was back then, like I really *was* someone else.

'Post-traumatic stress,' Dr Carmichael says. 'I imagine you were suffering greatly with it. After everything you'd experienced, it's not all that surprising that you'd go on to develop some kind of addiction in a bid to try and self-medicate those feelings.'

'I funded my habit through ill-gotten means as well.' I feel my skin bloom with shame. 'I capitalised on the skills I'd learned as a child. Shoplifting, picking pockets and handbags...' I think of Gabe then. What would *il mio caro marito* think of me if he knew what I was confiding in Dr Carmichael – if he discovered that his wife was a former thief and a drug user? It surely couldn't be any worse than what I think of myself.

'And how long did this continue – your drug habit and criminal activity?' She's starting to write in her notebook again, and I elongate my neck in a curious bid to see what. I imagine the words 'junkie' and 'thief' on the page and feel a stab of self-loathing, though they wouldn't be inaccurate.

'Around ten months, until just after my sixteenth birthday,' I say. 'Gina and I became good friends, partners in crime I suppose.' I snort ironically. 'She looked out for me, like I imagine an older sister would. I liked that feeling...' My voice trails off as I recollect. 'The feeling of not being alone, of knowing there was someone out there who had my back, even if it was so that she could continue to pump her veins full of muck. I was the bread-winner, you see – I possessed the skills to keep the cash coming.'

'Through stealing?'

'Yes.' I pause. 'And the irony was that I never got caught, not once, not even when I was high as a kite. Perhaps Fabienne was right and it really was all I was good at.'

'People who have suffered trauma almost always engage in negative, self-sabotaging behaviour if it's left untreated,' Dr Carmichael says.

'The nightmares were relentless.' I begin pulling at strands of my hair, and Dr Carmichael takes hold of my wrist; gently replaces it in my lap.

'Sorry,' I apologise quickly. 'I don't even realise I'm doing it most of the time.'

'PTSD,' she appraises. 'The nightmares, the OCD... all very indicative of childhood trauma.'

'I couldn't sleep without reliving it all; going over everything in my head. It was so... draining, the relentless racing thoughts that would send my heart rate stratospheric and cause me to break out in a sweat. Sometimes I found myself shaking uncon-trollably and couldn't stop, like I was having a heart attack.'

'Panic attacks, hmm, yes, of course, understandable...' She nods sagely.

'I could barely sleep, and I struggled to eat, to function normally, forever looking over my shoulder...'

'For him? For Alastor?'

I nod; can feel the horrifying sensation of that fear returning as I speak his name.

'Those words he said to me, the night I escaped: "*I will find you, Darcie. If it takes me a lifetime, I will find you.*"' I shudder as I repeat them. 'They tormented me.'

'Did you believe him?'

'Absolutely. For many years, it was my greatest fear that he'd come good on what he'd said. It was the conviction in his voice somehow – like he *really* meant it; like he'd make it his life's work...' I try to shake off the uncomfortable feeling that's descended upon me, but it's stuck to me like adhesive.

'The drugs were the only thing that helped back then – or so I'd convinced myself. Heroin was like a warm pair of arms around me – comforting, safe, like being gently caressed as you fall into the softest, happiest cloud. I'd never experienced a feeling as euphoric as the one heroin gives you – one that instantly erases the bad memories, all the horror and the fear of rejection, of being abandoned, and replaces it with... love I suppose, or what I thought love felt like, because I didn't know what it felt like, not until I met Gabe.'

'When did you decide to stop self-medicating?'

'It was decided for me really. The trap house was raided by the police.'

'*Wake up, Darcie... we've got t'get oot of here – the blues and twos are here. C'mon – get lively, hen.*'

'I had no choice but to run. The police would only ask questions, and of course there was the constant fear that I'd be placed into care. So I hopped a train to London. I was sixteen by then, my milestone birthday passing without fanfare or acknowledgement – with the exception of Gina anyway. She stole me a cupcake and a bottle of perfume from Boots. I remember it had one of those old-fashioned atomisers with the bottle, just like Fabienne used to use.' I can almost smell it on my skin as I speak, exotic and spicy.

'I arrived in London pretty much how I'd arrived in Edinburgh – with nothing,' I say. 'Only this time I resolved to do better, wean myself off the drugs, stop drinking and get a job, and start to rebuild my life, which is what I did.'

'That's very commendable,' Dr Carmichael says. 'Not many people can wean themselves off heroin without help,' she notes, adding, 'Not successfully anyway. That takes quite some resolve – some considerable determination and willpower.'

'I didn't want to be a victim anymore. I didn't want what had happened to me to destroy my life. I wanted *so* much just to be... normal.'

'Define normal, Darcie?' Dr Carmichael looks at me quizzically. 'Your definition of it anyway.'

'What I have now,' I say after a moment's thought. 'Being married to a man I love and respect, being a wife, a mother too I hope, and being free of the past, being myself, *being happy*.'

'And are you? Happy I mean.'

A sudden knock on the door startles us both, shattering the moment.

'Sorry to bother you, Dr Carmichael.' It's the snotty receptionist who always has a look about her that suggests she may have just trodden in dog shit. 'But your 3 p.m. is waiting.' She covers the side of her face with a hand and whispers, 'John's here.'

'Gosh, I hadn't realised it was quite that late,' Dr Carmichael says, suddenly glancing at the clock on the wall, which strangely no longer seems to be making a ticking sound. It's 3.50 p.m. Our session has overrun by almost an hour. I think about asking Dr Carmichael about the doll, the one I saw in her office on my first visit but haven't seen since. But I don't.

She closes her notebook; rests her pen top of it once more.

'This has been a very interesting session, Darcie,' Dr

Carmichael says as she stands, smoothing her satin palazzo pants out with her hands. 'Shall we continue next week? Alicia will book you in on your way out, OK?'

'Thank you, Dr Carmichael,' I say, adding, 'for everything. I'll see you next week.'

Only I know I probably won't ever see her again. I've told her everything. There's nothing more to say. What matters now is going forward.

John is hovering outside of Dr Carmichael's office as I exit, practically launching himself at me the second he claps eyes on me. Bloody hell.

'Darcie!' he says, placing a firm hand on my forearm. I glance down at it; notice the crescent of grime underneath his fingernails. 'So it's *you* who's been eating into my time with Dr Carmichael! I've been here for almost an hour, you know...' He looks agitated, distressed, perhaps even a little cross. He can't keep still.

'I'm so sorry, John. I got a bit carried away in there; didn't realise the time. Forgive me.'

His furrowed brow begins to soften slightly. 'S'OK,' he mumbles. 'I suppose I'll let you off, seeing as it's you.'

'Thanks, John,' I say, suddenly noticing that he's carrying something in his left hand. Is that...? Is that *the doll* I'd seen in Dr Carmichael's office?

Completely freaked out, I stare at its vacant-looking face, its dead eyes and painted red mouth. What's *he* doing with it? I tear my eyes from it; tell myself it's just a doll. It can't hurt me. None of it can hurt me anymore.

'Goodbye, John,' I say, moving past him. 'Take care of yourself now.'

'You too, Darcie,' he says without turning back to look at me. 'TTFN.'

TWENTY-SIX

DAN

Davis bursts into my office, her eyes alight, like a child on Christmas Day who's just realised she's been on the good list. 'We've got a hit with CCTV – a car, gov.'

'Go on...'

The phones have been ringing off the hook in the incident room thanks to the public appeal, and I'm silently praying that we'll get a lucky break or, with any luck, breaks plural, on the back of it. Appeals can often prove fruitful in tricky cases like this, though it's fair to say they can also be time-consuming. Every lead needs to be followed up, every avenue explored before you can call it a dead end. Anyway, I'm liking what I'm hearing so far at least.

'A white 2019 Nissan Juke,' she continues enthusiastically, 'seen driving along Mason's Hill, adjacent to the woods, on the morning of Darcie's disappearance. It's been picked up... twice.'

'Twice?'

'Yup.' Davis nods slowly. 'Parker says it took the route that runs almost the circumference of the woods – effectively went round in a circle, gov. *Annnnd...*' She deliberately leaves me hanging.

'*Annnnd...?*'

'And then it was picked up again a short while later!'

'Where?'

'Approximately five miles away, on the ring road, heading north out of town.' She raises an eyebrow.

'Really?' If I wasn't so exhausted, I'd be jumping up and down on the spot right about now. 'What time was that?'

'Around 8.25 a.m.'

I glance at Davis, and she nods in response, a silent exchange of understanding between us, because she knows as well as I do that if this is our perp's car, then there's every chance that Darcie Bonneville may well have been inside it at the time. It gives me a shiver.

'Did we get number plates? Can we find out who it's registered to?'

'Only partial plates, and we're running checks now, gov.'

'I want it recovered, pronto.' I feel a renewed sense of positivity flush through me, giving me a much-needed surge of energy.

She nods efficiently. 'We're on it.'

'Oh, and Lucy.' I beckon her further inside, away from the rest of the team. She leaves the door ajar as she takes a step forward. 'I need you to do something for me.'

'Not another charity-shop run is it, gov?' She shoots me a cheeky grin as she looks me up and down.

'Yes, very amusing, Davis,' I say, 'and no, it isn't, seeing as you did such a stellar job last time...' I adjust the large lapel of the bad seventies jacket I'm still wearing by way of demonstration. 'John Evergreen.'

'John Evergreen? Oh, you mean the bloke Shannon mentioned?'

'That's the one. I want you to run a check on him.'

'Why the interest, gov? You got a feeling?'

Actually, it's *more* than a feeling.

Delaney appears in the doorway then; hovers a little distance behind Davis.

'Something I saw on Dr Carmichael's desk when we went to visit her... It could be nothing, but there was a Post-it note from her PA asking her to urgently contact a John Evergreen – the same name Shannon mentioned.'

The name had set off an alarm bell at the time. I recognise it from somewhere, but as yet it hasn't come to me. They could be completely unrelated of course, maybe even a different person with the same name, but it's a coincidence, and in this game, it pays to be suspicious of those.

'No problem, gov.'

She turns to leave.

'Out of interest, what did you make of her?'

'Of who?'

I'm thinking aloud. 'Dr Carmichael, the celebrity psychologist...' I'm interested to get Davis's take on the enigmatic doctor. Female intuition isn't something to be sniffed at; this much I've learned over the years – and often opposite to the easy way.

She shrugs. 'Seemed very professional to me, clearly cares about her clients... She was pleasant enough, but ugh, that doll. It really gave me the heebie-jeebies! Why? You thinking of asking her to compile a suspect profile, gov?'

'Maybe,' I say non-committally, though frankly, as things currently stand, we could use all the help we can get because it's day three of Darcie's disappearance, and aside from this news about the vehicle being hopeful, we have no strong leads or a prime suspect, or any suspects at all for that matter.

I wonder if Dr Carmichael has checked over any notes she took during Darcie's sessions? Something tells me there could be something hiding within them that could prove useful at this stage, so I'd really like to get my hands on them – only Dr Carmichael put the kibosh on that, citing 'professional integrity' and 'client confidentiality'. Perhaps I'll pay her another visit; try and sweet-talk her. I'd rather not have to apply for a subpoena.

'Oh and, Davis, don't forget to run that check through the system will you.'

'Course, gov. John yeah? John Evergreen?'

'What about John Evergreen?' Delaney, who's been very obviously listening the whole time, suddenly pipes up behind her.

I blink at him. 'You *know* him?'

'Yeah, I know who he is – paranoid schizophrenic, tried to murder his own mother once – some years ago now though – did a fair stint at Ashworth Lodge psychiatric unit if I'm right in remembering.'

Of course... Now I remember.

'He thought she was plotting to kill him, his mother,' Delaney goes on, 'poisoning his food, so he got in there first – gave the poor woman a few doses of thallium in her breakfast. Left the poor sod with brain damage; almost killed her. I was working with DI Larry Bains at Kent constabulary at the time, earning my stripes with a bit of guidance from the best,' he adds in what I can't help thinking is something of a deliberate dig at me, or maybe the paranoia is catching. 'I never forget a name – not one like that anyway. Why you asking about him, Dan?'

'He's a patient of Dr Elizabeth Carmichael's,' I say. 'The psychiatrist Darcie Bonneville visited a few times some months back.'

'Really?' Delaney's eyes widen. 'You don't think he's got anything to do with her disappearance, do you? Not John... He was as mad as a rat under a bucket, but he's never reoffended, or at least not that I'm aware of. I wouldn't say he was the violent type either – bit of a pathetic character more than anything. It was a sad case really, because from what I remember, he loved his old mum, and she doted on him too – couldn't do enough for him. She didn't even want to press charges against him at the time; said he'd lost the plot when his pregnant wife ran off with the gardener and it led to a decline in his mental health...'

Well, I suppose that might do it. It could be nothing more than coincidence anyway – after all, Dr Carmichael is known and well established in her dealings with convicted criminals. John Evergreen can't be the only one she works with, I'm sure, and yet something is telling me to dig a little deeper. It's possible he may have met Darcie at Dr Carmichael's clinic. And the fact that Shannon Taylor mentioned him...

'Get on to Dr Carmichael's office,' I instruct Delaney. 'Tell them we want a list of anyone Darcie Bonneville may have come into contact with when she visited.'

He raises his eyebrows. 'You'll need a subpoena for that, Dan,' he says. 'They'll not hand over names willy-nilly – patient confidentiality and all that...'

I shoot him a forced smile. *Willy-nilly*?

'Well, in that case, Martin,' I say, 'get one.' There may be no connection, but I'm not taking any chances. 'And find out where Evergreen is, where he's living and if he's been in any trouble lately – see if we can't eliminate him if nothing else.'

'Gov.' Delaney nods, feeling like he has to add, 'But you're barking up the wrong tree, Dan. Evergreen might be a bit nutty, but he's harmless – hasn't been on the radar for years.'

'So he'll have nothing to worry about then, will he?'

My phone rings.

'Mitchell, you got something?'

'You want the good news or the bad news first?'

I sigh, wondering why the latter seems to always have to accompany the former.

'The bad first,' I say. After that, things can only get better.

'Darcie's pregnancy's been leaked to the press,' she says. 'I'm over at the forensics lab and I've just heard it on the news.'

'Perfect.' I start rubbing my forehead with a thumb and forefinger.

We'd strategically chosen not to announce the fact that Darcie is likely expecting. Not solely because it would put us under even more pressure from the public to find her, but because it could potentially be dangerous if indeed she is being held hostage somewhere. It could cause her abductors to panic; to do something rash. Archer's going to be apoplectic. We don't need this. I think to ask her where the leak came from, but in truth it doesn't really matter now. It's out there.

'I hope the good isn't going to be scant compensation,' I say.

'I don't know yet, gov, but it sounds interesting. Someone called Gina put a call in to the incident room,' she says. 'She saw the appeal on TV and claims she knew Darcie from years ago and that she's got some information. "Sensitive information" apparently; information she only wants to share with you. She asked for you by name, gov.'

My ears prick up like a dog's. 'You think she's legit?'

'Well, she knew that Darcie's maiden name is Vernier, and that's not information that's been released publicly, is it?'

Trapped butterflies of anticipation begin to dance inside my guts. 'Does Gina have a surname?'

'Didn't want to give it, boss, but she did leave an address of somewhere she'd like to meet. She's a bit reluctant to come down the nick.'

Something tells me this Gina character, whoever she is, might just be the break we're looking for. I've suddenly changed my mind about the bad charity-shop suit. I've got a feeling it might've brought me a touch of good luck.

'She's asked to meet you in Ladmore Grove... at the Brick-layer's Arms pub.'

'I'll be there in one hour, Mitchell,' I say before hanging up.

TWENTY-SEVEN

DARCIE

Am I dead?

It's the first thought in my head the moment I open my eyes, gritty and sore as they flicker back into life. *Where the hell am I?* That's the second.

A needle-sharp pain shoots through the back of my head as I make to sit up and, wincing, I instinctively bring my hand up to it; feel an egg-shaped lump on my skull, a congealing crust of something against my fingertips. *Is that blood?*

It's dark in the room but not pitch-black, and, disorientated and dazed, my eyes struggle to acclimatise. *Have I been kidnapped?*

Gabe's image explodes in front of me like a flashbulb – noodle head, *il mio caro marito* – and a small whimper escapes my lips as my memory slowly begins drip-feeding back to me.

I was walking Purdy in the woods... it was a cold morning... and I remember being suddenly aware of a strange presence; sensing that someone was there, lurking behind the trees. But after that, *nothing*.

I rub my temples with my forefingers, attempting to lift some of the fog my brain feels shrouded in.

Purdy! Oh no! What happened to my dog? Has she been taken too? I cry out again. I can't think; my mind feels fuzzy, like I have the hangover of ten men. Maybe she ran off, or perhaps she's been hurt?

More small, desperate whines escape my lips as I try to regulate my breathing. It feels short and laboured, like the air around me is rapidly disappearing in direct correlation to the rate my panic is increasing.

This is bad – *really bad.*

I can see a boarded-up window to the right of me, a thin, square outline of light escaping around the edges like lasers. I can just about make out what I think is a chair in the corner, a small chair, like a child's, and— I recoil as my eyes rest upon it. That doll! *Argh!* I cover my mouth with both hands to prevent the scream escaping.

The realisation hits me with such brute force then that I almost double over. *I recognise this place.* The bed, the window, *that doll...* I feel the hairs rise on my forearms, a rush of adrenalin spiking. It looks like that same room I was locked up in twenty years ago, in that horrible house. That isn't possible. *Was it?*

'No, no, no, no, no, no! Please God, no!' I whisper on a loop.

I make to get up off the bed, but when I try to swing my legs over the edge of the thin mattress, I feel some resistance.

When I pull back the bed sheets, I find a shackle on my right ankle – a metal cuff that's attached to a chain. My gaze follows it along the concrete floor – all the way to the wall next to me, where it's bolted to a hook. I gasp and start to pull at it, forcefully. I've been chained up like an animal!

Cold fear sweeps through me so violently that it takes the breath from me, forcing me, momentarily, to lie back down on the bed. For an all-too-brief moment, I think that perhaps I'm simply having a terrible nightmare; that I'm suspended somewhere between my conscious and subconscious mind, a twilight zone I'll eventually judder awake from. But then the physical sensation to empty my bladder shatters my wishful thinking. I need to pee.

I hoist myself upright and shuffle towards the door of what I assume is a bathroom, the metal chain clanking noisily against the concrete floor as it drags behind me, like entrails.

My heart still pounding in my ears, I quickly pull down my leggings and knickers and feel the relief as a rush of urine hits the pan. There's toilet paper and soap at least, a toothbrush and some unbranded toothpaste in a plastic cup on the side; a selection of sanitary products too. Not that I'll be needing those.

A small groan escapes my lips. *Oh my God, I'm pregnant!*

I run my hands under the cold tap, splash some water on my face and gulp back a few mouthfuls directly from the faucet. I just can't think clearly, can't hold on to a thought for more than a split second before it evaporates, like smoke. And then it occurs to me that I've probably been drugged.

'Helloooo?' I call out, finally finding my voice, though it sounds strangely distant somehow, like I haven't said it at all. 'Is anyone there?'

I begin walking towards the door to the room, but the chain I'm attached to stops me just short of reaching the handle, forcing me backward with the momentum. My throat makes a loud, dry clicking sound as I steady myself and try to process what's happening to me.

I'm locked in.

There's no concept of time. How long have I been here, in this room? A day or two? More? *Please, no more.*

Gabe will be wondering where I am by now. It's all coming back to me. Lunch at Bertollini's. I'd been due to visit my gynaecologist; had wanted to have my pregnancy confirmed by a professional before I planned to tell Gabe our good news over lunch – I'd been excited, full of anticipation. He'd be worried now though; he'd have called the police I'm sure. They'd be looking for me, wouldn't they? Yeah, yeah, of course they would.

It's a desperate struggle to stay calm, but then I'm distracted by remembering the note, the one that had been hand delivered the night of the dinner party with the Abberlines, and then the real panic comes for me as I remember the words: *FOUND YOU!*

If I'm honest with myself, somewhere deep inside me, in a place I didn't want to recognise existed, I'd known at the time who'd sent that note. Who else could it have been? Only, I'd tried to fool myself into believing otherwise. I mean, what were the chances, really? And now here I was, faced with the crushing reality of *where* I was, chained up inside a tiny, airless room that was just as I remembered it – my worst nightmare, my unhealed childhood trauma playing out in real time, like something from a bad horror film on repeat. He'd come good on the threats he made. *He'd found me.*

But then the questions started to come: *but how, why, what's he going to do to me?* Was I going to die in here, terrified and alone and *pregnant*?

I start to cry, frustration and despair rampaging through me; hot, salty tears slipping from my eyes and stinging my cheeks. I feel defective somehow. Who gets imprisoned by the same person *twice*? Why me? What have I done?

I flop back onto the bed and wipe my eyes with the sleeve of the running jacket I'm still wearing.

I have to stop with the self-pity. I've finally found happiness in my life, genuine love and connection and, perhaps above all, *normality*. It's everything I'd ever dared to dream of. I've worked tirelessly to become a better person, to atone for all my sins and wrong-doings, to forgive myself. I'm long clean of any substances and haven't broken the law in decades. I'm married, truly to the man of my dreams, I own a beautiful home, have money in the bank – a lot – and a baby on the way. And now that will all come crashing down around me. Because my abduction will invariably lead to an investigation, and that investigation will also lead to my secrets being exposed – *il mio caro marito* will discover the truth about my past and who I once was. And this is perhaps, truly, above everything, the worst fear of all.

Having exhausted any hope of finding an escape route, my thoughts torturing me on a loop, I lay my head on the flat pillow, defeated. This is all my fault. I should've had therapy years ago. I should've told people, told someone what happened to me back then, protected myself. Instead, I'd tried to outrun it. And now it's caught up with me, just as everything does eventually.

I must fall asleep, though for how long I don't know, but a sound disturbs me, and I open my eyes with a start. I hear something – the sound of a key jangling in a lock followed by the creaking of the door as it opens. I hold my breath.

Someone is here.

TWENTY-EIGHT

DARCIE

Something is amiss.

He brings me food and water regularly, though I can barely force anything down. I know I must though, for the sake of the tiny life growing inside me if nothing else.

The fact that he's bringing me sustenance indicates that he wants me alive, for now at least, and it gives me hope. But he says very little as he shuffles into the room and places the tray down next to me; barely engages at all, which is at once both unsettling and confusing.

'A-Alastor?' I stammered the first time. 'Is that you?'

He was wearing a black balaclava, his head cocking from left to right in a creepy motion as his eyes peered out at me through two black holes. I wanted to leap up, take a swing at him, give him everything I had and break the bastard's nose with any luck – only my body was paralysed. I was frozen ridged with fright at the sight of him.

He said nothing as he placed the plastic tray down onto the bed next to me, not a word. I glanced down at the bowl of grey, watery porridge and the bruised banana next to it and felt sick with despair.

. . .

It's been a couple of days – I think anyway – and I'm still none the wiser as to why I'm here or what his plans for me may be. I'm tormenting myself with questions I don't have the answers to.

'Please, Alastor, please just tell me what it is you want?' I've begged him numerous, countless times, but he remains largely unresponsive during our encounters, and as time ticks by, painfully slowly, little things are beginning to nag at me.

The balaclava bugs me. I already know what he looks like, though in truth, given that so many years have passed, I can't be one hundred per cent certain I wouldn't walk right past him if I saw him on the street today.

Why doesn't he want me to see his face? And why the silent treatment? The creep I remember was quite verbose at times, certainly no shrinking violet. *'We all have to learn the hard way...'*

There's something in his gait too, the way he shuffles when he walks, his shoulders slightly hunched over, and he seems smaller than I ever remember him being back then. He even smells different somehow.

It sounds crazy, but I'm beginning to question if it's actually Alastor at all. Only why would someone pretend to be Alastor if he wasn't really Alastor?

Something feels different; everything seems different. *He* is different. And yet I don't know how that can possibly be? My head is completely wrecked.

'Is it money you want?' I conjured up the bravery to ask him at one point. 'Because I have plenty of it. You can have it all. Take it – it's yours. I never wanted it anyway,' I said, mindful of my tone. I knew first-hand how he could suddenly switch, and I didn't want to trigger him. I had no choice but to follow his lead – to let whatever this was play out.

The question I *really* want the answer to though is, *how did he find me?* I'd done everything in my power to stay under the radar; remain anonymous, hidden and unreachable. I'd disappeared, used a different surname, acquired a new one when I'd got married. The only feasible conclusion I could reach was that it was thanks to my good deed that day outside the pharmacy, the day I'd haplessly rescued Dolly. Had he seen my face on social media and recognised me? It wouldn't have been too difficult to discover where I lived as the press, ever generously, had published nearly all of my personal details and general location in the aftermath. This type of breach of privacy was why I'd always eschewed any social media, which was no mean feat by today's standards.

Gabe once asked me why I had no online presence, and I made up some excuse about taking a political stance against 'Big Brother' and giant corporations who were watching our every move. I couldn't tell him that I hadn't wanted to be recognised, or contactable, and certainly not why. I didn't want any rude surprises from my shady past crawling out of the woodwork, though admittedly I do sometimes still think about Gina. I hope that wherever she is today, she's in a better place than I find myself now.

I lie on the small, hard bed in my cell and stare up at the ceiling. I can only speculate as to what may be happening outside this room – if the police are looking for me; if Gabe is too. I ruminate constantly on whether or not *il mio caro marito* knows the truth about his wife's dirty little secrets yet, if the police have been digging into my past, unearthing the boneyard of skeletons from my tightly closed closet. Maybe I'm front-page news already, my life laid bare for others to pick over and apart, to judge and condemn? Miserably, I know that whatever happens to me now, alive or dead, nothing will ever be the same again.

The sound of the door unlocking startles me, and I sit up.

Alastor, or whoever the hell he is, is back, and I feel my lower intestines contract in fear. I'm just so tired, so exhausted of being suspended in limbo like this, hovering precariously between what feels like life and death. I need to do something, but I don't know what. He's cautious enough to keep a safe distance from me whenever he visits, mindful perhaps of how I escaped him the last time, and ensure that doll stays out of my reach.

I sense it the second he enters the room. His demeanour is changed, his shoulders visibly sagging as he shuffles awkwardly towards me. He appears nervous somehow. I have no idea if this shift is a good or bad one yet.

'You've hardly touched any of your food, Darcie,' he says, his tone leaning towards concern rather than condemnation, as he stares down at the plastic tray of congealing food on the floor.

I'm stunned. It's probably the most I've heard him speak since he locked me in here however many fucking days ago.

'You really have to eat. You must, for the sake of—' He stops himself short.

'For the sake of what?' My brain instantly shifts up a few gears. Was he about to say 'the baby growing inside you'? Something tells me he might've been. But how could he possibly know I'm pregnant?

'I'm just not that keen on fish,' I say, staring at my untouched plate, not wishing to sound ungrateful. It's also a blatant, and deliberate, lie. Alastor would know I like fish. He served it to me often enough during my initial captivity, bland and unappetising as it was.

'How are you feeling?' he asks after a long pause.

Why the sudden concern?

'OK,' I say cautiously. 'A little tired perhaps, and it's cold.'

I toy with the idea of telling him about my pregnancy now that he seems to have been imbued with something resembling empathy. It's a risk though, one I keep swinging back and forth between like a pendulum. If he knows I'm pregnant, then his conscience might get the better of him, assuming he has one. Or he might just panic and kill me.

'I'll bring you some more blankets,' he says flatly.

'And maybe you could let me have the doll?' I say, a little too quickly.

He turns to look at me.

'It would be nice to have something to cuddle up to at night, and I can't reach her.' I rattle the chain in demonstration. That evil-faced abomination is the last thing I want near me, but, ever more convinced that this masked man isn't the real Alastor, I decide to test him.

He blinks rapidly behind his balaclava, clearly weighing up my request.

'OK then,' he says after a moment. 'Just for tonight.' He takes the doll from the chair, brings her to me and places her in my hands.

He's not Alastor.

'What's her name again? I've clean forgotten after all these years,' I lie.

He stares at me blankly.

'No, really,' I push him, 'I can't remember.'

I look down at her in my hands; notice the cracks on her face where it looks as if she's been carefully, painstakingly, glued back together. I pause for a heartbeat, wait for him to answer, but when he doesn't, I continue, 'Is it Rebecca...?' My voice almost shakes as I struggle to keep the one-sided exchange going. 'No... Felicity. Yes, that's right, isn't it? She's called Felicity?'

He nods.

'You have a good memory, Darcie,' he says.

I'm at once both grateful and despairing. He can't be Alastor. So then who the hell is he?

'Please,' I find myself saying, unable to prevent it, 'please, I just want to go home.'

It's no good – I just can't hold it together any longer. I break down into anguished, rasping sobs.

He begins to shuffle awkwardly from side to side as though my outburst is making him uncomfortable.

'Don't cry. I'll bring you some blankets,' he says, as if this will somehow mend everything.

He turns to leave, and it's all I can do not to throw myself at him, cling to his leg to prevent him from leaving the room. 'I won't be long. TTFN, Darcie.'

I stop crying. TTFN? Ta-ta for now... Why does this phrase sound so familiar to me? Where have I heard it before? Who have I heard say it, because I know *someone* has, someone recently, and—

Oh my God! I jump backward, my hands automatically shooting to cover my mouth. That man! The one I met at Dr Carmichael's office! Something to do with Christmas trees and—

'*John?*' I say, my eyes widening in horror and confusion. '*Is that you?*'

TWENTY-NINE

DAN

'Blimey, gov, I know where to come if I ever want to feel better about my life,' Davis comments sardonically as we walk through the door of the Bricklayer's Arms.

The scent of stale beer and regret hangs heavy in the air as I scan the old mahogany tables – largely occupied by grey-faced men of a certain age nursing their second pint of the day – and search for someone who could potentially pass for 'Gina'.

She doesn't yet know it, but a lot is resting on what Gina has to tell us, not least my career, as Archer made perfectly clear to me back at the nick. She's seriously vexed about the news of Darcie's pregnancy being leaked to the press, not to mention Gabe having since offered a reward of £500K for information that led to the safe return of his wife *and unborn child*.

'You do realise, Riley, that we'll have every crank crawling out of the woodwork now? She'll have been spotted everywhere from Scunthorpe to Sydney Harbour! And now that the pregnancy's been made public, we'll be under even more media scrutiny! The commissioner is breathing down my neck, and we *still* haven't got the first clue as to where she is, or even if she's still alive!' Her eyes were out on stalks.

'She *is* still alive, ma'am,' I said, watching as she brushed away an invisible layer of dust from the lid of her laptop. 'Someone has her; is holding her hostage somewhere.'

'And you know that for a fact, do you, Dan?' she asked tersely.

'I know for a fact that I *feel* it,' I replied. Pregnant women don't tend to up sticks and leave their affluent life of their own volition, especially without any provisions, and there's no reason to suspect she was anything other than elated about becoming a mother.

'Oh well, that's all right then. If Dan Riley *feels* she's still alive, then it must be true.'

Her facetious tone was so sharp I almost felt it slice my cheek. I opened my mouth to speak but didn't get there in time.

'I put myself on the line for you, Riley; convinced everyone at the top that you were the man for the job; that you'd get results quickly, efficiently... and here we are on day three with practically no leads whatsoever and now an unborn child in the mix to boot.' She raked an angry hand through her heavily styled hair, which magically sprang back to its original shape almost instantly. 'It's a disaster, Riley, an absolute bloody disaster. How on earth did you allow Bonneville to be so... foolish?'

'I didn't, ma'am,' I said flatly. 'You can imagine the emotional strain he's under. It's his wife and unborn child's life on the line, not to mention the mauling he's currently getting in the press and on social media himself. He'd do and say anything to get his wife back...'

'I think Martin Delaney should take over,' she said quickly. 'You should be on leave, on holiday with your family. I should've just let you go...'

A short, hot burst of anger exploded inside me.

Delaney? She wanted to oust me and stick that irritant Delaney in my place? Not in this lifetime!

'I think a fresh pair of eyes might be what's needed. It's nothing personal, Dan, you understand?'

'No,' I said sharply, 'I don't understand, because you know as much as I do that it *is* bloody well personal, and frankly, *ma'am,* you're mad if you think Martin's the right man for the job.' It was my turn to shriek. 'And we *do* have leads. A name has come up – someone of interest called Evergreen who appears to have met Darcie at the shrink's office where she was attending counselling sessions. He's got form,' I add, 'a paranoid schizophrenic who tried to kill his own mother some years ago; did a long stint at Ashworth... We've also picked up a suspicious vehicle on CCTV the day Darcie disappeared, *and* I'm on my way now to meet someone who called in following the appeal – sounds legit, claims to have some "sensitive" information on Darcie that could prove insightful...'

'We need more than insight, Riley; we need results,' she snapped back, clearly unimpressed.

Anger burned my earlobes. 'Well, if I don't stand around here chatting all day and am left to get on with it...' I said, causing her to look up at me. 'Look, the team is working on this round the clock, and no one's more aware than I am that the same clock is ticking, but I *will* find Darcie Bonneville,' I said, slamming the door so hard behind me that the glass rattled.

'Well, Davis,' I say now, with more than a hint of truth as we survey the less-than-exclusive clientele of the run-down pub, 'if we don't catch a break soon, it looks like I might be joining this lot in drowning their sorrows before 11 a.m.'

She gives me a curious sideways glance.

'Archer's threatening to take me off the case and put Delaney in my place,' I say, 'so let's hope this Gina's got something worth hearing, eh?'

Davis's eyes widen. 'She really said that?'

'Yes, Lucy, she *really* said that, and— Hang on, could that be her over there?'

I clock a lone female sitting at a table in the furthest corner of the pub, her face concealed by a mop of greasy brown hair. She looks up nervously as we approach.

'Gina?'

Her eyes dart left to right, furtively. 'Aye, I'm Gina. Are you that detective, the one off the telly who's in charge o' finding Darcie?' she says in a broad Scottish brogue.

'I am,' I reply, adding underneath my breath, 'for now anyway.'

We take a seat.

'DCI Dan Riley, and this is DS Lucy Davis.'

She swigs the last of whatever it is she's drinking, draining the glass.

'Another?' I ask.

She nods. 'Jameson's.' She pushes her glass towards me. 'A double, wi' ice.'

I nod at Davis to do the honours.

'It's ironic,' Gina says, displaying a set of neglected teeth. I notice that her fingernails are bitten to the quick too, and her clothes, though they appear clean, are clearly old and hanging off her emaciated frame. 'I've spent my life avoiding yous lot, now here I am inviting you oot for a dram!'

'Yep, it's a funny old world, Gina.'

'Nae offence,' she replies.

'None taken.' I clear my throat; get to the point. 'You called the incident room, Gina; requested to speak to me personally. Said you knew Darcie, that you had some information that might help us?'

She makes eye contact with me then, and I notice her pupils are the size of pinpricks. I suspect she's a user – heroin and crack probably; sadly, through experience, I can just tell.

'I couldnae believe it when I saw her picture on the telly... stopped me dead in ma tracks. I could never forget that wee face.' She picks at her non-existent fingernails; scratches the skin on her hands. 'She looked like one of them celebrities, you know, a model or an actress or summat.' She scratches at her hands again; twitches. 'Wee Darcie, eh, a doctor's wife, living in some posh hoose. I've spent years wondering what mighta happened to her on and off, but I've never forgotten her. You couldnae forget Darcie; she was just one of them people, ya ken?'

I nod; smile.

'But then when I heard she was missing...' She shakes her head; looks up at me with those pinprick eyes.

'How did you know Darcie, Gina?'

'Look, I dunno about this; I might be making things worse for her by telling yous... It seems like she's got her life sorted now; left it all behind her years ago, and I dinnae want to—'

'Left what behind her?'

Davis returns with a double Jameson's as requested and a couple of coffees; places them down onto the sticky table.

'Listen, Gina, whatever you tell us is in confidence, OK? You won't be in any trouble. We just need you to tell us whatever you can – anything you think might help with our investigation. Darcie has been missing for over two days now, and our concerns for her safety are at an all-time high, not least because...'

'She's pregnant,' Gina finishes for me. 'Aye, I heard it on the news. It's funny,' she muses, 'she was always adamant that she never wanted bairns – back then anyway – but only because of her own screwed-up childhood and that selfish bitch o' a mother of hers.'

I quickly glance at Davis. 'You knew Darcie's mother?'

'Me? No, no... never met the woman. Good job really, because I'd have given her a piece o' ma mind, dragging her young daughter all over the place like she did, all those different men...' She shakes her head. 'Some people shouldnae have bairns.'

She gulps a mouthful of neat whisky and pulls her lips over her teeth. 'Darcie was fifteen when I found her sleeping rough on a park bench in Edinburgh – that's where I live see, for ma sins, and I've plenty of those... Anyway, she was a runaway. One of her mother's fellas started noncing on her, didn't he, coming in her room at night and all of that? Poor wee thing ran off before he could do her any proper harm though, or at least I think so...'

Her voice trails off, but I stay silent; use the old psychological 'empty space' trick in the hope that she'll fill it.

'I took her in, took her back to the house I was staying in – a proper shitehole, but it was safer than the streets. She begged me not to get the authorities involved, tell the social and that. I spent my whole childhood in the care system and I wasnae about to put her through that horror, let me tell you, so she lived there with me, and a few others, for a good year or more.' She takes another sip on her drink; looks a little pensive. 'It was a trap house,' she says quietly. 'A drug den.'

'Did Darcie use drugs?' Davis seamlessly interjects. 'We're not here to judge you – or anyone else – Gina,' she adds.

'Aye, but you will,' she says, though there's no hostility in her tone.

Her legs begin to jiggle manically underneath the table. 'I'd been using for a good few years before she came along; the sickness had well and truly gripped me by then. I'm clean now though,' she adds brightly, as though she's trying to convince herself more than us. 'I was clean for seven months last year... Had a little relapse when my wee dog died. Been in and out of rehab all my life.'

I try not to show the pity I feel as I look at this poor wretch of a woman who seems worn out with the constant battle she's clearly been fighting most of her adult life.

'Darcie never injected though – just chased.' She appears

almost proud of this fact. 'Heroin takes the pain away, see. And like me, she was in a lot o' that when our paths met.'

'I'm sorry to hear that.'

'Heroin doesn't abandon you like people do, Detective,' she says ruefully, 'but it makes you abandon yourself in the end – that's the horrible irony.'

'So tell us about Darcie, Gina?' Davis smiles at her warmly.

'Well,' she says, 'Darcie was a wee live wire – all five foot nothing o' her.'

She laughs as she remembers, and I'm struck by the sound of it, pleasing on the ear, somehow incongruous to the rest of her.

'She was rebellious, spirited, thought she was invincible, as you do at that age. She was fifteen going on thirty though, an old soul I used to say, a smart head on her, fiercely intelligent, fierce full stop, though it got her in a bit o' trouble sometimes.'

'And do you think this has something to do with what's happening to her now?' Davis enquires. 'That it could be someone from that time in her life with a vengeance against her perhaps – someone she upset, owed money to, wronged in some way? Or this ex of her mother's?'

Gina shrugs. 'She was a good little thief was Darcie, a natural; had a real talent for it – for many things actually. We lost touch when we had to do a moonlight flit though. The house, it got raided one night... She went on her toes and I never saw her again.'

'And you've no idea where she went?' I ask.

'This is it, see; this is the thing I wanted to tell you, why I came here in the first place. I felt I had to because... well, it stayed with me all these years, what she told me, and then when I saw what happened to her on the telly... I dunno.' She shakes her head. 'It could be nothing – could be just a story, you know? She was good at telling them – stories I mean. Sometimes I couldnae work out what was truth and fiction with Darcie...'

My heart is banging against my ribs, my hands lightly shaking in anticipation as I take a sip of my lukewarm cappuccino. 'So, this story she told you...'

Gina sips her whisky and smacks her thin, dry lips. 'The fella – her mother's fella – she didnae like him; said he was strange, that she didnae like the way he looked at her... and so she ran away. Only he found her – hit her wi' his car.'

'What, he ran her over you mean?'

'Aye. But he didnae take her back to her mother. He locked her up, kept her prisoner in a wee room in the house.'

A rush of cortisol explodes in my prefrontal cortex. 'Do you know where this house is?'

Gina shrugs. 'Some remote mansion in the Highlands I swear she said. I dinnae know where exactly, like; cannae remember if she even knew hersel'.'

My throat is so tight I can barely swallow.

'She said summat about him having a doll and that she'd hit him wi' it , and that's how she managed to escape – something mental like that...'

'A doll?'

'Aye. One o' those old-fashioned ones wi' the china faces.'

'Gov,' Davis whispers; turns to me, wide-eyed.

'I thought she was talking a load o' shite, didnae take much interest at the time... It all sounded a bit mad – just one of her stories.' She shrugs. 'It's not that Darcie was a straight-up liar or nothing; she was just a teenager at the time, and you know how teenagers like to... What's the word?' She sighs apologetically. 'My brain isnae what it used to be, but then, to be fair, it wasnae all that to start with.' She giggles, like self-deprecation is second nature to her.

'Embellish?' Davis offers helpfully.

'Aye, aye, that's the one – embellish. She just wanted attention really; she'd never had none her whole life, you see, poor wee hen...' Her gaze drops back to the table. 'I know it was years ago now, but I loved her like a wee sister; we were thick as thieves. Ha!' She smacks her forehead. 'Nae pun intended. Darcie was a streetwise lass, but underneath all that bravado, she was just a vulnerable wee girl really, abandoned and lost...'

Her voice trails off into a whisper, and instinctively my hand slides across the sticky table onto hers. She doesn't move it away.

'Did she tell you who this man was – give you a name, an address, anything about his identity?' Davis asks.

She comes back to herself. 'Aye. It's funny what you remember, eh? I forget what I did yesterday, what day of the week it is, yet some things just stay wi' you.'

She sits back in her seat then; drains the last of her whisky.

'She called him Alastor.'

Davis scribbles in her notebook. 'Alastair?'

'No, no, not Alistair – Alastor. I definitely ken that because I made the same mistake mysel', and she corrected me. I thought it was strange – we have a lot o' Alistairs up our way. But Alastor... It's Ancient Greek, you know?' she says, looking a little pleased with herself. 'I looked the name up – dinnae know why now, but I guess something inside me musta told me to – and it's funny what it means.'

'And what does it mean, Gina?' I ask, intrigued.

'It means "he who never forgets".'

THIRTY

Davis and I are silent as we leave the Bricklayer's Arms in haste, both of us seemingly needing a moment to process what we've just heard.

Davis eventually breaks it. 'What you thinking, boss?'

I take a sharp inhale. 'Here's what I'm thinking, Lucy. I'm thinking that you need to get back down the nick lively. I want to know everything there is to know about this "Alastor" character, so get the team on it straight away. Names, locations, anything we can find that might identify him. Gina said Darcie thought she'd been taken to a location somewhere in Scotland, somewhere remote, so let's identify those areas and start there.'

She raises a brow. 'Most of Scotland is remote though, isn't it, gov?'

'Have you ever actually *been* to Scotland, Davis?'

'No,' she says. 'I've heard the weather's bad.'

'No such thing as bad weather, Davis,' I say, 'only inappropriate clothing.'

'And you would know, boss.' She smirks as she gives me the once-over.

'Touché, Davis,' I say. 'You can mock my suit all you like –

you chose it! Anyway, I've grown quite fond of it actually. I think it may have brought us some luck!'

'You're getting all hokey in your old age, gov,' she says cheekily.

'Less of the old,' I say, mock offended as I straighten the oversized lapels of my jacket – which, to be fair, *is* probably as old as me. 'Anyway, as Gina said, Alastair is a pretty common name in Scotland, but maybe the unusual spelling will help.'

'Assuming Alastor even exists, gov. I mean it sounds a bit implausible, doesn't it? And you heard what Gina said about Darcie being a bit of a fantasist, an attention-seeker even... and she was very young at the time, and on drugs. It could be a WGC.'

'A what?'

'Wild goose chase,' she says. 'And Gina could have ulterior motives for coming forward – the reward Bonneville's offered.'

She catches the look I don't even realise I'm giving her. 'Come on, boss, she's a junkie, and as nice as she seems on the surface, them lot would confess to killing a classroom full of kids to fund their addiction.'

'I never knew you were so cynical, Davis,' I say. 'I thought she was legit; telling the truth...'

'How could you tell, boss?'

'Years of listening to a million lies I suppose, Davis.'

Gina may have been reluctant to speak to us at first, but the concern she showed, and her fondness for Darcie, appeared genuine to me. I thanked her for her time and for coming forward, then shook her small, bony hand before we left.

'It could all just be something and nothing, you know, a made-up story,' Gina said, apologetic, like she felt she might be wasting our time. 'But it stayed wi' me all these years. And it does seem a wee bit strange, don't you think, to have made up something like that?'

'Did *you* believe her, Gina?' I looked into her pinprick eyes, and a silent moment passed between us.

'Maybe not at the time,' she said eventually, 'but now... now I'm not so sure.'

'And' – I turn to Davis – 'it would explain a lot, about the holes in Darcie's history, her lack of cyber footprint and social-media presence... All these years, I suspect she was in some kind of state of semi-hiding, fearing that it might all come out and that if this Alastor character could somehow locate her, then he'd come looking for her.'

'Assuming it's him, how do you think he did find her then, boss? I mean, she's done a good job of reinventing herself, keeping her profile on the down-low...'

'The YouTube video,' I say. 'The one where she saved Dolly from being hit by a car.'

It's only then that the irony strikes me. Darcie told Gina that she'd been hit by a car the night she'd run away – that a stranger, this 'Alastor', had knocked her over and taken her back to his house before locking her up. She'd been a hero that day on the high street, saving Dolly from what would have almost certainly been a fatality, according to witnesses. The video had gone viral, her name and identity revealed in the press. How ironic that her act of bravery might have put her wherever she is now. It certainly adds weight to the saying that 'no good deed ever goes unpunished', that's for sure.

'Maybe he watched it, recognised her, found her location, started stalking her...'

'Jesus.' Davis shakes her head. 'And what about the doll, gov? Gina mentioned something about a doll.'

I nod. 'It can't all just be coincidence. And where have we seen one of those recently – one of those porcelain dolls that, to use your exact words, "weirdos" collect?'

'Carmichael,' she says without missing a beat. 'In Elizabeth Carmichael's office.'

'Hmm, and who else is a patient of Dr Carmichael's?'

It's a rhetorical question but she indulges me anyway.

'John Evergreen.'

'Exactly.'

'But what could Evergreen have to do with all of this? By all accounts, he's just some harmless oddball now... and he's not Scottish.'

My brain is going off like a box of faulty fireworks.

'I wouldn't call someone who attempted to murder his own mother "harmless" myself, Davis.'

'Yeah, but you know what I'm saying, gov. What's his motive? It can't be money, because there's been no ransom, no demands...'

'I don't know,' I exhale, trying to rearrange my thoughts into some kind of order. 'But we need to eliminate him if nothing else.'

Hopefully Delaney's found an address for him already.

Davis is right though. If Evergreen is somehow involved in this, then why? Money, sex and revenge are the top three motives for murder – for most crimes in fact – but I'm fairly certain we can cross money off the list. As Davis rightly stated, there's been no ransom demand, so that leaves sex or revenge, and with Evergreen having no history of sexual violence, my instincts are steering me towards the latter. But why would someone like Evergreen want to take revenge on Darcie? What for?

'I guess the only way to find out is to pay him a visit, and—'

Davis's phone rings, and I watch her expressions carefully as she takes the call.

'You're not going to believe it, gov.' She's beaming at me. 'The car, the white Nissan Juke that was picked up on the ring road the morning of Darcie's abduction...' She's almost hyperventilating. 'They've done a search on the partial reg – tried out a few combinations for the missing digits – and guess who comes up as owning the exact same model, same colour?'

'Evergreen?'

'Boom,' she says.

'Get back down to the nick, brief the team, put an APB out on John Evergreen, and you and Parker go to his address. Let's bring him in.'

'Gov.'

'And get Mitchell onto the name Alastor – see if we can't corroborate some of what Gina's told us. We may need to bring her in too; get her to make a formal statement... Find out where Delaney is with the subpoenas for Carmichael's notes on Darcie and the other patient details, oh, and give Archer the heads-up – I don't want to come back to the nick to find Delaney swanning around like he owns the place even more than he does already.'

I'll resign before I ever refer to him as 'gov'.

'Oh and, Davis, when you get a minute, I want you to go through your notes meticulously – every statement, everyone we've spoken to so far in this case...'

'OK, boss. Why?'

'I don't know,' I say. 'Just do it.'

Davis rolls her eyes. It's adding to her workload, I'm aware, but... my instincts are telling me we've missed something – a thread, a missing link, a connection... *Something*.

'So, I'm guessing you'll be going to the Bonnevilles' now then, to speak to Gabe? What you going to say, gov?'

I pause for thought.

'Let's see if we can corroborate Gina's story in some way before I drop the bombshell on him that his wife's a former heroin user, eh?'

'And a thief,' Davis says. 'Don't forget thief. Christ, you think you know someone... No wonder she wanted to keep it quiet.'

'Well, you can't go forward in life if you're always looking in the rear-view mirror, Lucy. Maybe it won't make the slightest bit of difference to how he feels about her.'

'Yeah.' She pulls a face. 'But, I mean, there's telling little white lies about your past, and then there's out and out whoppers.'

'But she hasn't told him anything about her past, has she? So technically she's not lied about anything.'

Davis pulls her chin to her neck. 'If you say so, gov. Shall I take Martin too – when we bring in Evergreen?'

It pleases me that she's used the word 'when' and not 'if'. It's one of the many things I like about my work wife – her unwavering positivity.

'No, just Parker – he should be enough backup. I don't want to talk about Delaney,' I say, 'not after Archer's threats.'

She's silent for a moment; looks at me tentatively. 'So, have you spoken to Fiona yet, gov?'

'On second thoughts, let's talk about Delaney,' I reply. 'I'll see you and the team back at the nick in an hour or so.'

'Where you going, boss?'

'I've got a doctor's appointment.'

THIRTY-ONE

I march right past the snooty young receptionist as I head towards Dr Carmichael's office with purpose.

'Wait!' she calls out to me as she looks up. 'Sir! You can't just go in there!'

Oh no? *Watch me.*

'You need an appointment... She won't see you without an app— Sir!'

Dr Carmichael's eyes widen in surprise as I open her office door while simultaneously knocking on it, the flustered receptionist in hot pursuit.

'I'm so sorry, Dr Carmichael,' she says apologetically, a little breathless as she catches up with me. 'He just walked right in, and I couldn't stop him, and—'

'It's OK, Alicia,' Dr Carmichael says reassuringly, shooting me a cursory glance. 'It's OK.'

'I need to speak to you urgently, Dr Carmichael,' I say. 'It can't wait.'

'So I see,' she says with a raised brow. 'You'd better come in then, hadn't you? Alicia, hold my calls and push my one o'clock back, will you?'

Alicia nods, looking at me and then her boss before closing the door behind her.

'Perhaps you might've called first, Detective... Riley. That's right, isn't it?'

'Yes, Riley – Dan Riley,' I say. 'And I'm afraid there just wasn't time.'

'Well,' she says breezily, sitting back in her plush leather chair, affording me a waft of her distinctive, expensive perfume, 'I'm glad you came actually. I've been meaning to call you myself.'

'Oh?'

She smiles affably. 'I fear I owe you something of an apology.'

'You do?'

'Yes, for not being as forthcoming as I now feel I should've been during our last encounter.'

Well, this is something of an about-face, and a turn-up for the books – I was expecting another brick wall to be fair; came prepared for battle.

'I saw it on the news, the appeal,' she says. 'And then about Darcie being pregnant...' She lowers her eyes slightly. 'Client confidentiality is extremely important to me, Detective Riley – you do understand that, don't you? But I think, given the information that's come to light, that I can make an exception in this case.'

'I'm happy to hear that, Dr Carmichael. Although actually, I'm not just here to talk about Darcie.'

'I wasn't entirely open with you,' she continues, 'about Darcie's sessions – about the things we discussed during them.'

'Oh? Are you telling me that you *lied*, Dr Carmichael?'

'Not exactly,' she replies carefully. 'You see, there are two primary ways to lie, Detective Riley: to conceal and to falsify. Concealing involves withholding something without actually saying anything untrue. By falsifying something however, an additional step is taken. Not only does one withhold true information, but one presents false information as if it were true.'

Is she trying to bamboozle me? If so, it isn't an altogether unsuccessful attempt.

'Which did you do, Dr Carmichael?'

She cocks her head to one side. 'I never made any untrue statements during our first meeting, but admittedly I *did* conceal. I felt it was my professional duty to protect my client, you see.'

'Go on.'

'If anything, it is, in fact, Darcie herself who is perhaps, regrettably, the liar among us.'

She has my full attention now, and I sense she knows it. 'How so?'

'Darcie Bonneville was – is – an interesting case.' She picks up a gold pen from her desk; begins pushing the button on it. *Click-click-click...* 'She came to me initially for help with the claustrophobia she was suffering from...'

'I remember you saying.'

'I suspected this was merely a ruse though and only part of the issue... one of many issues in fact.' She looks at me with gravitas. 'Darcie was – is – a very damaged individual. Her childhood, her relationship with her mother, who was clearly highly narcissistic... it was obvious during our first session that Darcie experienced some rather extensive neglect, abuse even, during her formative years.'

'I'm aware of her relationship with her mother – or lack of it.'

'Oh?' She looks surprised. 'What is it that you know, Detective?' *Click-click-click...* The sound of her pen seems to go right through me.

'Much the same as you I imagine,' I reply. 'That she was shunted around a lot; was largely ignored by her mother, who, it seems, was solely committed to her own interests, largely men and money by all accounts...'

Dr Carmichael nods, impressed. 'Yes,' she replies, 'to put it succinctly – and perhaps mildly – that's correct.'

She pauses; audibly draws breath. 'When Darcie came to see me, I noted some obvious personality issues, or certainly obvious to the professionally trained eye and ear.' *Click-click-click.* 'She exhibited all the signs of someone suffering from HPD.' She glances at me. 'Histrionic personality disorder,' she explains. 'Individuals afflicted by HPD frequently lie to get attention, and in severe cases, the lies may be prolific enough to resemble pseudologia fantastica.'

Click-click-click...

I shrug. 'Pseudo whatitca?'

She flashes me an almost pitiful smile. 'Pathological lying, also known as mythomania and pseudologia fantastica, is a chronic behaviour in which a person habitually, and often compulsively, lies. These lies they tell are often severe, with no obvious purpose other than to paint oneself as a victim or hero, depending on the individual's circumstance.'

'And in Darcie's case? In your professional opinion obviously?'

'Both actually,' she surmises. 'Victim and hero respectively in her case.'

'I see. And what exactly is it that you believe she lied about? Her mother's treatment of her?'

'No, I think she was telling the truth about her mother's abuse, though to what extent I'm unsure. It was clear Darcie held an enormous amount of resentment towards her; that she'd been damaged by her neglect as a child, which is when I suspect she began "acting out" by telling lies.'

A phone rings somewhere, and she quickly glances at the expensive-looking designer handbag on her desk. Ignoring it, she continues, 'It was clear from our sessions together that she desperately needed to expunge some of the negative emotions she felt towards her mother – and consequently herself – and that they'd become detrimental to her life and her ability to form relationships. She found it incredibly challenging to talk about – to verbalise her inner emotions and the anger she'd buried deep. I concluded,' she states, 'that she would most likely benefit from talk therapy and hypnotherapy, to help her relax and therefore be more able to recall and release these experiences, those negative thoughts and feelings.'

I swallow dryly. I'm desperate for a glass of water but loath to interrupt Dr Carmichael's flow.

'So that's the route I took with her, during which she began to tell me a rather far-fetched tale – to give you the edited version – of how she ran away and how her mother's husband at the time came looking for her. She said that he'd run her down with his car then taken her back to his mansion and subsequently imprisoned her.'

I try not to let my thoughts show on my face. This sounds just like the story Gina told me not an hour ago.

The phone rings inside her handbag again, and she places the bag down on the floor by her feet.

'And you didn't believe her?'

'No.'

'Why not, Dr Carmichael?'

'I believe that *Darcie* believed it was true, that her being held captive by her mother's lover actually did happen all those years ago, but really I think it was nothing more than a metaphor for something else and that she *wanted* to believe it had happened in a bid to convince herself that all the other things that occurred prior – and after – didn't really happen at all. Does that make sense, Detective?'

'Not entirely,' I reply.

She gives me another pitiful glance. 'A smokescreen if you will, a mental diversion to distract from the painful truth of her fractured childhood, her abandonment issues, her drug use and criminal acts... It makes sense if you think about it. By concocting such an outlandish, implausible and frankly bizarre tale, one could expect to garner much sympathy and attention, admiration even – not least because she's both the victim and the hero of the story by managing to escape her captor's clutches. I surmised that she was shifting the focus onto a fantastical story to avoid facing reality. It's really very classic behaviour from those with HPD and avoidant cluster B types.'

'I see,' I say. Though I don't, not really, because if Gina is telling the truth, then Darcie has told this same story before, almost twenty years ago. Why would she maintain such a fantastical lie for all that time, and, moreover, to what ends? Surely she would've confessed the same story to others if Carmichael's theory is correct and it was attention or a reaction she was seeking?

Click-click-click... The sound of her pen is distracting me, so much so that I have to rub my temples to try to maintain focus.

'So why has she been at pains to keep her identity on the down-low throughout her adult life?' I say. 'Why, if this was the case, would she have no social-media presence and practically go into hiding after she rescued that little girl from being hit by a car? If it was attention she was after, then that would've guaranteed her a pretty healthy supply of it. It doesn't make sense.'

'Potentially, the idea for such a story may even have come from that exact incident with the toddler,' Dr Carmichael offers.

Only she's wrong. Gina claims to have heard this 'story' decades before the incident on the high street. Clearly, Dr Carmichael doesn't know this however, and I'm reluctant to tell her. I don't want to undermine her for one thing, and for another... Well, like I say, my instinct is telling me to keep schtum.

'So are you saying that you think there's a possibility Darcie could've staged her own abduction and that she's not really missing at all? You think she's capable of that?'

I hear Dr Carmichael suck air in through her thin nose. She pauses for a moment.

'I'm not saying that she has, no, but do I think she's capable of it? Well, then, the answer would have to be yes.'

Click-click-click. I rub my temples again. I feel confused; a touch disorientated. I wish she'd stop doing that...

'John Evergreen,' I say, suddenly remembering why I'm here.

Her eyelids flicker in quick succession as she looks up at me. *Click-click-click.*

'What about him?'

'I need to know as much about him as you can tell me, Dr Carmichael.'

'Why?' she reiterates. 'What's John got to do with any of this?'

It's my turn to exhale. 'I'm afraid I'm going to have to exercise my own professional integrity now, Dr Carmichael, you understand?' I smile at her, guiltily feeling a slightly childish sense of schadenfreude. *Got you back.* 'But they met, didn't they, Darcie and John, here at your offices, in the waiting room, perhaps on more than one occasion? Do you know if they spoke – if Darcie ever mentioned him? If he ever mentioned her to you?'

'I have no idea, and no, not that I can recall, from either of them.'

'John's a regular client of yours though – that's right, isn't it?'

'Yes, absolutely,' she says. 'John's been coming to see me for years. I was instrumental in his rehabilitation when he left Ashworth psychiatric hospital years ago. I've been treating him ever since. Surely you can't think John has anything to do with Darcie's disappearance though?'

I say nothing; hold eye contact for a moment, playing a little psychological trick of my own.

'John's absolutely harmless, Detective Riley – wouldn't hurt another soul.'

'But he did try and kill his own mother, didn't he?'

'Yes, but that was decades ago – before he underwent treatment for paranoid schizophrenia and the mental-health issues he was suffering at the time – and he's undergone something of a total transformation since then. I can confidently say that he's no longer a threat to society – to anyone really.'

'Not even his own mother?' I say dryly. 'When was the last time you saw John, Dr Carmichael?'

Her phone rings again, and we both glance at the handbag on the floor.

'You're not going to answer that?' I find myself asking.

'It can wait,' she replies, quickly adding, 'whoever it is.'

'Sounds urgent.'

'Everything is urgent when you think about it, isn't it, Detective Riley?'

'I suppose so. John... the last time you saw him?'

'Last week, usual time – 1.30 p.m. on Wednesday I think.'

'And he seemed normal?' I ask. 'Well, as normal as someone who's tried to kill their own mother can seem.'

She casts me a mild look of disdain. 'Like I said,' she says tightly, 'John's harmless.'

THIRTY-TWO

DARCIE

His eyes widen beneath the balaclava, the whites of them highlighted in the darkness of the room as he takes a sharp step backward, a reaction that only serves to confirm the fear that I'm right. I try to stifle the gasps as they come, but I can't seem to stop them slipping through my fingers like gas. *Oh my God, it's* him! It's the guy... that odd guy from Dr Carmichael's waiting room. But no... no, how can it be *him?*

My whole body is shaking so much I'm practically dancing on the spot. My mind flashes back to the moment when I first met him, recalling his awkwardness, his dishevelled appearance, his odd inflection as he spoke. '*I'm John by the way... John Evergreen – you know, like the Christmas tree?*'

When I'd next seen him a week later, again at Dr Carmichael's office, he'd seemed genuinely pleased that I'd remembered him. Had he become fixated and started stalking me? Was that what this was all about – some kind of obsession?

It's a strange sensation, but now that I'm pretty sure my abductor is the guy from Dr Carmichael's office, I realise that I'd somehow recognised him all along only couldn't place him, and then it hits me, like a door slamming in my face: if he's John

Evergreen, then *he isn't Alastor*, and so, then, who is he and how does he *know* about Alastor?

I rub the sides of my head in sheer confusion and frustration. I want to scream to release some of the pressure inside me, but I can't; I feel paralysed and mute, my mind like a ball of wire wool on fire.

I swing my head up to look at him; meet his eyes, and suddenly, almost palpably, like a switch being flicked, everything seems to shift in an instant.

Quite suddenly, *he* looks scared, terrified even, as he backs away from me and I think he's... I think he might even be crying. Yes, I hear him wailing, audibly distressed. This is my chance. *Carpe diem.*

'John, John...' I hold my hands out to him, my arms outstretched as I address him gently. 'John... It's OK. It's OK...' I gradually lower my voice, sing the words soothingly. 'It's *OK*...'

He stops still, like a musical statue. I swallow dryly. I can't think too hard about what to say next; I just have to trust myself.

'It... It is you, isn't it, John? The guy I met at Dr Carmichael's office? John Evergreen, like... like the Christmas tree?'

His silence speaks volumes.

'I thought so,' I say softly. 'I know you...'

'Y-You... remember me?'

I nod slowly. 'John... John, listen to me. You need to tell me what's going on. Why am I here? Why are *you* here?' I'm careful to keep my tone level – I'm still in chains, and I don't know if he has weapons, or access to them. I don't want to spook him. 'John... how do you know about Alastor?'

Randomly, the note pops into my head, that horrible note that was slipped through the door of my home the night the Abberlines came to dinner and those two foreboding words it contained, the note that's ripped my life apart and changed it forever. Hell, if I wasn't already a basket case before all of this, then it's a dead cert now.

I glance at the chain around my ankle. I have a baby inside me – Gabe's baby, *our* baby. One way or another, I have to somehow survive this.

'Who sent the note, John?' I can hear the anger simmering just below the surface of my voice. 'You delivered it that night, didn't you, to my house?'

He's little more than a shadow in the corner of the room, but I can still see him twitching manically. 'Why, John? Why did you do that?'

'I... I don't know. I just...'

'Did someone ask you to deliver it? Did someone put you up to this? How did you know where I live?'

Questions... there's so many I can't put them in any kind of order that the answers might ever start to make sense. None of it makes sense.

I'm as close to him now as the chain will allow me to go. 'Please, John...' I open my palms out around me. 'Look at me. Look at us – where we are, what's happening to us... John, listen to me: you need to let me go.'

I can hear his distress better than I can see it, but it's there – I sense it from him like sonar.

'I can't do that, Darcie,' he says, still crying. 'You've got it wrong. I'm... I'm not John Evergreen; I'm... I'm Alastor.' But there's a lack of conviction in his voice.

'This is bullshit!' I'm unable to contain my anger any longer, even though I know he has the upper hand.

On first meeting John Evergreen at Dr Carmichael's office, I'd found him to be awkward and maybe a touch odd I guess, but I'd felt nothing sinister from him, nothing malevolent. If anything, I'd sensed he was a little sad, lonely and in need of human company. I don't remember feeling frightened of him, and if I should've been, then I'm pretty convinced I would've been at the time. Life has taught me to trust my first instincts about people, and I'm not usually wrong.

He's trying to speak. 'H-How... how did you know it was me? What gave it away?'

I can still see him in the shadows, shuffling from foot to foot. His tone is soft, nervous even, but I mustn't be misled; mustn't let my guard down, even though I've spent my whole life wishing I could.

'TTFN,' I say, hoping he can see, or at least sense, the smile I force myself to give him. 'You said that to me, instead of saying goodbye – you always said, "TTFN, Darcie."'

I wonder if the police are close by now. Have they worked it all out yet? Are they staking us out right now, in this moment? God help me, I hope so. *I pray so.*

There's more silence, but neither of us, it seems, can be still. He keeps rocking from side to side, and I'm still dancing on the spot.

'John...' I say carefully. 'John, this is really serious...'

'I know,' he interjects quietly.

'The police are going to find us, John.' I'm getting tired of using his name, but something inside keeps willing me to say it, to keep reminding him of who he is – that he's a human being; that he's someone. 'John... how do you know about Alastor?'

There's a long pause.

'I saw the thing.' His voice is a nervous whisper.

'What thing, John?'

'On the TV – the policeman...'

My ears prick up.

'The policeman... and your husband. On the TV.'

A rush of adrenalin fuses me to the spot. *Gabe?* Gabe made an appeal on television? The mention of my husband's name sends my heart rate into orbit. Does that mean he still loves me; wants me home? A whimper escapes my lips.

'What did he say, John? Did he talk about me? Does he want me to come home?'

'I know... I know you're h-h-having a baby,' he stammers. 'It said so – on the radio.'

I'm suddenly aware of tears streaking the contours of my cheeks, hot and salty as they sting my skin and slip into the corners of my dry mouth.

Gabe knows I'm pregnant with his child, with *our* baby, which means the police must know too! They'll be here soon; they'll find me, won't they? In this moment, it's the only thing that matters. Everything else... *Please dear God, just let them find me.*

'Yes, John.' I start nodding uncontrollably, like my neck has been replaced with a slinky. 'I'm having a baby – and that's why I need to get out of here; why you need to unlock this chain and let me go. You can do that, can't you, John? For the sake of my baby?'

I hear a clicking noise coming from somewhere and immediately freeze. I can't identify the source exactly, but, instinctively, like an animal, I sense immediate danger.

'John... what's that noise? Is – is that a...? John, do you have a *gun*?'

There's that clicking noise again.

'Please, John.' I strain my eyes to see him, to see if he's holding a weapon, but it's just so freakin' dark in this godforsaken room. 'Please don't kill me and my baby.' My voice is high and tight and strained with fear and desperation. I can feel myself wanting to give up, give in, but I just need to hold on.

'Whoever's put you up to this, John, they're using you. You'll be the fall guy – you'll go to prison for the rest of your life, John. But if you let me go now, if you let me and my baby go—'

'Stop!' he wails. 'Please stop! I didn't know about the baby. I'd never hurt' – I can hear the mucus thick in his throat – 'a child. I was just doing what I'd been told to, to take you and bring you here... It was supposed to be a game. Just a game...' he wails. 'I didn't think I would have to—' He breaks down then; starts really sobbing.

'You didn't know what, John?' I hear the urgency in my voice. 'What didn't you think you would have to do?'

'Kill you,' he says between sobs. '*I didn't think I'd have to kill you.*'

THIRTY-THREE

DAN

Davis calls me as I hastily make my way back to the station from Dr Carmichael's office. 'There's no sign of Evergreen at his address, gov. We took uniform along, and they used a Halligan bar to get inside the property, but when we went in, it looks like he hasn't been at home for a while – no sign of any recent occupation. There were a few old coffee cups by the sink with mould on them, and the bin was full. I'd say he hasn't been back there for a good fortnight or so – the place stank. Still, SOCO are there now to check if there's any trace of Darcie having been inside the property.'

I exhale heavily. Part of me hoped that we'd strike lucky and find her there, but I suppose it would've been too good to be true. *Christ, where the hell has he taken her?*

'OK, Lucy... I'm on my way back in to give the briefing. Let the team know – *let Archer know.*'

I hang up, frustrated. At this stage, I'm almost certain John Evergreen has Darcie Bonneville held hostage somewhere, that he's responsible for her abduction, but aside from the question of where he may have her holed up, the real head scratcher is *why?* What motive could John Evergreen have to abduct a pregnant housewife? Had he met her at Carmichael's offices and suddenly, after so many years being on the straight and narrow, liked the look of her and decided to snatch her? It's not impossible, but it just seems so... unlikely. Dr Carmichael couldn't even be sure the two of them had even met. She insisted that John Evergreen was harmless, that he wasn't a danger to women – to anyone anymore – hadn't been for years. She was adamant in fact, and I'm guessing from all her experience, she'd be able to call it.

'Our sessions together are somewhat cursory now,' she explained about her weekly appointments with John. 'Generally, we just talk. Sometimes, if he's feeling particularly anxious, I may engage him in a little hypnosis to help him relax, but he's not undergoing any specific therapies. His condition is managed with drugs, specifically chlorpromazine, a very common antipsychotic drug,' she said, as if most people knew this, or at least should. 'They keep his mood stable, help with the anxiety, deter any manic episodes, hallucinations, that kind of thing.'

'And you prescribe him these drugs?' I asked.

'Yes, I prescribe John's medication. He's on a low dosage now though; he's come such a long way from when I first began treating him. He's definitely one of my successes.' She smiled proudly.

'But if he were, say, to stop taking his medication...?'

Dr Carmichael looked at me a little wearily, like she'd had enough of the conversation already.

'Well, it's not something I would ever advise him to do, Detective Riley. Stopping any medication of any sort suddenly is always inadvisable. Potentially, it could cause a relapse, even tardive psychosis, which, before you ask,' she quickly added, 'means he could experience new psychotic symptoms which can begin after taking antipsychotics for a while; a delayed effect of the medication itself even.'

'When did you last prescribe his medication?'

She shook her head as if to recall. *Click-click-click…*

I felt exhausted all of a sudden, though it was hardly surprising, because I'd barely had a moment's shut-eye in days. I decided I'd go home after the briefing, have a hot shower, eat something and then sleep… I just wanted to sleep.

'Are you OK, Detective Riley?' She was looking at me, her head cocked in mild concern.

'Yes…' I shook myself out of it. 'I'm just a little tired. What was I saying?' I struggled to remember. 'Oh yes, medication. When did you last write John a prescription?'

'About a month ago, or thereabouts,' she said. 'I've no reason to believe he'd stopped taking it – I saw no change in his behaviour, his moods, which I'm certain I would've done if he had.' She paused. 'You really can't think that John has anything to do with this woman's – with Darcie's – disappearance…'

I put my foot down on the accelerator as I think back over the conversation I had with Dr Carmichael. Certain things are beginning to bother me, nagging at me like a demanding child pulling at my trouser leg – like my Pip sometimes does when she wants my attention.

I try not to think about her, my Pip, or about my new son Jude, or Leo and Fiona; forcibly push them from my thoughts. I've got no choice but to see this thing through now. I'll have to find a way to make it up to them when all this is over, if they'll let me…

As I was leaving Dr Carmichael's office, the receptionist – Alicia – gave me the side-eye, clearly unimpressed by my earlier blatant disregard for protocol, when I'd burst into Carmichael's office unannounced.

'Sorry about that,' I apologised. 'Urgent police business.'

She managed a cursory smile. ''S'all right,' she said. 'Is it about that woman? That one off the telly – the one who's missing? Is that why you're here?'

'Yes,' I said. 'Darcie Bonneville – you remember her?'

'Oh yeah, I remember her,' she said. 'She was pretty, and she was wearing those trainers I want – the Balenciaga ones,' she said, as though she only remembered attractive faces and designer labels. 'Have you found her yet?' she enquired.

I shook my head. 'Not yet, but we will. Listen, did you ever see her talking to anyone when she was here – anyone in the waiting area? Did you ever see her talking to John Evergreen?'

'*Him?*' She reacted as if the mere mention of his name irritated her. 'Yeah, well, *everyone* knows John; everyone talks to him. You can't *not* really.' She shot me a look that suggested she viewed him as something of a pest. 'He's Dr Carmichael's *biggest fan*,' she said sarcastically. 'I think he's in love with her myself. And yeah, I think I do remember seeing them chatting together, now you mention it... He was probably telling her how great Dr Carmichael is, how she saved his life, how she's this and she's that.' She rolled her eyes. 'John, he's like a puppy dog – was in here all the time, every week without fail since I can remember. He used to turn up sometimes an hour, two hours even, before his appointment and just sit there, gazing over at her office with these big eyes. Used to give me the creeps a bit, but he's not the worst one. We get some real nutters in here, which is why I've got an alarm under my desk – you know, just in case one of them flips out.' She lowered her eyes suddenly, like she realised she'd been a bit too candid.

'He *used* to? You said he "used" to...'

'Yeah, well, I haven't seen him for a while now – a few weeks actually. He missed his appointments, which is unusual – unheard of in fact... I thought maybe he wasn't well or something. John's a nuisance but he's harmless really, and I'm a good gatekeeper you see.' She gave me the once-over before adding, 'Usually.'

My brain instantly slipped into overdrive. Dr Carmichael's phone had been ringing during our conversation – twice, three times in fact. She'd ignored it, which wasn't strange in itself – I did it to Archer all the time – but... the Post-it note on her desk, the one I'd seen when Davis and I had first come to her office, waiting for her, had read, 'John Evergreen called FIVE times – says it's extremely urgent.' What was so urgent that he'd needed to get hold of his therapist so desperately just a few days ago? It struck me suddenly that I didn't remember seeing the doll either – the one that had given Davis the fear when I'd waggled it in her face before Dr Carmichael had come in and caught us playing silly beggars.

'The doll.' I looked at Alicia, who'd gone back to scrolling through Instagram on her laptop.

'Sorry?' She looked up at me once more.

'The doll – the one in Dr Carmichael's office. The porcelain doll...'

She looked miffed for a moment, but then a flicker of recognition appeared across her face.

'Oh yeah, that one.' Her brow furrowed slightly. 'What about it?'

'Did John give it to her? Was it a present – from her *biggest fan*?' I shook my head, conspiratorially.

'No... that's Dr Carmichael's doll.'

'A present from another client?'

She shrugged. 'Not sure,' she said, rapidly losing interest as she turned her attention back to Instagram. 'Don't think so. It's been here since I can remember, ever since I started anyway, and that was over five years ago now.'

'I see. Thanks, Alicia.'

We'd been trying to call John Evergreen's number of course, but the line appears to have been disconnected, the last hit pinging off a mast close to his address, over a week and a half ago, before Darcie went missing, yet it's clear he *has* tried to contact Dr Carmichael since then. Did Dr Carmichael lie to me about when she'd last seen John or was it just an oversight?

My head feels fried by the time I stand in front of the team for the day's briefing, so much so that it's a struggle to arrange my thoughts in any kind of concise order, the clicking noise of Dr Carmichael's pen still persisting in my ears as I address them.

'So, we're pretty certain that John Evergreen is our guy and that he's holding Darcie at a location as yet unknown. We've already put an APB out on him, but we need witnesses, last sightings of his whereabouts, names and addresses of any family, friends, anyone he may have contacted or who may be harbouring him – harbouring them both in fact.'

'His resident address was empty,' Davis continues. 'No obvious signs of John or Darcie having been there recently, though forensics are going over the property now. It's possible she was there at some point and that he's moved her to a different location.'

'We've got the car though,' Delaney says, ever the bearer of good news. 'We've impounded it.'

I nod, barely able to keep my eyes open.

'Harding.' I look over at him. 'I want you to check out John Evergreen's local pharmacy – find out where he went to get his prescriptions and check when he last picked anything up. As we know, Evergreen is a paranoid schizophrenic and uses medication to control his symptoms. It's possible that for some reason he could have stopped taking his meds and therefore has had a relapse. Dr Carmichael doesn't seem to think so, but I want this checked out.'

'Yes, boss.'

'Gov,' Mitchell pipes up. 'I've got something of interest about the name you gave me to look into – "Alastor".'

'And…'

'Well,' she says, 'it's a bit of a needle-and-haystack job. There's around 194 men with the name Alastor – spelled in that way – currently residing in or around Scotland, but as yet no one of interest, no one with any convictions, any previous, and most of them are of a young age, kids and teens, *but...*'

I raise my eyebrows, trying to shake off this feeling of malaise.

'... I did find a *house* of that name.'

THIRTY-FOUR

So it's a *house* called Alastor.

Apparently, according to Mitchell's findings, it stands alone on a hill on one of the remotest islands in Scotland. 'You could get to it by car eventually – there's a village elsewhere on the island with a small road bridge to the mainland,' she explains, 'but by all accounts, the fastest way to get there would be by boat as it's pretty much surrounded by water.'

A boat. Mentally, I'm already packing a suitcase for an impromptu trip to Scotland. Not that I have a suitcase, or any clothes to put in one – Fiona took almost everything I own to Sandbanks with her.

'It's got to be the same house,' I said. 'The one Darcie told Gina and Dr Carmichael about.' I'd briefed the team on the information Gina had given us, about the admittedly macabre and somewhat unorthodox story Darcie had told to her all those years ago – and more recently to Dr Carmichael too.

'Carmichael seems to think it's the work of an overactive imagination,' I explained. 'She diagnosed Darcie with something called pseudologia fantastica, or chronic pathological lying to you and me. She claims Darcie made the whole story up in a bid to gain attention and portray herself as a victim to gain sympathy, apparently to fill some kind of emotional void from her traumatic childhood – or at least in her opinion.'

'Her *professional* opinion,' Delaney piped up. 'Carmichael's one of the top psychiatrists in the country, Dan – she knows what she's talking about. I see her on that Crime Inc channel all the time. She's quite fit as well, for an older woman... I certainly wouldn't say no.' He sniggered.

Davis gave a little eye roll in response.

'So Carmichael reckons that all this is some kind of ruse then?' he continued. 'That Darcie's staged her own abduction and that she's not actually missing at all? Because that kind of makes sense, doesn't it? It's certainly an interesting theory...' The corners of Delaney's mouth turned outwards. Somehow I knew he'd favour the idea Dr Carmichael had thrown into the ring about Darcie being a compulsive liar.

'Ordinarily, I'd agree with you, Martin,' I said, which statistically isn't true, but anyway, 'only Gina claims Darcie told her about the hit-and-run abduction almost twenty-odd years ago now, long before she ever sought counselling with Dr Carmichael. And as we know, she's done her best to keep her identity on the down-low all these years – didn't want any notoriety from the incident with the toddler she rescued; didn't want her details released to the press; no social media either... It doesn't strike me as someone who compulsively lies for attention and sympathy.'

Now, I rub my temples, my foggy mind wandering. I really need to go home and get some rest. I almost feel as if I'm in some kind of trance I'm so sleep-deprived.

I turn to Mitchell. 'So, who lives there now, at this house? We got any names yet?'

'Hmm, well, actually no one lives there now, gov.'

I mentally start unpacking my suitcase.

'It burned to the ground some eighteen years ago.'

'Any fatalities – anyone in it when it burned down?'

'Yes,' she says. 'According to the press cuttings I dug up, the owner, someone called Mikhail Carson. He was a doctor apparently.'

'Christ, another one?'

She raises a brow. 'It was an heirloom, the house – or mansion really when you look at it...'

She hands me the cutting, a photo of an old, foreboding house of some considerable size perched on a small grassy hill.

'Been in the Carson family for years, so it says here. According to this article, it wasn't until someone from the village saw smoke and raised the alarm that anyone realised it was on fire. By that time however, the whole place was an inferno – nothing left of it when they finally arrived.'

'Jesus.' I scan read the newspaper article.

'Nothing left of Carson either apparently. They identified him from his dental records.'

'Was it an arson job?'

Mitchell shrugs. 'Doesn't appear to be any evidence suggesting the fire was started deliberately, boss, though rumours were rife. Some local residents said at the time that Carson was a recluse – that he'd lived there alone for most of his life, didn't bother anyone and no one bothered him.'

'Most of his life?'

'He supposedly had a wife and daughter at some point, but apparently, she and the girl, who was about ten at the time, left him years ago and he'd remained there ever since, alone – kept himself to himself, only visited the village every once in a while for provisions and was rarely seen on the mainland either.'

I stare at the photo, the ramshackle windows of the house staring back at me ominously, like eyes. It's given me the wiggies a bit, and I think of Darcie, just fifteen at the time she claims she was taken there, and how utterly terrifying it would've been, trapped somewhere like this, somewhere so remote and sinister looking.

'The fire service conducted an inquiry after the blaze, gov,' Mitchell continues, 'which, according to their findings, seems to have started in an upstairs bedroom – one of the eight bedrooms – most likely from a naked flame. A candle probably. There were no electrics at the property either; everything was heated by fuel – coal and open fires. Somewhat behind the times.'

'How old was he when he died?'

'Forty-five, boss.' She swings her laptop round towards me, displaying a picture of Mikhail Carson on screen. He looks unremarkable, just your average middle-aged man, his face staring to drop, his hairline receding. He's smiling, a little crookedly, in the picture, though it doesn't appear to quite reach his dark eyes somehow.

'Mikhail... that's not a Scottish name, is it?'

'Russian by origin,' Mitchell, the human encyclopedia that she is, replies.

'What was his wife's name – and the daughter? Are they still alive? Can we locate them; get some details?'

Mitchell flicks back through her notes. 'The wife's name was Harriet, and the daughter... Ah, there it is, yes, Betsy. Harriet and Betsy Carson.'

I instruct Mitchell to do her best work in tracking them down. Assuming they're still alive, it could be extremely useful to speak to them; find out more about their late husband and father. The house burned down eighteen years ago in 2006, two years after Darcie claims to have been taken there and held hostage. I also ask Mitchell to dig deeper – to find out what kind of doctor this Mikhail Carson was, and, specifically, if he ever owned or collected porcelain dolls.

After we wrap up, I head back to my office, Davis following.

'You sure you're OK, gov?' she asks, looking at me with light concern as I grab my laptop from the desk. I want to go through everything – every statement, every bit of intelligence we've got so far – in minute detail. It won't make for light reading, but I'm convinced there's something there, in among it all, a golden nugget that we've inadvertently overlooked.

'I said I'd go through that lot,' she reminds me. 'You should go home – get some rest. You don't look yourself, gov, I have to say.'

She's right – I don't look myself. I don't feel myself either. Perhaps I'm coming down with something. Great. Just what I need – another reason for Archer to push me out and put Delaney in my place.

'I think Dr Carmichael may have lied about when she last saw John Evergreen,' I say exclusively to Davis as she walks me to my car. 'She said he'd attended his weekly appointment last Wednesday, at 1.30 p.m. – their usual time. Only when I spoke to the receptionist, Alicia, she told me that he hasn't been in for a few weeks; that he never misses his appointments – he's Carmichael's biggest fan apparently.'

'Why would she lie, gov?'

I shrug. 'Could be just an oversight,' I say, unconvinced. 'But you remember, when we went to her office the first time... I saw a Post-it note on her desk saying that Evergreen had called her no less than five times – said it was "urgent". And then today, earlier...'

Davis looked at me intently.

'... Carmichael's phone was ringing in her handbag – her personal mobile I assumed – two or three times... and she ignored it. I even asked her if she needed to take the call. It sounded like the caller really wanted to get hold of her...'

'But Evergreen's number's no longer recognised, gov. It last pinged over a week and half ago.'

'He could have another phone, a burner even.'

She nods. 'I'll look into it, boss.'

I pause for a second.

'Go round there – pay her a visit.'

'To Carmichael's office?'

'To her home address,' I say, thinking out loud. 'Surprise her, catch her off guard, make it look and sound like a routine visit. Ask her about when she last spoke to Evergreen again. Tell her we've traced a number...'

'Lie to her, you mean?'

'White lies, Lucy, white lies... I think it'll be better coming from you. I get the feeling she's not that taken with me personally. Maybe the female touch is what's needed. Go in gently though – don't spook her. If she has lied to us, then we need to know why. I think maybe she's protecting him, Evergreen, in some way.'

'OK, gov.' Davis nods. 'I'll drop by her address on my way home.'

THIRTY-FIVE

There's a heavy sensation in my chest as I pull up outside Colville Terrace. I told Davis I was heading home, but first I need to have this conversation with Gabe Bonneville. One I'm not looking forward to. He's owed the truth, but I intend to keep the information I give him to a minimum; spare him from hearing too many of the more unpleasant details about his wife's past and what she might have endured. Then I can finally go home myself and snatch a few hours' sleep before it's back on the wheel.

We corroborated Gina's story in as much as there's evidence to suggest that Darcie did indeed once reside in a trap house in Edinburgh, sometime back in the early 2000s. There's a photo Gina produced for one thing, and another witness who called in following the appeal who'd known her from around that time, though as for the rest of it, well, only Darcie can really answer that, and as I'm painfully aware, she's still very much unable to.

'You look how I feel, Dan,' Gabe says with a weary smile as he welcomes me into his stunning home. He looks distressed beneath the forced smile though, his eyes rimmed red, and he's sporting a five o'clock shadow.

The dog, Purdy, scoots up to greet me as I enter; begins licking my shoes as she looks up at me with sad brown eyes as if to ask, 'Have you found her yet?'

'No offence,' he adds. 'I know you're all working tirelessly. And I really do appreciate it, everything you've done – that you're *doing* – to find her.'

'I know, Gabe.' I return his smile. 'And none taken.'

'I know why you're here,' he says. 'Why you're both here.'

'Both?' I hear the sound of a toilet flushing, and my heart sinks as Delaney exits the bathroom, doing his zipper up. I didn't even notice he'd left the office. And now he'd beaten me to it.

'Martin's been bringing me up to scratch.'

How thoughtful. I'll bet he could hardly wait to inform Gabe of his wife's past discretions. He's nothing if not a Job's comforter.

'So I see,' I say tightly. 'Martin.' I acknowledge him with a stiff nod.

'I was just bringing Gabe up to speed on where we are with the investigation, Dan,' he says.

'So I'm guessing Martin has told you about...'

'Yes.' Gabe nods; lowers his eyes slightly. 'He's told me about the time Darcie lived in Edinburgh, about her being a heroin user and about the things she supposedly had to do to survive.'

Delaney is watching Gabe with a sense of what I can only describe as exaggerated sympathy.

'She never told you anything about that time in her life?'

He shakes his head. 'No, never,' he sighs. 'Not a word to me about any of it...' His voice trails off. 'I know— well, I always sensed her relationship with Fabienne – her mother – was strained. She rarely, if ever, mentioned her, and as for a drug habit...' He collapses down on the sofa. 'Darcie never touched drugs – certainly not since we've been together.'

'That you know of,' Delaney interjects.

Gabe glances up at him then looks back at me. 'She never touched – never touches – drugs. She rarely even drinks alcohol. When we met, all I knew – all she told me – was that her mother was dead, that they were never close, and that she'd left home when she was very young and came to London.'

'And you never thought to probe any further?' Delaney offers.

'No.'

'Why not?'

He pauses for a brief moment.

'Because I figured if there was anything she wanted to tell me, then she would've done. And,' he adds, 'I'm not in the habit of forcing people to talk about things in their past that they might not want to.' He smiles thinly. 'Unlike you I should imagine, Detective Delaney... in your line of work I mean.'

I inwardly smile.

'Did Darcie ever mention the name Alastor to you, Gabe?' I ask. 'Did she ever tell you a story about being held captive in an old house, somewhere remote?'

He shakes his head again. '*Captive*? No – never!'

'Look, Gabe,' Delaney interjects once more. 'I know this must be difficult for you, learning about your wife's past, about the drugs, the thieving. It must be a bit of a shock to your system, realising that she isn't who you thought she is, but if you could really think hard...'

Gabe runs his hands through his mop of ringlets.

Though he's careful to conceal it, I get the sickening sense that Delaney's actually getting off on Gabriel Bonneville's obvious discomfort.

'Like I say, she never told me about any of it – assuming it's all true of course.'

'Oh, I'm afraid it is,' Delaney replies quickly. 'We've spoken to a woman who lived with Darcie during that time, and further confirmation came from other sources following the appeal, and of course, her therapist, Dr Carmichael – she claims she diagnosed your wife with a condition called...?' Delaney looks over to me for support. I don't offer it. 'Well, anyway, it was essentially something to do with pathological lying. Was Darcie a liar, Gabe? Did she ever tell lies, aside from the obvious ones we've already mentioned?'

'Yes, thank you, Martin.' I shoot him a hard look that silences him immediately.

'If you're asking me if I think my wife has a pathological need to tell lies, Detective Delaney, then the answer is absolutely not. Darcie is honest – sometimes too honest in fact. She's never told me any "stories"; anything that would ever lead me to believe that she suffered with any such condition to the one you say this... this psychiatrist claims she has.'

'I'm sorry, Gabe.' I look directly into his blue eyes; make sure he knows I mean it at least – because I am, truly.

'Well,' – Delaney's tone lifts an octave – 'I suppose we all have secrets from our past, don't we? Though some with more far-reaching consequences obviously. Sometimes, we think we know those closest to us, only to discover we never really knew them at all...'

It's all I can do not to shake my head at Delaney in contempt.

'But I *do* know Darcie,' Gabe says, ignoring Delaney and addressing me personally. 'I know everything I need to know about her. Look, I can't say I'm not a little shocked by all of this, but the truth is, I don't *care* about her past – that's not where we're living.' He adds poignantly, 'And if you think learning that my wife ran away when she was just fifteen and became a drug user, stealing to support her habit – and *if* it's true that she was held captive then – she's even more remarkable, even *more* incredible than I already think she is.' He draws breath. 'To have experienced all of that horror... to have survived all of that and gone on to become the person she is – a brilliant, resilient, kind, loving, empathetic and capable woman – only proves to me that I know *exactly* who she is, and in fact' – he looks over at Delaney – 'it makes me love and admire her even more than I already do.'

He audibly exhales, but he isn't finished.

'*And* if you're also asking me if I wish she'd told me about it all, then the answer is yes, of course. I'm gutted she didn't trust me enough to tell me, because I can only imagine what she went through back then, as a young teenager. And it makes me want to hold her, comfort her, tell her it's all going to be OK. I just pray I get the chance to do that,' he says, standing now. 'As for the diagnosis, the one from this Carmichael woman' – he looks over at Delaney – 'it's called pseudologia fantasia by the way – well, I'll be asking for a second opinion. I might not deal with diseases of the mind, but I do deal with ones of the heart, and my heart is telling me that my Darc is no pathological liar.'

I nod at Gabe, silently agreeing with him. But I know one thing: Darcie Bonneville may not be lying, at least not anymore, but I'm sure as hell that *someone* is.

THIRTY-SIX

My earlier malaise seems to have waned by the time I finally make it home, and I'm hit by something of a second wind. I shower, savouring the sting of the soapy hot water against my skin as I try to wash away the last few days' debris from it.

I dress in a pair of boxer shorts and a white T-shirt – pretty much the sum of the clean attire I have left in my cupboard – and whack the central heating up as far as it'll go. Then I hang my charity-shop suit on the back of the chair in the bedroom before making my way through to the kitchen and opening the fridge. I scan the contents for anything that could pass for a late dinner, only there's not much doing – a couple of slices of ham and some eggs whose sell-by date I daren't look at.

I throw together an omelette, staring into the pan as the runny yellow contents spits and splutters onto the hob, my thoughts drifting until the smell of burning reaches my nostrils. *Shit!*

I scrape the black-and-yellow contents of the pan onto a plate and head to the sofa; place it next to me alongside my laptop. I hear a squeaking sound I'm pretty sure hasn't come from me as my backside meets the cushion and fish whatever it is out from beneath me.

Ah, it's one of Pip's toys – Bit-Bit, a soft fluffy rabbit with an overbite that she drags around by the ear everywhere she goes. She'll be upset this has been left behind.

I bring Bit-Bit up to my nose and give it a deep sniff, closing my eyes for a moment and savouring my daughter's innocent scent on its fur.

Sighing, I flip open my laptop and begin reading, while simultaneously shovelling burned offerings into my hungry mouth. Remarkably, the omelette tastes better than it looks.

I go through the statements one by one, studying them meticulously, unsure of what it is I feel I may have missed. It's on the reread of the reread that I spot it, my fork clattering against the plate as I abandon it in haste. Something Anita Abberline said, something innocuous at the time, so much so that I don't even recall her saying it, yet it's here in black-and-white in front of me.

Anita told us it had been she who'd recommended Dr Carmichael's services to Darcie, describing, so it says here, the eminent celebrity psychiatrist as being 'an absolute miracle worker'.

'Darcie told me she suffered from claustrophobia, so I suggested she go and see her, although I thought they may have already met.'

I'm already dialling the number as I think about putting in the call.

'Anita Abberliiiine…' she sings her own name down the line as she answers, surprisingly chirpy for someone whose friend is missing. 'Detective Riley!' She seems thrilled to hear from me.

'I'm sorry to call you out of the blue, Anita…'

'Ohhh, no problem – no problem at *aaaalllll*,' she says. 'How utterly bizarre though! I was only just talking to a girlfriend about you, on the phone! We saw you, on TV, on the appeal yesterday. It's all over the news; *you're* all over the news.'

She pauses, her voice dropping an octave or two. 'It's just awful though, isn't it? I was in floods of tears watching it... Then to learn that Darcie is *pregnant* – I mean, pregnant *and* missing!' I hear her take a large breath. 'And my poor, poor Gabe, what he must be going through, what with people pointing the finger. I've been trying to contact him but he won't pick—'

'Anita,' I interrupt, 'I wanted to talk to you about the statement you gave us, specifically when you mentioned you'd given Darcie Dr Carmichael's business card – that you'd recommended her services, for her claustrophobia?'

'Yes...?' she says, slightly cautiously.

'You said that you thought that perhaps Darcie and Dr Carmichael already knew each other. What made you say that?'

'Did I say that? Oh, well, ummm, Dr Carmichael... When I went to see her for help, we talked about my social interactions – hobbies, gym, clubs I belong to, that sort of thing. We got talking about my yoga class if I remember rightly... Anyway, when I was leaving, she offered me some of her business cards, in case I ever wanted to refer her to a friend. She said I'd get a twenty-five per cent discount off a single session if a booking came directly from one of my recommendations, and an M&S voucher... Anyway' – she draws breath – 'she specifically insisted I give her card to Darcie; made a bit of a thing about it.'

'A thing?' I look down at my half-eaten plate of burned eggs, my appetite rapidly vanishing.

'Yes, she mentioned Darcie specifically by name, as though she somehow knew her, even though I don't recall ever telling her Darcie's name, so I just thought perhaps they'd already met... I thought perhaps she may have seen Darcie from all the video clips that were circulating online and in the press – you know, from when she saved that little girl on the high street?'

She pauses. 'Perhaps I should've asked her at the time; didn't really think to, to be honest, and anyway, I got my discount for the referral, and an M&S voucher thrown in too!' she adds breezily. 'I... I hope it wasn't anything important?'

I thank her and hang up. Something isn't sitting right in my gut, and I don't think it's the burned eggs.

I stare at the laptop screen so hard that my vision blurs and the words on it begin to soften around the edges and... my phone rings.

'Lucy...'

'Did I wake you up, gov?'

'Yes,' I lie. 'I was blissfully in the land of nod.'

'Sorry, but as you always say, there's no rest for the wicked.'

'Ain't that the truth?' I say, shovelling the last of the eggy mess on my plate into my mouth.

'We've got the info in now about John Evergreen's prescription – for the antipsychotics Carmichael prescribes him – well, his local chemist hasn't seen a doctor's script for around six months, gov. We've checked out all the chemists within a ten-mile radius of Evergreen's address and... nothing.'

'*Six* months ago?'

'Yep,' Davis reiterates, 'just shy of six months. On the off chance, I asked if they still had it on file – you know, kept hold of the script like chemists used to do before it all went digital. It was a long shot, but would you believe, they only fully switched to paperless scripts just under six months ago and managed to locate it – the last prescription Evergreen presented to them, signed and dated by Dr Elizabeth Carmichael.'

My mind is suddenly spinning out of control.

'It could prove that Evergreen hasn't been taking his medication, boss. I'll send it over now.'

'Do that, Davis,' I say. 'And when you visit Dr Carmichael, keep it as informal as possible – make it seem as if she's being super helpful; kiss her arse if you have to... metaphorically speaking.'

'*OK*,' Davis says, drawing the word out. 'I'm getting ready to head over there now, gov.'

'And in the meantime, ask Mitchell to run some checks on Dr Carmichael – just some general background stuff,' I say. 'Just so we know exactly what we're dealing with. Like I said earlier, she may have lied about when she last saw John Evergreen.'

'Or just forgotten?' Davis says.

'Quite possibly,' I reply, a trickle of unease travelling the length of my spine. 'Call me back if you get anything else, and let me know how the visit with Carmichael goes. Use this prescription business, the concern that John hasn't been taking his meds, as an inroad if you like, but, Davis,' I say, 'go gently, yeah?'

'Yes, boss, kiss her arse... I've got it.'

We hang up, and I start reading through the email Davis has pinged over to me, stifling a yawn. It's a standard doctor's script from what I can see, with the name of the recipient, John Evergreen, his address and the medication name and dosage in faint type. Dr Carmichael's handwritten signature is at the bottom, somewhat florid and distinctive – especially the swirling E and C. It's dated almost six months previously and—

Hang on.

I rub my gritty eyes and pull up the info we have on Dr Mikhail Carson. *Mikhail Carson.* I stare at the name. Mikhail... the Russian version of Michael.

'Michael Carson, Car-son... Mikhail... Michael...' I repeat the name out loud to myself over and over. 'Michael Carson... *Carson... Michael, Car Michael!*'

I leap forward on the sofa with such impact that it upends my plate, sending it clattering to the floor. My fingers are vibrating as I pull up the note on my computer screen – the handwritten note Darcie received the night before she was abducted – and drag a copy of the doctor's script that Davis just sent over, bringing them together on-screen, side by side.

'Well, what do you know...' I whisper as I stare at the handwriting. I'm no handwriting expert, but then again, you wouldn't need to be – the style is so distinctive.

They look identical.

Then it occurs to me. During our first encounter at her office, Dr Carmichael wrote something down on a piece of paper for me, the name of her agent. I think... I'm sure it's still in my jacket pocket!

My heart is banging painfully against my ribs as I stumble over myself in haste, snatching the jacket from the back of the chair in the bedroom where I threw it earlier.

It's here, in the inside pocket of my charity-shop suit!

The paper dances in my hand as I unfold it and hold it up close to the screen, comparing it to the anonymous note that was sent to Darcie; to the writing on the prescription. I zoom in on the image, as close as it'll allow. The paper it's written on appears similar in colour and thickness – cream, embossed, expensive looking. I study the writing, my eyes manically darting from screen to paper, paper to screen.

'Emma Gardiner Management Company,' it reads, followed by a phone number. I cross reference the E and the C with Dr Carmichael's signature – the elaborate, swirling E; the curling C...

Blood pumps furiously through my body, forcing me to exhale heavily.

Mikhail Carson... Carmichael...

I click back onto the press cutting Mitchell discovered, struggling to keep focus as I speed-read it again.

'Dr Carson's estranged wife, Harriet, and their daughter, Betsy...'

Betsy. Betsy is short for Elizabeth!

Dr Elizabeth Carmichael is Betty Carson. *She's his daughter*!

'Yes! Yes!' I shout, euphoric. 'You son of a bitch!'

But then it hits me, and my euphoria evaporates, killed stone dead in a flash of horror as it dawns upon me...

'*Davis!*'

THIRTY-SEVEN

DARCIE

In that second, my whole life flashes before me. Tiny microsecond snippets of it all spliced together, random stills of people and places and faces, sights and sounds and smells that have fused themselves into my subconscious memory; are flashing through my mind on fast forward.

'John... John, please listen to me. You don't have to do this...'

My hands are out in front of me, pathetically trying to create some kind of barrier between us. I try to keep my voice calm, but it sounds broken. All I can think about is Gabe and Purdy and this baby inside me, a baby I'm growing convinced will never take its first breath or see its mother's face. And as small as this world of mine is, I realise just how perfect it is; how it's all – everything – I've ever wanted.

Please don't take it all away from me, not now that I've finally found it. I'm begging you, please.

'You don't have to do this. You can let me go, John,' I say as he hovers in the corner of the room. 'We can work this out. I know you're a good person, John – I sensed it the moment I met you. You can let me go; you can say I escaped. I... I won't go to the police. *We* can escape – we can escape together, John; go somewhere together. I can help you, John. This can all go away – you can *make* it all go away. Please don't do this. Don't let me die like this; don't let my baby—'

'I'm sorry. I'm sorry,' he wails between breaths. 'I... I don't want to kill you. I don't want to hurt your baby. I... I never meant for... I didn't know... I thought...'

I hear that clicking sound again, like the cocking of a gun, amplified in the dark, and instinctively I jump sideways.

'Is that a gun, John?' I ask again. I hear the urgency, the desperation in my voice. 'John... do you have a gun?'

'No...'

There's another voice, a different voice, and I gasp, turning sharply to my left. I see a sliver of light as the door opens, and my eyes widen. *Oh thank God. Thank you, God – thank you, thank you, thank you!* I drop to my knees, relief flooding through me, the force of it causing my bladder to collapse. I don't know why she's here, but in this moment, it doesn't matter. All that matters is that she *is* here.

Instinctively, I rush towards her, but I'm stopped short by the chain.

'He has a gun, Dr Carmichael!' I scream, convinced he's going to shoot her, shoot me, shoot us both. 'John has a gun!'

A sudden stillness falls, the briefest second of it, just like it did before he abducted me in the woods.

'No,' she says. Her voice sounds soft, almost ethereal. 'John doesn't have a gun, Darcie... *but I do.*'

I see a flash of light, then the sound reaches my ears like an explosion, like a bomb detonating next me, and instinctively I cover them with my hands. A high-pitched scream is burning through my brain, ringing painfully in my ears, a continuous, sharp flatline sound vibrating through me. I'm rendered momentarily blind and deaf, the cold concrete burning my knees as I fall on them, struggling to breathe. *I've been shot! I've been shot!*

But I feel nothing, no pain, except for the ear-splitting scream that's reaching a crescendo inside my head. I look down at myself, my eyes stinging with tears and mucus. There's no blood – I see no blood on me...

I look up, look over at Dr Carmichael, though she's nothing more than a moving blurred image before me now. There's a thick fog around me before I'm hit by a sharp, smoky smell of black crackling powder, a scent I'm unfamiliar with yet somehow recognise as the harbinger of something powerful and harmful, something malevolent.

The smell of death.

I see him slumped in the corner of the room, his legs splayed out before him in a V shape, his chin touching his chest and—

Oh God, oh God, oh God. The top of his skull is gone, and white globules of fat, grey tissue and blood so dark it's almost black runs down his face. The whites of his eyes, juxtaposed against the blood and brain matter, are wide in alarm and surprise, and his mouth is open, the shape distorted and unnatural, displaying his decaying teeth – the ones I couldn't help but notice when I first met him. The image looks unreal, like it's been staged, and I tell myself he's just an actor from a film; that it's just a part he's playing, and the blood and brain just gruesome special effects.

Still crouched on my knees, I turn towards Dr Carmichael in slow motion. 'Y-Y-You shot him!' I stammer. 'You killed John!'

I can feel the shock and confusion as it begins to claim me; my heart is beating so rapidly I'll surely die right here on this spot.

'Who the hell are you? Why are you doing this?'

THIRTY-EIGHT

DAN

'C'mon... c'mon... Answer the phone, Lucy. *Answer the goddamn phone!*'

I balance it between my ear and shoulder as I haphazardly throw on my clothes, my hands shaking as I struggle with the buttons. I check my watch. Has she already left the station? Is she making her way over to Carmichael's place right now? *Or is she there already?*

Frantic, I try to calculate the time it could take for her to reach Carmichael's address in Hussywell Hill, another notably affluent area of North London. I estimate forty minutes tops on a good day maybe, if the traffic isn't against you. *Oh please, please let the traffic be against you...*

I hit her number again, but it rings out.

My mind is racing as I get into my car. I curse on a loop under my breath; feel panic swelling inside my guts. Where does John Evergreen fit in to all of this? Carmichael hasn't been operating alone, and I'm certain Evergreen was the one who abducted Darcie from Ravens Wood – under Carmichael's instruction I now suspect.

'John's absolutely harmless, Detective Riley – wouldn't hurt another soul.' It was all to try and put me off the scent. She's been using him.

'Everyone knows John... He's Dr Carmichael's biggest fan... He's like a puppy dog... He used to turn up sometimes an hour, two hours even, before his appointment and just sit there, gazing over at her office.'

Carmichael's own words, and those of her assistant's, resonate. She recruited John to do her dirty work for her, his mental-health challenges and his obvious affection for her making him vulnerable, the perfect target, more open and susceptible to manipulation. And she's pretty good at it too – I'd go as far as to say expert in fact.

I think about how I felt only hours earlier when I'd been in her company, the *click-click-click* sound of that pen as she pressed it up and down with her thumb, the same pen I feel sure now was used to write that anonymous note to Darcie. Is it some kind of psychological trick – one she uses to confuse and subdue? A form of hypnosis maybe? I know it's *something,* because I left there feeling different somehow, my thoughts marred and my concentration impaired.

Carmichael hasn't been protecting John at all, like I thought she might've been – she's been protecting *herself.* Only there's still a gaping hole where an explanation should be in all of this. Why would Carmichael want to harm Darcie in the first place? Even if she is, as I also suspect, Betsy Carson, Mikhail Carson's daughter, the press cutting claims that she and her mother left that old house, and him, years ago, long before Darcie claims to have been taken there and held against her will. I can't quite piece it all together.

I weave in and out of the trawling traffic at speed, my blue light on. If I really put my foot down, I'm sure I can make it there in thirty minutes.

Would Davis have taken someone with her to Carmichael's place – Parker perhaps; Delaney even? I pray to

God that she has, but then again, why would she? She said she was going to drop by on her way home. She'll be alone. She's going to turn up at Carmichael's house, impromptu, and *alone*.

I call the nick.

'Incident room, DC Parker speaking.'

'Parker! Parker! Oh thank God.' I'm breathless with adrenalin as he picks up.

'Hey, gov... I thought you were supposed to be at home, getting some kip. I—'

'Parker, shut up and listen to me very carefully. Is Lucy still there? Has she left the building yet?'

'Umm...' I hear him on the other end of the line; imagine him doing a 360 turn as he scans the incident room. 'Er, no, gov – not by the looks of it. I think she left already.'

'Shit. *SHIT*!'

'Gov? You OK?'

'How long ago?'

'What?'

'How long ago did she leave?'

'Umm... I dunno. I—'

'Was she with someone? Did anyone leave with her?'

I hear him muttering to someone in the background, clearly detecting my sense of urgency.

'She left about forty minutes ago, boss. Yeah, Mitchell's saying forty minutes or so, and she was alone. Why, gov? Is everything OK?'

I drag my hand down my face as I press my foot further down on the accelerator.

'I need a tactical unit sent down to 16 Alexander Park, N10 2BA – that's November one zero, two bravo alpha. Right away, Parker – *immediately*.'

'PTU? Why? What's happened?'

'Elizabeth Carmichael – I think she could be holding

Darcie hostage at her home, and... and Lucy's on her way over there now. She may already be there.'

Parker's silent, but I can hear the increase in his breathing down the line as he processes what I'm saying.

'Elizabeth Carmichael is Betsy Carson, Mikhail Carson's – *Alastor's* – daughter. I'm almost a hundred per cent sure of it. The handwriting; the note... She wrote that note to Darcie and got Evergreen to deliver it. She's the one pulling the strings. She's the—'

'Slow down, gov,' Parker says. 'I can't understand what you're saying. Carmichael is who? You're breaking up a bit – the line's really bad.'

I shake my head in frustration. 'Jesus, we haven't got time! Just get Archer to sanction PTU to Carmichael's home address as quick as you can. I think Davis could be walking into something bad – something potentially dangerous.'

I hear Parker talking to someone in the background again. It's starting to rain now – fat drops of it, hard and heavy, battering the windscreen. I switch the wipers on.

'Gov!' Mitchell's voice comes on the line.

'Mitchell! Mitchell! Listen to me, I think Darcie Bonneville is at Carmichael's address over in Hussywell Hill. We need PTU there right now.'

It suddenly hits me just how foolish I've been. While I'd begun to question Dr Carmichael's authenticity, I certainly hadn't thought she'd had any malevolent part to play in all of this. My focus has been purely on Evergreen being the puppet master, only it seems he was only the puppet.

'Boss. *Boss...*'

I hear the gravitas in her voice as she addresses me, instantly alerting me that she's about to tell me something I'm fairly certain I don't want to hear.

'I've been doing some background checks on Carmichael, like you asked me to, and...'

The inflection in Mitchell's voice is starting to scare me.

'And it's come up that Carmichael has a gun licence.'

'She has a *what*?' But I've heard her perfectly clearly. 'Ah, no, Mitchell, no, no, *no*!' I bang the steering wheel hard with my palm three times in quick succession. 'A *gun* licence? How the hell does a celebrity psychiatrist get a gun licence, for Christ's sake?' I make a sharp right turn, tyres screeching as I rake my left hand through my hair.

'The certificate was first issued back in the late nineties, and she's renewed it every five years since. On the most recent application, it states that she requested it for her own safety, and that her profession puts her at high risk from potential stalkers, obsessives and the like... It was signed off by her local police department – by someone called Jack Coggins.'

'I need to speak to Archer.' My voice sounds alarmingly calm considering what I'm feeling right now.

'She's right here, gov, next to me. I—'

'Riley!' Archer's sharp voice batters my eardrum as she snatches the phone. 'For the love of God, you'd better tell me what the fuck's going on.'

'Carmichael – Dr Elizabeth Carmichael. She's not who we thought she was, ma'am. I think she's holding Darcie Bonneville prisoner at her home address – that she recruited John Evergreen to abduct her and take her there.'

'Oh come off it, Dan,' she snaps. 'We both know the Bonneville woman is already dead. It's been three days with no sign of her, no proof of life. You know he'll have killed her by now; disposed of her remains.'

'She's there, ma'am,' I say flatly. 'I know she is, as is Evergreen no doubt and... and *DS Lucy Davis*.' I close my eyes for a second longer than the right side of road safety. 'And if Carmichael has a firearms licence, we need SCO19 down there, ma'am. *We need them now*.'

I hear her suck air through her nose so deeply I imagine all the oxygen draining from the incident room.

'Ma'am...?'

She's silent for a painful second longer.

'You'd better be right about this, Riley, or I'll have your badge.'

'If I'm wrong, I'll give it to you willingly.'

'If they show up mob-handed and it turns out that one of your hunches hasn't paid off, then it'll be *you* who'll be paid off – and not handsomely either, I might add.'

'It's a potential hostage situation, ma'am. Carmichael's licensed to have a firearm on the premises. Lucy could be walking straight into—' An image of Davis, my trusted colleague, my work wife, ringing the door of Carmichael's home only to be greeted by a bullet straight in the chest flashes before me, and I grip the steering wheel so hard my knuckles turn white.

'I want you back here at the station, Riley,' Archer says. 'Right now. We'll deploy armed response and bring in a negotiator.'

'But I'm a trained negotiator,' I say.

'You're a bloody liability is what you are, Riley. Get yourself back down to the station and let the pros deal with it. This is out of our remit. Do you hear me, Riley? I'm instructing you to return to the station *immediately*.'

'I'm doing a U-turn as we speak, ma'am,' I lie. I have neither the time nor inclination to argue with her. I'll just have to deal with the consequences in the aftermath, or in the afterlife perhaps. But either way, I know one thing: Darcie Bonneville is there at that house and I'm not leaving Davis on her own.

Over my dead body.

THIRTY-NINE

DARCIE

'Well, someone had to put him out of his misery, didn't they?'

I blink at Dr Carmichael, paralysed with shock and disbelief. Initially, it was an indescribable relief to see her – a friendly, familiar face; the psychiatrist I'd met some months ago and genuinely warmed to, opened up to, put my trust in. Only now I'm sensing something altogether quite different from her as she stands in the doorway, still pointing the gun at John's lifeless body and holding something – I can't see what – in her other hand.

'Dr Carmichael?' What has she got to do with any of this? I remember John speaking so highly and so fondly of her, and I could tell it was genuine. Did he confess to her about abducting me? Has she taken it upon herself to intervene? Is that why she's here, wherever here is? I'm overwhelmed with fear and confusion. Where are the police?

In my peripheral vision, I can see John's bloodied corpse. I open my mouth to speak when a woman – a stranger I don't recognise – appears quite suddenly from behind Dr Carmichael. Her eyes widen as she sees me, and I recoil out of instinct, taking a step back. *Can someone please just tell me what the hell's going on?*

'Dr Carmichael? Darcie! Darcie Bonneville, I'm Detective—'

I hear the sound of the gun discharging again and throw myself to the floor, clutching my ears as I crouch up into a ball, as tight as my body will allow.

Oh God. She's shot her, hasn't she? I'm too terrified to look.

'Well,' Dr Carmichael says, clutching her heaving chest, visibly surprised. 'She came out of nowhere, didn't she?' She collects herself, sighing heavily as she looks at her on the floor.

'Is she... is she dead?' The words spill out of my lips involuntarily as I glance down at the body.

'Rotten timing.' Dr Carmichael turns, smiling professionally, as if she's about to initiate one of our sessions. 'I suppose I'd better get on with it now then, hadn't I?' Her tone is unnervingly calm. 'I think she was merely a harbinger. This particular breed are like cockroaches. Where there's one, you can be sure others aren't far behind...'

'Get on w-wi-with what?' My larynx is so tight it feels like it might snap in half. I know what she's implying though.

'Dr Carmichael.' Somehow, miraculously, I find my voice again. 'Please tell me what's going on...' My eyes dart around the room, searching for a place of safety, only there isn't one.

'You know, we could've been sisters, you and I,' she says. 'So much in common, so many shared life experiences... D'you know, Darcie, you really don't look so different to the first time I ever saw you.' She cocks her head from side to side as she watches me, crouched on the floor, hugging my knees to my chest.

'You've barely aged a day. Must be good genes,' she muses. 'From that deceitful bitch of a mother of yours I suspect.'

I will myself to shrink, to become as small as I can so I might disappear.

'It was one of the first things I thought when I saw your picture on TV, after you so *bravely*, so *selflessly*, saved that little girl's life.' She brings her hands to her chest; flutters her eyes dramatically, mocking me. 'How instantly recognisable you were, like I'd seen you only yesterday. For years – *years* – I'd thought of you, wondered what you might look like now, if you were still alive even, and then suddenly *boom*! There you are! In my front room, on my TV, acting coy for all those idiots with their camera phones in the aftermath, all that false modesty... I couldn't believe it! You'd been so close all this time... so near, so accessible. I never even knew your name until I saw that TV footage – no chance of locating you without a name was there? But God is good – He provides...'

I've no idea what the hell she's talking about.

'Why? Why are you doing this?'

'Do you know, I'm really quite hurt that you don't remember me.'

'I... I *do* remember you, Dr Carmichael,' I protest. Salty mucus is running from my nose and into my mouth. My whole body feels like it's melting in terror. 'I came to your office a few months ago... We spoke...'

She snorts then wags a finger. 'No, no, no, Darcie, I mean when we *first* met. I suppose it was a fair while ago now though. What? Twenty years?'

I stare at her blankly. I have no idea what any of this means. I can't seem to connect the dots.

'You knew my father,' she says flatly.

I think of Gabe then, his handsome face flashing in front of me, and I close my eyes, trying to hold that image of him there. Trying to hang on.

'Don't you remember him, Darcie? You certainly seemed to when you came to see me, crying for help, wanting to be exonerated for all your sins, all your dirty little secrets and lies. Poor little victim/hero Darcie...' She sticks her bottom lip out; pouts like a sulking child. 'Should she tell that handsome husband of hers about the drugs she smoked and snorted to mask the pain of all that rejection from... what was her name... Fabienne? *Will he still wuv me if I tell him I'm a lying, thieving, deceitful, drug-taking bitch?*'

I wipe the mucus from my nose with the back of my hand. It's covered in filth and grime, and I think I see blood on it.

'The day you arrived at the house was one of the happiest days of my life, you know – of our lives in fact – not that you knew it; not then anyway, but I'd been waiting, hoping for that day to come for a very long time...' She inhales deeply. 'He promised to let me go, you see, once he found a "suitable replacement". Those were his words. And I believed them; held on to them tightly.'

I'm shaking uncontrollably. I want her to shut up, want it to stop – all of it just to stop – and yet at the same time, I want her to keep talking, to hear an explanation – to try to understand.

'Papa was a doctor too, you see, like me – or, more accurately, *I* am a doctor like *him*. He was also a psychiatrist. I guess the apple never fell far from the tree after all. *Anywaaaay...*' She pauses. 'He was really quite brilliant was Papa, or at least he started out that way. His understanding of the human mind was unparalleled for the time, his theories and methods of treatment, though some might describe them as unorthodox, were highly respected and lauded among his peers. The first ten years of my life were wonderful – "normal" you might say. We lived alone, the three of us – me, Mother and Papa, happily, in that grand old house...'

My heart almost stops beating. Grand old house? Her father? Is she talking about that house – the house *he* took me to all those years ago?

My head explodes. '*You're Alastor's daughter?*'

She claps her hands together slowly. 'Bravo, Darcie, bravo. I knew it wouldn't take you long to catch on, smart girl like you.

Only Alastor wasn't my father's name; it was the name of the house I grew up in – the house you came to that night.'

I'm saying the word 'no' under my breath on repeat.

'My father's name was Mikhail – the brilliant Dr Mikhail Carson,' she says with a theatrical bow and simultaneous wave of the hand. 'Until that brilliance was diminished by his steep decline into complete insanity of course.' She sighs heavily again. 'Mental health is such a drag, such a precarious thing, Darcie. You know, the mind's brilliance is most often found in its fragility. But unlike a broken arm, or a fractured femur, it's sometimes unfixable once it's broken. You can't put titanium rods in the mind, can you?'

I glance down at the woman behind her, the one she's just shot. I think I see her hand moving, and I silently pray it's not just wishful thinking. Dr Carmichael's right though, if she is – *oh God, maybe* was – a policewoman, then others will come now, won't they?

'I suspect that my mother never really left my father like he told me,' she continues. 'I was ten years old at the time she allegedly walked out. According to Papa, she just woke up one morning and... poof! Gone! Never saw her again. I can't be certain, but I think he may have killed her, probably in a psychotic rage. He really was quite insane,' she says, smiling, matter-of-fact. 'He told anyone who asked that she'd left him and taken me with her. No one disbelieved him, not Dr Carson. And so for the next eight years of my life, I remained there, a prisoner in my own home.'

'He... he im-imprisoned you? Hi-His own d-d-daughter?' I'm struggling to hold it together. I can't stop shaking; can't concentrate on what she's saying.

'Oh yes,' she says almost jovially, swishing her perfectly styled hair from her face. 'His psychosis had a firm grip on him by then, claiming the last pieces of my once sweet, clever father – and leaving a true abomination in his wake.'

'I'm sorry.' I don't know what else to say.

'Oh please, Darcie, spare me the disingenuous platitudes.'

She shifts, and, with the light coming through the door, I see she's holding something in her other hand. *Oh God, it's that horrible, creepy doll!*

'He kept me hidden in a room upstairs; locked me away twenty-four-seven with nothing but dolls for company – dolls like this one!' She cradles it in her arms like a baby; looks down at it lovingly. 'Tabitha was my favourite though... Say hello to Tabitha, Darcie. Tabitha, say hello to Darcie, but' – she slaps her forehead – 'silly me, you've already met, haven't you? He gave her to you when you arrived – he gave you my favourite doll.'

'Dr – Dr Carmichael, what... what do you want from me?' I sense it would be futile to start begging for my life now, plead with her not to harm my unborn baby, however instinctively I might want to. It's patently clear that ship has already sailed, if it was ever seaworthy to begin with. She's just coldly executed two people in front of me, and I don't need letters after my name to know that I'm next. Are they dead because of me? Because of something I've done – something I did all those years ago? I feel her eyes upon me, studying me intently, as though she can read every thought in my head.

'You know, I actually quite like you, Darcie. You have chutzpah; you have... *character*. If things had been different, perhaps we could've been friends?'

'We still can be,' I reply quickly. 'Friends I mean.' Suddenly, my body can't seem to produce any more fear. It's transcended above and beyond it somehow – reached a pinnacle and plateaued into something else.

'Are you going to try and reason with me; tell me to put the gun down, beg for your life and that of your unborn child; appeal to my better nature?' She smirks a little, and I remind myself that she's a psychiatrist, a professor of psychology, someone with hundreds of letters after her name who's supremely intelligent, as well as insane. I doubt I could psychologically outsmart her even if I wanted to.

'No,' I say quietly, and she nods succinctly, seemingly glad we've got that out of the way. 'But I do want to know why I'm here – why you're going to kill me.'

She looks almost impressed by my directness, by the acceptance of my impending fate.

'He had this fear, my father,' she replies, clasping her hands together, like a teacher addressing a classroom of pupils, 'of abandonment, you know? Of course you do,' she answers for me. 'After all, you suffer with the same affliction. He couldn't bear the thought of being alone... Only you knew, didn't you, Darcie? You knew *I* was there, in that house. You heard me – you *saw* me!'

I begin to rock back and forth on the floor, clutching my knees. 'No, no, I didn't see you; I didn't see anyone. It was only ever him – him and the doll. Dr Carmichael, *please*. Two people are dead. You have to stop this.' I'm crying now – fat, desperate sobs. 'Please just stop this.'

'*Tap, tap, tap...* those noises you heard, the scratching and tapping and what you thought were footsteps above you, you remember? The ones you never investigated... And that night, the night you escaped, after you'd wounded him with our dear friend Tabitha here...' She holds the doll up like a trophy. 'As you were rowing away from the house, you looked up at the round window, didn't you, the one right at the top, and you *saw* me.'

Groans are escaping my lips now, involuntary noises coming up through my diaphragm and into my throat, because I *do* remember, God help me. I think I do.

'No. No I don't,' I wail in protest. 'I don't remember anything. It's all just a blur, like a dream. I... I thought I imagined it all – that it wasn't real... None of it was real.'

'He promised to let me go,' she says. 'Swore that if he found a replacement for me, then he would turn me free – and *et voilà*! There you and that conniving, criminal mother of yours were, like a gift from the gods! Do you know, Darcie, that not long after you ran away, your whore of a mother disappeared and never returned? Apparently she told my father she was visiting her sick mother in Paris and that was the last he ever saw of her.'

My chest is heaving so violently I fear I'm going to pass out.

'No,' I say, 'I never knew that she didn't return.'

'But you knew that's what she did, didn't you, Darcie? That her plan was always to marry my father, abandon him and steal half his fortune – you told me yourself.'

'I couldn't do anything about it,' I say. 'He'd locked me up in that room by then. If I'd told him what I suspected she'd done, he might have killed me.'

'Hmm, yes.' She nods, smiling at me just as she used to in our sessions together. 'I can see your rationale I suppose... Did you know, Darcie, that Fabienne inherited everything my father owned – not just half, but *everything*?'

I hear the click of the gun as she points it directly at me, and for a split second I entertain the thought of lunging forward and snatching it clean out of her hand; smashing the butt of it in her murdering face! Would my reactions be fast enough before it went off? Can I take the chance?

'Eight whole years,' she says with a glazed expression, 'locked away in that house like a ghost, hidden from the rest of the world, denied and deprived of my freedom and liberty, of fresh air and flowers, of friends and sunshine and...' Her voice is becoming increasingly more animated – more manic and disturbed. 'But you outsmarted him, didn't you – the great Dr Mikhail Carson? You incapacitated him and escaped – after only twenty-seven days! Quite incredible – commendable even.'

I don't know what to say to her, what words I could use that would potentially precipitate the best outcome.

'I was overjoyed that you'd escaped though, euphoric beyond measure, because you would, of course, go straight to the police, immediately alert the authorities of my predicament, of your suspicions, tell them that a madman had held you captive in his house and that you suspected there was another person held hostage there, wouldn't you? Oh, how we hugged each other relentlessly that night, Tabitha and I, overjoyed and overcome with emotion. Weren't we, Tabitha?' She addresses the doll like a human being. 'Soon we'd be rescued, freed from the nightmare of our hellish existence; soon we'd be safe. Only that never happened, did it, Darcie?'

She pokes the end of the handgun into my sternum, causing me to gasp and recoil. I screw my eyes tightly together.

'I... I didn't think you were real. I thought my mind was playing tricks on me. I was just a child myself...' None of it's a lie, but I don't think it matters now.

'Papa was incandescent with rage and inconsolable when you left. He blamed me of course, convinced I was somehow responsible for you managing to do in a matter of days what I never could in eight years. He starved me of oxygen and light; denied me food and water. He tortured me because of what you did, escaping like that. And he vowed every day thereafter for weeks, months, years even, that he would find you – bring you back.'

I keep my eyes on the gun.

'Two more years passed,' she says, 'another 730-odd days... Every one of them I waited, hoping that today would be the day someone would come for me; that you'd told people about us, about what had happened to you, and they would find me, release me from my nightmare prison... but no one ever came, and slowly, day by day, my hopes diminished until they ceased to exist at all.'

I want to cover my ears; place my hands over them like a child and go, 'La-la-la-la.' But instead, I look up at her, meet her eyes, show her that I'm prepared to listen to what she has to say, to try to understand. Is this how she's going to kill me? Is she going to keep me here, starve me of food and water, torture me like he did to her?

Suddenly I feel angry. I feel betrayed and violated. How can she punish me for what her father did to her – what he did to *me*?

'Once I realised there was no cavalry coming to my rescue, I made a vow to kill him,' she says bluntly. 'Kill him and then make my escape; after all, you'd managed it, so why couldn't I? And so I bided my time, something I'd been forced to become very adept at doing, and I waited, waited for an opportunity to arise, prayed for one every day and night, and then, a little more than a year later, that moment finally came.'

FORTY

She lowers the gun slightly. I suspect she's unable to hold it up in the same position – directly at my chest – any longer, though I've no doubt about her pulling the trigger.

'I think he had a conscience sometimes,' she says. 'He wasn't a complete psychopath, not entirely, not in the truest sense of the word anyway. I think it was the reason he started bringing me books, one after the other; books on psychology mainly – the study of the human mind and condition, medical books, case studies, papers and theses he and others had written. And I devoured them, one by one, the demand outweighing the supply, so much so that he was forced to buy more.

'It's fair to say,' Dr Carmichael says, with more than a hint of pride, 'I was – am – an exceptionally well-read individual and a master student. By the time I came to study for my first degree just a few years later, I'd practically written the exam paper myself. But again, I digress.' She smiles and, for a moment, appears almost normal, like we're simply chatting amiably in her office.

'The only stipulation was that I was forbidden to read at night. This would mean supplying me with light of course –

Papa didn't like electricity; said it was the work of the devil – and that it presented the risk of someone seeing me from the outside, a lone night fisherman on the lake perhaps. But I begged and pleaded with him, wore him down eventually until he presented me with a tiny candle, one I lit every evening while I studied the works of Freud and Jung and William James and others...'

She draws breath. 'One night, when I was sure he was asleep – because even the insane must rest sometimes, Darcie – I took that candle and set fire to my bed sheets. Only the room was ablaze within minutes; the fire took hold far quicker than I'd envisaged, giving me no time to escape. I began banging on the walls, calling for his help. "Papa! Papa! Open the door! The room is on fire! I can't breathe." And a few minutes later, I heard the keys rattle in the lock and he opened it. I seized the moment.'

She lunges forward in demonstration, causing me to gasp and recoil.

'I snatched them from him as he entered, then I ran from the room and shut him in, locking the door from the outside.' She stares straight ahead, lost in the memory.

'Do you know, I stood and watched that house burn to the ground, every last brick of it, until it was nothing but dust?' She snaps out of her thousand-yard stare. 'And then there you were, all those years later, right there on my TV screen, in my front room, larger than life itself. Darcie Bonneville, a national heroine – no pun intended.' She smiles at me, displaying her neat teeth. 'Selfless, beautiful, brave, altruistic, fearless Darcie... and it transpired you were married to a doctor no less. Oh! The irony.' She starts to laugh, but it sounds hollow and sinister, and it sickens me. 'A handsome surgeon and his hero wife, living together in their perfect home, planning to start a family, leading a happy, normal, privileged life thanks to my father's stolen inheritance...'

'So that's what this about,' I manage to croak. 'Some kind of revenge? You think I deliberately abandoned you, left you there, captive, and took your father's money?' I try to swallow, but it feels like rocks are lodged in my larynx.

'I was scared, just like you, locked inside that room... I didn't know that what I was hearing was real; what I thought I might've seen. Please – you have to believe me. I'm sorry, Dr Carmichael. I'm so sorry... I was traumatised after I escaped. I was too frightened to tell anyone; frightened that no one would believe me even if I did, and I was scared he'd find me, that he'd come after me... I've spent my whole life being scared and—'

'The best things always come to those who wait, Darcie.' She holds the gun up to me again with a shaking hand – it's inches away from my face – and... that's when I look up and see him, standing in the shadows behind her.

FORTY-ONE

DAN

I have a very bad feeling as I pull up outside Dr Carmichael's impressive-looking house. I can see no lights on from within the property, yet I get a sixth sense that there's someone inside. There's no sign of Davis, or her car, as I make my way round to the back of the property via the side return. I can only hope that she's been held up somewhere and hasn't arrived yet, or parked out of sight around the corner perhaps – but deep down I know that's just wishful thinking.

I thought of ringing the front doorbell, of portraying blind ignorance, like I'd just turned up on her doorstep unannounced to pay her an informal visit, greet her with a friendly smile, appear none the wiser, *act*. Perhaps she'd even voluntarily let me through the door if I could pull it off. Only I know that years of experience has bestowed Dr Carmichael with the ability to be able to read people extremely efficiently. Even if I put on an Oscar-worthy performance, I can't guarantee she won't be able to see right through me. If Carmichael's armed, then I can't risk spooking her, potentially precipitating a terrible tragedy.

A sensor-operated security light trips as I creep down the side return towards the gate, and I curse under my breath as it illuminates the entire left side of the building. I press my back against the wall of the house; can hear the sound of my own breathing as I stay frozen, wait for it to switch itself off and praying that she hasn't been alerted. SCO19 will be here soon – in minutes I imagine, *I hope* – but I can't wait for them, not when I know Carmichael could be armed and that Davis and Darcie may be inside. If it costs me my career, then so be it. If anything happens to either of these women, I'll hold myself personally responsible. Archer's going to have my head for it, but nothing else matters in this moment; nothing but getting them out of this house and bringing them to safety, even if it means jeopardising my own.

My phone vibrates in my pocket. *Shit.* I've switched it to silent mode, and Archer's calling me. I cancel it then try to open the side gate. It's unlocked, and I wonder if this is usual as I walk through it or if it indicates something more sinister.

I can see that the bi-folding doors to the back of the house are open. An exposed thin gauzy curtain gently rises and falls in the cold night breeze, like a ghost's breath. I slip inside quickly, praying I won't trip another sensor and flood light into the kitchen, where I now find myself.

The house is eerily silent as I take tentative steps through the room. I stop, listen, hoping to hear something, anything that may give me an indication of human life. Yet there's nothing but the sound of a clock ticking; the low hum of an electrical appliance. I look for something that could be used as a weapon – scan the kitchen for a knife block perhaps... only I can't see anything on the work surfaces, and I can't risk turning on a light to search. I carefully open a drawer, wincing as it squeaks, punctuating the deathly silence. Blindly, I feel around inside. There's a large metal slotted spoon, a whisk... and, ah! A wooden rolling pin. It's the best I can do.

Cautiously, I navigate my way out of the room; open a door that brings me out into a large hallway and to the front of the house. To the left of me is a big winding staircase. Could they be up there?

I'm already two steps up when I spot the small slim door, almost hidden, in the hallway next to a console table. Instantly, I'm drawn towards it.

I back up, creep across the wooden floor, bring my ear close to the door and listen.

I hear something! The low vibration of voices. I'm pretty sure this door leads to a basement and that behind it I'll find Darcie Bonneville and Dr Carmichael. I can only hope that Davis isn't down there with them too.

The door is unbolted from the outside, and I brace myself, acutely aware that timing is crucial. If I open this door too quickly and startle Dr Carmichael, it could cause her to spontaneously react – pull the trigger to that gun she could be holding.

I'm grimacing, holding my breath, my palms sweaty and slippery as I grip the handle and turn it slowly, millimetre by millimetre, until I feel it give. I inch it open. It's all I can do to stop myself from screaming Davis's name, from calling out to Darcie, but I press my lips together; say a silent prayer to a God I'm not sure exists instead.

The door opens to a stairway, and I slip through it. The staircase itself is dark, but there's a dim light source at the bottom. A lantern perhaps? I take tentative steps down, using my left hand to steady myself against the wall, my right arm holding the wooden rolling pin aloft, poised to strike if it comes to it.

It's Dr Carmichael's voice I hear first. I think I see the shadow of her as I stealthily navigate the stairs and—

My hearts drops like an elevator from top floor to basement. There – at the bottom of the stairs. She's lying on her side, her face turned away from me, her hair fanning out across the floor, and I see blood.

Lucy.

I feel the emotion rise like a tsunami inside me, zero to one hundred in a tenth of a second. *No, no, no, Lucy! Not my Lucy!*

It's difficult to breathe. The sheer brute force of adrenalin causes my knees to almost buckle underneath me, forcing me to grip the rolling pin tighter. *She's killed her. She's killed Lucy!*

I cover my mouth to prevent my scream from slipping out. I want to run to her, crouch down and tend to her, comfort her, but excruciatingly I know I can't. I mustn't. If Carmichael sees me, it could get us all killed.

'I didn't know that what I was hearing was real; what I thought I might've seen...' I hear who I think is Darcie speaking. 'Please – you have to believe me. I'm sorry, Dr Carmichael. I'm so sorry... don't do this...'

I can smell gun powder as she keeps talking – the distinctive, bold, acrid scent of sulphur and ammonia lingering in the air as I continue my careful descent. I can see her now, Dr Carmichael, the back of her head, her perfectly styled strawberry-blonde hair, as she comes into view. She's standing in the doorway of a basement room, holding a gun, pointing it at Darcie Bonneville's chest as she says, 'What goes around always comes back around, Darcie, eventually.'

My eyes dart around what I can see of the basement room, scan it for... Suddenly, I spot a pair of legs on the floor, splayed open. He's slumped forward, and I can see immediately that the top of his head is missing, open like a tin can, the contents spilling down his face, blood and bone and brain everywhere.

John Evergreen.

She briefly looks up then, Darcie, and her eyes widen like dinner plates as they meet mine. My finger instantly shoots up to my lips as I shake my head. *No.* If she alerts Dr Carmichael to my presence, we're toast, and I'll never see my wife and kids again.

Where the hell is SCO19? Frustration and panic burn through me. I've had Uber Eats turn up faster.

'Why didn't you say anything, Darcie? Why did you leave me there to rot – trapped in that room? You knew I was there; you could've told someone. The police, a teacher, someone you trusted! Eight years – eight years of my life...'

Dr Carmichael's hand is shaking as she grips the gun, the tip of it only inches away from Darcie's head. I can hear the growing mania in her voice, the anger and rage building and... it's now or never.

In one quick, fluid move, I leap down the last few stairs and bring the rolling pin down onto the back of her head with all the physical force of someone who probably should go to the gym more. It makes a sharp crack on impact, the sickening sound of bone breaking. She collapses like a Jenga tower, falling forward onto the concrete.

'I'm sorry.' Darcie is still on the floor, her eyes closed as she grips herself, crying, shaking, 'I'm so sorry.'

FORTY-TWO

DARCIE

I don't remember everything that happened in the moments that followed Dr Carmichael collapsing, but suddenly the room was filled with people wearing dark vests and holding guns and shouting a lot. At first I was terrified, automatically assuming they were there to cause me harm after everything I'd been through, but of course, they were the police – they'd come to rescue me. *They'd found me.*

I do remember Detective Riley – Dan – as I now know he's called, pulling me up off the floor and sweeping me out of the room in what had felt like one graceful, fluid movement, and placing me in the care of one of the officers. I remember how he'd smelled, fresh like Marsala, as he'd placed a protective arm around me, offering me words of comfort. It had reminded me of the French soap I used to use as a child. In hindsight, in that brief, subconscious moment of recall from my childhood, I realised I hadn't thought of Fabienne. And it felt sweet some-how, like progress.

'It's OK now, Darcie.' Those were Detective Riley's words as he scooped me up off the floor, and he spoke them in such a way that it had left me in no doubt whatsoever.

'I'm DCI Dan Riley of the Met Police, and you're safe. It's over.'

As I was being whisked away, I turned to look behind me; saw Dr Carmichael lying face down on the floor, a circle of guns pointing at the back of her bloodied head. She was still holding the doll, Tabitha, as they began pulling her arms behind her and placed cuffs on her. I heard her groan, murmuring incoherently, as she struggled to regain consciousness. She was still alive and, for reasons I can't explain, I felt relieved. There had been enough death already.

'I get to meet you properly at last!' Detective Riley sits at the side of the hospital bed next to me now, his hand resting on top of my own. 'I feel like I already know you,' he says. 'You've been the only woman in my life for some time now, Darcie – and a remarkable one at that.'

I look up at him and smile; I figure I owe him that much at the very least. I get to see his face properly then, as if for the first time, without the filter of fear discolouring everything, and I'm struck by how attractive he is – for a policeman anyway. Though perhaps it's simply the fact that he's rescued me that makes me think so. He has the kind of face I think he deserves somehow.

'How are you feeling?'

Remarkably, I left that horrific basement room pretty much as I entered it, physically at least. There was barely a mark on me, aside from a few bruises and abrasions; the small cut to my face I must've acquired when John abducted me from the woods.

John. I've since discovered that Dr Carmichael has confessed to recruiting him into following her wicked plan. Detective Riley told me that she manipulated him, groomed him to abduct me and, eventually, kill me. She spent the past six months coercing and brainwashing him into doing what she wanted him to do, lavishing him with praise and promises of her affection, of companionship. She told John it was all just an elaborate game, a test of his loyalty towards her, proof of his affection and dedication.

She advised him to stop taking his medication too, fully aware of the potential ramifications – how doing so could affect his mental and physical state. She deliberately fed into his paranoia, his confusion – encouraged it even – told him she had a special mission for him, one she trusted only him to complete. She had him eating out of her hand, her slave, a puppet whose strings she could pull at will. And once he completed that mission – abducting me and holding me prisoner – she upped the ante and instructed him to finish the job for her, to kill me. Only when it actually came down to it, he couldn't do it – John just didn't have it in him to pull the trigger. Seems Dr Carmichael's 'magic' wasn't quite as potent as she believed.

John is a victim in all this too – a sacrificial lamb – and whatever else he was, he was a vulnerable person who didn't deserve to be brutally murdered by someone he believed in and trusted. He didn't deserve to be murdered at all.

'Nervous,' I reply and he looks at me knowingly somehow, as if this is the answer he expected. He smiles softly and taps my hand, and a moment's silence passes between us.

'How did you find me? How did you know where to look?' I have so many questions, though I'm not sure I'll ever get all the answers. Somehow I'll have to learn to accept that maybe there aren't any. Maybe I'll just have to answer them myself.

'Gina,' Dan says. 'Gina was the catalyst to piecing it all together. She came forward, after we put out an appeal. She remembered what you'd told her all those years ago, after you'd escaped – about the house, about Alastor, about the doll...'

I smile. *Gina.* All those years ago, she rescued me from the park bench I was sleeping on, and even though my drug habit followed, I can't help but think that somehow she's rescued me again – by remembering, by coming forward and having the courage to *tell the truth*. She looked out for me back then, and, it seems, once more all these years later.

They say we all have guardian angels in life – some heavenly, some earthly. I believe she's one of mine. I'd like to see her again, to thank her. I hope I get the chance to.

'We'll need to talk more,' Detective Riley says, 'when you're up to it of course, and we've placed a couple of officers outside the room. We want you to feel safe, Darcie, and to keep the reporters from getting to you. As you can imagine, there's been substantial interest in your story, and by substantial, I mean absolutely off the chart.'

He grins at me then, and we both briefly, gently laugh. It feels good to know that I still can – that I'm still capable of it.

'Trust me they're a... resourceful lot, journalists. I should know – I'm married to one. Though I'm not sure for how much longer.'

I give him a puzzled look, and he shakes his head, wrinkling his nose and smiling.

'Doesn't matter,' he says. 'All that matters now is that you and that little baby inside you are safe and well. Everything else... well, we'll just have to take one day at a time, won't we?'

I like the fact he used the word 'we', like we were somehow in this together. I suppose we were really. In fact, there's no real suppose about it.

It was the first thing I'd asked as I was admitted to hospital – was my baby still alive? I was convinced that the poor tiny thing must have died of shock inside me during my ordeal. How could it not have? I'd almost died of it myself.

I felt numb as the nurse placed the ultrasound transducer on my stomach; held my breath and closed my eyes, hoping for the best and expecting the worst. But then I heard it, the whoosh and throb of a heartbeat, and it sounded strong! Strong and loud and proud, and I started to laugh and cry at the same time.

'It must take after its mother,' Detective Riley continues. 'It's a survivor – a fighter.'

'Your colleague?' I ask. 'Is she OK?'

He lowers his eyes but not before I catch the depth of emotion in them. He has such nice eyes – kind.

'She will be.'

I nod, grateful and relieved. I don't think I could bear another death on my conscience.

'What will happen to Dr Carmichael?' I didn't want to ask the question; I didn't want to care. She'd had me kidnapped and chained up, murdered John Evergreen in cold blood, almost killed Detective Riley's colleague, and she'd wanted to lock me inside a tiny room until I went insane like her. And yet, somehow, I still did. I understood what she'd been through, and perhaps I really was somehow to blame, for all of it...

Detective Riley takes my hand in his own then. 'You're a good soul, Darcie,' he says. 'You did nothing to deserve any of this... whatever she said to you, however she tried to convince you otherwise. You were a survivor then, and you're a survivor now. You mustn't let her get inside your head; mustn't let her live there. She's good at doing that – she almost managed it with me too.'

'But she was right,' I say. 'All those years ago... I *could've* told someone; I *should've*. Maybe if I had, then none of this would ever have happened. If I'd just told the truth back then, gone to the police and explained what had happened to me, maybe her life would've been different – maybe all of our lives would've been.' I hear the crack in my voice; feel the tears come.

'Shhh.' He links his fingers into mine and squeezes tightly. 'Dr Carmichael is a very disturbed woman, Darcie. A disturbed and dangerous woman who's extremely mentally unwell and expertly adept at hiding it. Maybe she's a psychopath,' he says with a gentle sigh. 'After undergoing psychiatric assessment, she'll go to trial, and I suspect she'll plead insanity on the grounds of diminished responsibility.'

'Do you think she'll fool them – the doctors?' I ask.

'Quite possibly,' he replies with refreshing honesty. 'She fooled everyone else after all, myself included – for a while at least. I imagine she'll spend the best part of the rest of her days in a secure psychiatric unit – she may never be released.'

I have an image then of Dr Carmichael – the attractive, stylish, professional and intelligent woman I first encountered – caged in a cell, the doctor having become the patient in a bizarre role reversal, no longer studying others but being studied herself. I try not to feel sorry, to feel empathy, for her, but I just can't help it; it's impossible. Her story is a tragic one.

'The damage was done a long time ago, Darcie,' Detective Riley says, as though he's read my thoughts. 'Long before you came along. Perhaps it was always there to begin with, in the DNA.'

I nod; try to convince myself that he's right. Maybe in time I'll get there. *Maybe with therapy*.

'There's someone here to see you,' he says, his tone lightening. 'He's been waiting patiently. Shall I show him in?'

My stomach shrinks. I know who he's talking about. *Il mio caro marito. Gabe*.

I ache so much to see him, but I'm convinced my heart will shatter the moment I do and that not even he will be able to mend it. I'm terrified. He knows everything now. It's all been exposed – *I've* been exposed – in the most horrific and public way. The boil has finally burst. I've spent my whole adult life being afraid of this happening, forever fearful of my past catching up with me, always trying to outrun it. Now, at least, at last, I don't have to run anymore.

I've gone over and over it in my mind, lying in this hospital bed – what I want to say to Gabe and how I want to say it – but however I framed it, I couldn't get past the shame. The shame of lying to him, the fear of his rejection, of him looking at me differently to the way he's always looked at me – the way I know I'll never tire of. How could he not?

I remember asking Dr Carmichael, during one of our sessions together, when I'd been blissfully unaware of who she was and her intentions towards me, whether withholding something from someone is the same thing as lying. For a long time I'd convinced myself that it wasn't, that if I admitted nothing, then it wasn't a lie as such. But she never gave me a definitive answer to the question. Perhaps, knowing what I do now, she didn't know the answer herself.

A minute or two passes after Detective Riley says goodbye, for now at least, before I see the door handle turn. I hold my breath. I want to close my eyes; pretend to be sleeping. But I have to face it – to face him. I've faced everything else, haven't I?

I see his silhouette, the shape of him instantly recognisable, as he appears in the doorway – his mop of noodle curls. But I'm too scared, too much of a coward, to look directly at him, to look into his eyes, because if I do, I'll know in an instant what he's thinking – what he thinks of me – and I'm not sure I can cope with what I might see.

Only then he's in my arms, and I'm in his. He wraps them around me, and I feel the strength of them as he holds me. His skin as it touches mine smells how I imagine pure joy might smell if it were tangible, perceptible to touch, and I bury my nose into his clavicle; inhale him deep down into my lungs, until it feels like he's part of me.

I'm crying as his lips find my cheeks, my hair, my neck, until they reach my own, and we say nothing as our eyes connect. And the answers I need, the ones I've been so afraid of seeking, are right there in them, in that perfect moment of silence.

FORTY-THREE

DAN

'Come on, sweetheart – wake up... Wake up now. Yeah, I need to go home – get out of this awful suit.'

I've been at her bedside on and off since she was brought in to the hospital together with Darcie; haven't wanted to leave her on her own. Not after what she's just been through, not after everything.

I've just sat here talking to her, willing her to come round, praying that she'll be OK. *Just let her be OK*. I mop her brow every few minutes, scrape her hair back from her face, touch her hand.

It's no exaggeration when I say that walking into that basement and seeing my colleague, my trusted number two, *my Lucy*, on the floor, injured with a gunshot wound has to be one of the worst experiences of my life – and trust me when I say I've had my fair share.

My first instinct was to rush to her, try to save her, to do something, anything, but the situation dictated that I couldn't. I felt so helpless, so angry and guilty that I wasn't there to protect her, that I hadn't gone with her, *that I hadn't gone myself*. It was going to be tough dealing with those emotions, a long road ahead.

When SCO19 finally made an appearance and I could be sure Darcie Bonneville had been safely removed, I rushed to Davis's side; felt for a pulse.

'C'mon, c'mon, c'mon. Please... Please, Lucy, don't you die on me – don't you dare die on me. You hearing me, Davis? Don't you leave me – that's an order, do you hear?' I could see she'd been hit in the right shoulder, just above her chest; saw the blood, fresh and glistening from the wound. I put my hand on it.

'Officer down, officer down!' I called out to no one, to everyone, to *anyone,* my voice breaking with emotion, my heart threatening to follow suit.

'Paramedics are on the way,' one of the SCO19 team said, squeezing my shoulder. 'She'll be OK.'

'No thanks to you!' I shot back. 'What took you so long, eh? Stopped off for a pint on the way, did you?' I was angry, upset, traumatised.

After what feels like forever, I see her eyelids gently flutter open. I pull my chair in closer to the hospital bed.

'Hey... hey, Lucy. Lucy, can you hear me?'

She blinks; turns her head slowly towards me.

'Gov...'

And I break down then – that one word undoes me completely – and drop my head onto her arm, covering my eyes with my hand, not wanting to cry in front of her but unable to stop the emotion – my tears have their own agenda. This girl isn't just a colleague; she's become family to me over time, like the little sister I never had but kind of always wanted. She's even a godparent to Jude, our latest addition, a suggestion my good lady wife had wholly supported. 'She'd make a fantastic Godparent,' she'd agreed, adding, 'After all, if she can keep *you* in check, Daniel Riley, then she's as good as got the job.'

'It's going to be OK,' I say. 'You're going to be OK; it's all going to be OK... Except for when I get back to the nick and Archer sacks me,' I say, and she smiles; manages a whisper of a laugh.

'I'm so sorry, Lucy; I'm so, so sorry, sweetheart.' I take her hand in both of mine and I realise, staring down at her then, just how young she looks, her whole life and career in front of her, and how easily it could all have been taken from her, from me, from a world where more people like Lucy Davis are needed.

She places her hand on my arm, like she wants to say something. I lean in closer to her.

'You're... you're a hero, boss.' Her voice is a dry rasp, but still I can hear her wry tone in it, even now.

'You know, I love you, Davis.' I squeeze her hand.

'Love you too, gov.'

I enter the station via the back entrance, trying to avoid the world's media, who have congregated en masse, like a circus that's come to town, a colourful convoy of them all, waiting to pounce on me with their plethora of unending questions. I know I'll have to face them at some point, but there are more pressing matters at hand.

I'd decided I was going to jump before I was pushed – that I'd give my verbal resignation to Archer there and then and spare us both. I knew she would be left with no option but to, at best, suspend me or, at worst, discharge me from all duties with immediate effect. I'd blatantly disobeyed her orders by not returning to the nick and allowing SCO19 to take over, and I'd jeopardised the safety of my fellow officer, my second in command, my dearest Davis, who was now in a hospital bed, recovering from what could've been – but praise be to God thankfully wasn't – a fatal gunshot wound. Lastly, I'd put Darcie Bonneville's life at risk by attending the property unarmed and without backup to a hostage situation that I wasn't sanctioned to attend, potentially precipitating a blood-bath. My actions, and the decisions I'd made, could've got us all killed. And yet if I ask myself whether, with the benefit of hind-sight, I'd do the same again, I can't deny that the answer is an unequivocal yes.

I can't bring myself to look at my team as I walk via the inci-dent room towards Archer's office, but I can feel their eyes on me, watching through the glass in a sombre silence.

I took a deep breath, bracing myself for what I knew had to happen. Perhaps it was for the best anyway. I've always fancied getting into gardening.

Archer has her back towards me as I enter. She's peering out of the window, no doubt surveying the sea of reporters that's surrounded the building. She doesn't turn around immediately.

'Ma'am.'

'Take a seat, Riley,' she says after what feels like a long pause, her back still to me.

I clear my throat. 'Before you say anything, ma'am, I'd like to speak, if I may.'

'Well, I suppose it wouldn't matter even if I were to say no, would it?' she says. 'All things considered.'

It's a fair enough comment I suppose... *all things considered*.

'How is Lucy Davis?' she asks tightly.

I exhale. 'She's doing OK. The bullet entered through her right shoulder and exited just above her collarbone. The doctors say she'll make a full recovery – could be back in the office in a couple of weeks even, on light duties. She was lucky really. If the bullet had been just a few inches lower...'

She turns around then, finally.

'Yes?' she says, her tone sharp. 'And it's all thanks to you.'

I drop my head. 'I know, ma'am,' I say. 'That's why I'm here to give you my verbal resignation and—'

'I think you've misunderstood me, Dan,' she says. 'It's *all* thanks to you. Darcie Bonneville is alive and safe, rescued unharmed... Have you seen the news? Have you heard what they're saying?'

I blink at her, confused. 'No, ma'am, I've been at Lucy's bedside all morning – done my best to avoid the reporters...'

She looks at me intently. 'They're saying you're a hero, Dan. That you risked your own life to ensure the safety of your colleague's and to rescue Darcie Bonneville *and* her unborn baby in the process. The commissioner wants you put forward for a National Police Bravery Award; maybe even a King's Police Medal. The press are going bananas over it, over you and your selfless actions, and what they resulted in.'

I stare at her, dumbfounded.

'But I thought... I was expecting...'

'Of course, it could all have been very different, if you'd followed orders and done what I'd commanded you to do. Ordinarily, your defiance would have earned you an early retirement, only... well, the commissioner and I are aware of *public feeling* about this, about... you, and so *we* feel it's in the Met's best interest, publicly, not to make any official reprimand... on this occasion.'

I stare at her, lost for words, genuinely unsure if this is all some kind of prank.

'Looks like it's all turned out well for you, Riley.'

I can't tell from her tone if she's pleased or irked. Perhaps it's a little of both.

'I... I don't know what to say, ma'am.'

She raises an eyebrow. 'Well, I suppose there's always a first for everything. You know, aside from everything, from everyone else involved, *you* could've been killed, Riley. Your own stupid —' She stopped and took a breath; corrected herself. 'Your own *ill-advised* actions could've seen your wife a widow, your children fatherless...'

I drop my head again. She's right of course, and the reality of it is only really starting to kick in.

'It was rash, impulsive, reckless even... and it was also *extremely brave.*'

'Thank you, ma'am,' I say quietly. *I think.*

'We'll need to give a press briefing before you go off and take that holiday you were originally supposed to be on. It's been organised for 1 p.m. – in an hour's time. Your fans await,' she adds wryly.

'Yes, ma'am.' I stand.

'Oh and Riley,' she says, just as I'm leaving. 'Wear a decent suit this time. Please.'

FORTY-FOUR

I text Fiona just as I begin the drive to Sandbanks.

I'll be there in approx three hours, traffic depending.

She hasn't replied by the time I hit the M3. I've been beyond lucky over the past twenty-four hours in one way or another, and I'm really hoping my luck hasn't finally run out.

I think about Darcie, about Davis and John Evergreen, as I follow the signs towards Poole. I think about Dr Carmichael too. I know this case will leave an indelible scar on everyone's lives – the ones that weren't taken anyway. I hope we can all recover respectively from it somehow, even Carmichael herself.

Are people born bad or mad, or do they become that way through the things they see and hear, through their life experiences? Do we all have predilections towards certain things, certain behaviours and traits when we're born that we can't foresee – no options or choices? Is what we are and what we become in our DNA, simply preordained no matter what?

When you look at a newborn baby, at its purity and innocence, it's virtually impossible to imagine that nature could have any responsibility for someone becoming a murderer; an insane, deranged criminal with evil intent. Is it nature or nurture, or a combination of both? Or is it circumstance that dictates who we are at the end of the day and what we become? I doubt even Carmichael herself has the answers, but she'll certainly now have the time to reflect on them.

I feel a deep exhaustion by the time I pull up to the address at Sandbanks, the kind of mental and physical fatigue that seems to penetrate right through your bones and into your soul.

She's standing in the doorway of the – admittedly impressive – house; a house I should've spent the past few days in with her, together, with my family, her arms folded across her chest, her poker-faced expression giving nothing away.

She'd said I had a week to resolve this case and 'get my arse to Sandbanks', otherwise she'd be straight down to Kingfisher's solicitors for a decree nisi. Admittedly, part of me had even believed her. I know I've let her down; let my Pip and Leo and my almost still brand new Jude down too.

I feel it acutely as I approach her – the regret, the apology, the turning back of the clock we all would sometimes like to do but aren't capable of.

'Well, what do you know, you're early for once,' she says wryly as I follow her through the front door into what can only be described as a lavish entrance lobby, with its high, vaulted ceiling and shiny marble flooring.

'This has got some serious wow factor going on,' I find myself saying. 'And the house looks pretty decent too.' I flash her a cheeky grin. I'm pushing my luck.

I can't gauge her mood as I follow her into the grand room, replete with its own well-stocked bar and sleek black couches, in keeping with the whole swanky-hotel vibes I'm getting. I sense things might be a little chilly, despite the roaring open fire that's filling the cold January night with heat.

'Where are the kids?' I ask. 'I've missed them.'

'Mimi has them. She's watching them this evening to give us some time alone, to sort things out.'

I feel my heart deflate a touch.

'Drink?'

She's wearing a red dress, her lips crimson to match, offsetting her dark hair. She looks... beautiful. She pours me a large brandy without waiting for an answer and hands it to me.

'Courvoisier,' I remark, checking the bottle. 'The good stuff, eh? What are we celebrating?' I hear the hopefulness in my own voice; wonder if she hears it too. She has no idea how truly happy I am to see her.

'Listen, Fi, I...'

She sits down on one of the couches and crosses one leg over the other, affording me a glimpse of her thigh. She pats the space next to her; gestures for me to sit. I feel a flicker of hope reignite inside my chest.

'I know you're mad at me, and you've every right to be. I should've been here. I should've been here with you all from the beginning. I know I've let you down; let the kids down... I shouldn't have got involved. I should've just walked away... I should've put you all first and I'm sorry. I'm so—'

She leans in close to me, places a soft finger on my lips and starts to smile. 'That's a lot of should'ves,' she says. 'Oh, I can't keep this up any longer.' She throws her arms around me. 'You're impossible to be mad at for long – do you know that, Daniel Riley?'

I close my eyes as relief floods through me, warm and soothing, and welcome her embrace.

'Oh God, Fi... I don't know what I was thinking, going into that house, unarmed, no backup. I know I could've been killed. Archer was right – it could've ended badly; I could've left you with our three children, alone to cope on your own. It was selfish. It was reckless. It was—'

'The bravest, most heroic thing I've ever heard – not to mention your *job*.'

The emotion I feel in that moment hits my eyes, and I take a large swig of brandy to try and disguise it; buy myself a diversion. I should've known really, that out of everyone, Fiona would just *get it* without explanation. I feel bad for underestimating her, because in that moment I feel more understood than I ever have before – by anyone. It's a money-can't-buy feeling.

'So you're not going to divorce me, then?' I ask, resting my head on her shoulder.

'Kingfisher's has closed down anyway,' she says, giving me a sideways smile. 'They've built a Starbucks in its place.' She sighs. 'Sign of the times.'

God, I love this woman.

'Thank you,' I say, placing my hand on her thigh as I look at her.

I see something in her eyes then – a certain look, one I've seen before. At least twice before anyway.

'There's something I've been meaning to ask you, Dan.' Her voice is heavy with gravitas. 'Something that's bothered me since I saw you give the appeal on TV. Something I just don't understand, can't seem to come to terms with... or get my head around.'

'OK?' I reply cautiously.

'Just where, in the name of Tom Ford, did you ever find that *suit*?'

'What this?' I pull at the lapel, mock offended. 'Lucy got it for me, from the charity shop down the high street. You'd packed everything else and taken it with you. Anyway,' I say, 'it's grown on me. It's my lucky suit.'

'Yes,' she says, edging closer as she starts to undo the buttons, 'I think you might be right.'

A LETTER FROM ANNA-LOU

I want to say a huge, warm thank you, dear reader, for choosing *The Housewife's Secret*. I really hope you enjoyed Darcie's story – and Dan's valiant attempts at finding and rescuing her!

If you did enjoy it, it would be so wonderful if you would be generous enough to leave a review saying why. Reviews are a fantastic way of introducing new readers to my books, and I'm always very grateful when people take the time to write them and share the love!

If you want to keep up to date with all my latest releases, just sign up at the following link. Your email address will never be shared with anyone, and you can unsubscribe at any time.

www.bookouture.com/anna-lou-weatherley

I'd love to hear what you thought of *The Housewife's Secret*. I always adore hearing from my readers and do my best to reply personally to every message – you can get in touch with me on Facebook: Anna-Lou Weatherley Author, or X: @annalouwrites

Thank you again and much love,

Anna-Lou

KEEP IN TOUCH WITH ANNA-LOU

facebook.com/annalouweatherleyauthor

x.com/annaloulondon

instagram.com/annalouwrites

ACKNOWLEDGEMENTS

I'm always mindful of missing someone out when it comes to thanking people, so a big thank you to whoever I may have missed! Big thanks to my fantastic publishers, Bookouture and all the fabulous gang I'm so, so proud and honoured to be part of: my fellow authors; my editor, Jennifer Hunt; and Kim, Noelle and Peta. Annie, Bridget and Bob, Amanda, Mo, Natalie, and Jan and Lawrie – all the J Road gang who're such lovely people and so supportive of my work – thank you! Also thanks to my lovely new friend Helen. Thanks to Stevie P, Lacey, Jac and Sean, Greta, Stacey, Emma, and Marieke and all the PW crew. Thank you also to my wonderful friend, Qefs.

A big shout-out to Kelly and the girls and Tony, to Sue Traveller (or is it Headley now?), and to John and Sam. As always, I want to thank my truly amazing mummy, my inspiration on so many levels, for all your support and guidance and for always being there for me – I'm so glad you're nothing like Darcie's mum! Thank you to my sister and brother, Lisa-Jane and Marc-Paul! I'd also like to mention Jan and Mick – wishing them both well. Thank you also, DC. My boys, Louie and Felix, Philip Joe, PJ, Joey D! And lastly, but by no means least, to my fabulous agent, 'best in the business' Mr Darley Anderson – thank you so much for all your support, your valuable words of wisdom and guidance (plus our wonderful lunches together) and to everyone at the Darley Anderson agency, especially my fellow frizz sympathiser, Rebeka Finch (thank you *so* much for all your hard

work on my behalf; it has meant so much to me!) and to the
wonderful Rosanna too.

PUBLISHING TEAM

Turning a manuscript into a book requires the efforts of many people. The publishing team at Bookouture would like to acknowledge everyone who contributed to this publication.

Commercial
Lauren Morrissette
Jil Thielen
Imogen Allport

Contracts
Peta Nightingale

Data and analysis
Mark Alder
Mohamed Bussuri

Editorial
Jennifer Hunt
Sinead O'Connor

Copyeditor
Laura Kincaid

Proofreader
Claire Rushbrook